UNDER COVER
OF THE NIGHT . . .

It seemed even darker in the parking lot without Ruth. And once she was gone I felt the watcher's presence again. Forget it, I told myself. But I couldn't stop the trembling that took over my body . . .

Get back to the light now, my mind screamed. I inhaled deeply and took a step back to safety, stepping heel first as in tai chi.

Then I felt something slip lightly over my head . . .

THE LAST RESORT
A KATE JASPER MYSTERY

Don't miss Kate Jasper's
first exciting adventure . . .

ADJUSTED TO DEATH

A visit to the chiropractor—who has a corpse on the examining table—teaches Kate a valuable lesson: A pain in the neck may be pure murder!

"A FUNNY, FUNNY BOOK!"
—SUSAN DUNLAP,
author of *PIOUS DECEPTIONS*

THE LAST RESORT

JAQUELINE GIRDNER

BERKLEY PRIME CRIME, NEW YORK

This Berkley Prime Crime Book contains the complete text of the original edition.

THE LAST RESORT

A Berkley Prime Crime Book / published by arrangement with the author

PRINTING HISTORY
Diamond edition / June 1991
Berkley Prime Crime edition / December 1993

ISBN: 0-425-14431-3

Berkley Prime Crime Books are published by The Berkley Publishing Group, 200 Madison Avenue, New York, New York 10016. The name BERKLEY PRIME CRIME and the BERKLEY PRIME CRIME design are trademarks of Berkley Publishing Corporation.

PRINTED IN THE UNITED STATES OF AMERICA

10 9 8 7 6 5 4 3 2 1

– Prologue –

SUZANNE WAS RUNNING the perimeter of the spa in the cool night air. Her long smooth legs were the metronome for her breathing. Step, breathe in. Step, breathe in deeper. Step, breathe out. Step, force the last breath out. She wasn't going to be one of the pack in this year's Bay to Breakers race. She was going to be a contender! She pumped her arms as if propelling invisible ski poles and lengthened her stride, gliding past early primroses and outdoor mud baths. In. In. Out. Out. Back straight under streaming blond hair. Shoulders down.

She rounded the curve toward the section of the spa under construction, her arms and legs a study in symmetry. This lousy spa, she thought. In. In. We could have gone to one of the first-rate resorts. Private hot tubs, room service, haute cuisine. Out. Out. No haute cuisine here. Raw vegetables, brown rice, carrot juice. In. In. She was thin, young and healthy. She didn't need that garbage. Out. Out. And the rooms. Dark paisley wallpaper, decor by Charles Manson.

As she neared the rubble of the old solarium she saw a solitary figure at the entrance. Jesus Christ, one of the local inmates. In. In. A hand waved at her, beckoning. No way she was going to stop and talk. Out. Out.

Time to ramp up the speed, she decided, and then felt the sudden jerk around her neck. Her long body slammed to the ground. Scream! she told herself. But there was no air for a scream. Breathe! she commanded. No air. She clawed at the thing around her neck. No air.

No more air.

- One -

I HAD JUST ripped open the envelope when the telephone rang. I unfolded the enclosed document and read as I walked to the phone. Two days ago, on Monday, October 10th, a Final Judgment of Dissolution had been entered in the Marriage of Craig and Kate Jasper by the Clerk of the Superior Court of California, County of Marin. The attorney for Craig Jasper was listed as one Elias Rosen of Rosen, Chang and Ostrow.

Fourteen years of marriage finally ended. My feet stopped moving. I ignored the second ring of the telephone and stared at the words of the decree, trying to analyze my feelings.

I didn't hate my ex-husband, Craig, anymore. Not that I wanted to be married to him. Never again. It was just impossible for me to hate him for very long. Even in his upwardly mobile incarnation, he was a warmly enthusiastic and funny man, incapable of intentional malice or cruelty.

But unintentional cruelty, that was another story. After years of our on-again, off-again, mismatched marriage, Craig had finally severed the bond and found a more suitable woman by the name of Suzanne Sorenson. She was an up-and-coming attorney with Rosen, Chang and Ostrow, as driven to success in her own field as Craig was in his thriving computer business. And she was beautiful. Model-thin, tall and elegant. Sultry Scandinavian features under flowing angel-blond hair. A far better match for Craig's long, lean good looks than I.

I'm short, dark and A-line, myself. And, as far as my own gag-gift business goes, I define success as solvency. Plus enough salary to keep me in tofu burgers.

I probably would have hated Craig for a lot longer if I hadn't found my own someone to love. But I had. A shy, homely and quietly intelligent someone—Wayne Caruso. And once I had found Wayne, Craig and I had unaccountably become good friends. Strictly platonic, but still closer to each other than we had been in all the years of our marriage. Much to Wayne's muted unease and Suzanne's shrill dismay.

The piercing insistence of the telephone's fifth ring ended my abstraction. I sprinted the last two steps to my favorite naugahyde easy chair, plopped myself down and picked up the receiver. My cat, C.C., jumped into my lap just as I said "Hello."

"Kate, is that you?" asked a familiar voice, tuned to an unfamiliar pitch of hysteria. It was my new friend and ex-husband, Craig. His voice was high and trembling. Had the end of our marriage upset him that much?

"Yeah, it's me," I answered. "Who did you expect? C.C.? Meow, meow?"

He didn't respond to my invitation to lightness. He didn't respond at all. The only sound that came over the phone line was his raspy breathing. C.C. flexed her paws and purred.

"Are you all right?" I asked impatiently. C.C. sank a claw into my thigh. I plucked it out. Then I heard what sounded like a muffled sob over the line. Good God! I had never heard Craig cry before. What was wrong with the man?

"Craig?" I prompted anxiously.

"It's Suzanne," he said. He drew a deep ragged breath. "She's dead."

My mind couldn't assimilate it. "Your Suzanne?" I asked stupidly. C.C. raised her claw for another dig. I caught it midair.

"And they think I did it!" He wasn't holding back now. His wail was a hurt child's.

"Did what?" I asked in my calmest voice, while my stomach tightened with dread. "How did Suzanne die?"

"She was murdered."

Three hours later I was sitting in a front aisle seat of a Southwest Air flight approaching San Diego, my head buzzing as loud as the turbo jets. San Diego had the closest airport to Spa Santé, where Craig and Suzanne were staying. Or, more accurately now, where Craig was staying. Suzanne was in the Lakeside County morgue. I was only able to get a few more details out of Craig by phone. That he had found Suzanne face down in a Spa Santé mud bath, for one. And that he would pick me up at the airport if I would fly to San Diego, for another. It was his final tearful "please" that snagged me.

I accepted what was to be my lunch from a smiling Hispanic stewardess. Tomato juice and salted nuts. At least it was vegetarian.

It hadn't been easy to tell my sweetie, Wayne Caruso, that I was flying to San Diego for Craig's sake. On a workday yet. I sipped at my tomato juice and sighed. Wayne. A homely man from the neck up, but beautiful from the neck down. Not to mention the inside out. He was a man who liked me, even loved me, exactly the way I was. A powerful aphrodisiac after years of not meeting Craig's standards.

Wayne hadn't even objected to my trip. Instead, he had expressed his concern quietly and offered to feed C.C. Whatever jealous torments he was going through, if any, he had kept them to himself.

"My name's Krystal, what's yours?" squeaked a voice to my left. I turned my head and saw a small freckled face with intent hazel eyes scrutinizing me.

"Kate," I answered cautiously.

"I'm six. How old are you?"

"Thirty-nine." Might as well be honest.

"Oh." She considered for a moment, furrowing her freckled brow. Maybe she was trying to count that high. "Grandma's older than you," she said and tugged the tweed sleeve of a well-groomed woman who was busy reading on Krystal's other side.

The woman gave me a brief unfocused smile, before sliding her eyes back to *Queen of the Damned.*

"I'm going to see my daddy and his girlfriend in San Diego," Krystal continued. "Who are you going to see?"

"My ex . . . my friend," I answered.

"Oh." She considered again. "My daddy misses me. He wants me to live with him again. Does your friend want you to live with him again?" Her clear hazel eyes glommed onto mine knowingly.

"God, I hope not!" I replied.

My comment popped Grandma back out of her book.
"Krystal, that's enough! Buckle up. We're almost there."

It certainly was enough. Krystal's question had opened a
Pandora's box of doubts in my mind. And tensed all my
shoulder and back muscles in the process. As the plane began
its descent, I thought enviously of C.C., probably digging
her claws into Wayne's well-muscled thigh at this very moment. What was I going to do down here? Comfort Craig?
Find out what happened to Suzanne? Or get myself in a lot
of trouble? But it was too late to turn back. The plane was
bumping down the runway, and suddenly I was feeling air-
sick.

Craig was waiting for me in the crowd at the gate. His
lean, handsome face no longer looked lean and handsome. It
looked gaunt and aged under dark stubble. His large brown
puppy-dog eyes were bleary, red and swollen. His broad
shoulders were hunched inward. Splash on a little eau-de-
vino and he wouldn't have looked out of place sitting on the
curb drinking Thunderbird out of a paper bag. A far cry from
the man who might have modeled for the cover of *Inc* magazine the week before.

"She's dead, Kate," were the words he greeted me with.
He held out a hand for my suitcase, ever courteous, even in
his disheveled grief. Empathetic tears surged up unexpectedly
behind my eyes.

"I know," I replied inadequately. I gave his outstretched
hand a platonic squeeze before letting him have my suitcase.
Only the echo of six-year-old Krystal's question kept me from
wrapping my arms around him. No use encouraging him if
he did harbor any illusions about marital reconciliation. The
crowd surged around us as I stared at him, formulating questions that couldn't wait any longer. Krystal waved at me as
her grandma hustled her down the corridor.

"Tell me what happened," I said finally.

Craig stared down at the airport floor. "She was murdered," he said softly, as if he still didn't believe it.

"How?" I asked firmly. "How was Suzanne murdered?"

Craig raised red eyes full of panic to mine.

"I . . . I found her, Kate. She was . . ." He dropped his
eyes again. I could hear his breathing as he tried to calm
himself.

''What happened to her?'' I asked again, unable to keep the impatience out of my tone.

''I don't know!'' he yelped. Curious faces turned our way. Damn.

I patted Craig's shoulder uneasily. What was it that he couldn't, or wouldn't, tell me? ''Are you all right?'' I asked after a few moments.

''I'm fine,'' he insisted in a voice two octaves too high. ''Fine.'' He brought his head back up, but his eyes weren't seeing me. They were looking through me.

''Did you call the police when you found her?'' I asked.

He shook his head slowly. ''Fran called the police,'' he murmured.

''Who's Fran?'' I asked.

''She's the lady that runs the spa,'' he answered quietly. ''When I found Suzanne last night . . .'' he began. He took a breath and continued, his voice a little stronger. ''When I found her body I ran and pounded on the doors of the main building. Pretty soon the lights and the sirens came. Then everyone from the spa was out there milling around. And Chief Orlandi . . .'' Craig's face paled beneath its stubble.

''Who's Chief Orlandi?'' I asked.

''He's the chief of the Delores Police Department.'' Craig's eyes focused on mine suddenly. ''Kate, he thinks I did it.''

''He thinks you killed Suzanne?'' I prodded.

''Yes.'' Craig swallowed. His eyes went wild again. ''He questioned me for hours! He had our room searched. They took my clothes for lab tests. They took my fingerprints. Orlandi told me I had to stay at the spa!''

''Did they just take your fingerprints?'' I asked. ''Didn't they take anyone else's?''

His eyes refocused. ''No, I think they took everyone's. They would have searched all the rooms too, but Terry McPhail—he's one of the guests—asked the cops if they had a search warrant and started squawking about constitutional rights.''

''Are the police still at the spa?'' I asked, wondering why they had allowed Craig to drive to the airport.

''No,'' he said. Then he sighed. ''At least they weren't an hour ago. They left right before I drove out to pick you up. They'd been at the spa since I found Suzanne last night— actually it was this morning, just after midnight—asking questions, measuring things, searching." Panic was seeping into his voice again. He picked up speed. "Chief Orlandi said he'd be back this afternoon. I didn't like the way he stared at me when he said it."

Craig looked at me, his fear fully evident in his red, swollen eyes. He didn't just look like a wino anymore. He looked like a man on the run. Why was he so afraid? And why did the police think he killed Suzanne?

I cleared my throat and looked straight into his frightened eyes. "You didn't kill her, did you?" I asked.

"No!" he yelped. The intensity of his answer turned the heads of the last of the disembarking passengers.

"No," he repeated in a deeper, modulated tone. He closed his eyes for a few heartbeats. When he opened them again they were clear of panic. Then he straightened his shoulders. The wino persona dropped away. He began to look like a corporate leader again, albeit a rumpled one.

"Kate, look at me," he said in a nearly steady voice. "I've made mistakes. I've treated you badly, for one. I shouldn't have taken Suzanne to Spa Santé, for another. But I did not kill Suzanne. Believe me."

I looked into his sincere red eyes and believed him completely. Well, almost completely. "Then, who did?" I asked.

He began to crumble again, shoulders first. "I don't know. I don't know! I can't even believe it happened . . . but I saw her body. And the police! They haven't charged me, but I know they think I did it. I can see it on their faces." His voice was leaping in pitch with each word, his eyes darting wildly.

"Craig, we'll figure out who did this together," I promised rashly. Anything to alleviate his mounting hysteria. "But I'll need your help. Let's get the car and you can fill me in on the way."

The driving seemed to calm him. So I let him be as he guided the rented silver Toyota northeast on Highway 15 from San Diego to Lakeside County. But after twenty miles of brown hills and low dry shrubs, my need to know what had happened overtook my more tender sensibilities.

"So why do the police think you did it?" I asked.

"Because no one else makes sense," he answered after a moment of continued silence. I was relieved to hear the steadiness in his voice. "Spa Santé is pretty isolated. It's unlikely that a stranger would have been on the grounds last night, and none of the others staying at the spa knew Suzanne.'' He paused. ''Except for me,'' he added bitterly.

''Who are the others?'' I asked. ''Run them down for me.''

He sighed before speaking, but complied. ''First, there are the owners. Francisca and Bradley Beaumont. She's friendly, competent. From Hawaii originally.'' He pointed out the car window toward some orange groves that glittered in the mid-day sun before going on, more comfortable as a tour guide than an interrogatee. ''Bradley's a bit strange,'' he said.

''What do you mean 'strange'?'' I probed hopefully. ''Strange like Ted Bundy?''

''No, I don't mean that kind of strange,'' Craig snapped. He looked over at me with sudden anger in his eyes. The speed of the Toyota was accelerating with his temperature. ''It's bad enough that the police suspect me. I don't want to slander anyone else.''

''Damn it. Why did you ask me to come here?'' I asked sharply. I was getting angry myself. I didn't need to be here in the middle of nowhere, receiving a lecture on ethics from my ex-husband.

He turned his eyes away from me, pressing down on the gas pedal. The orange groves disappeared rapidly behind us.

''Craig?'' I had to know the answer.

''Because I need your support!'' he exploded.

''Is that all?'' I probed, all the while watching the road nervously.

Suddenly, he threw his head back and laughed shrilly, pressing the gas pedal even harder. Laughter had always been his way of coping. Nervous laughter, that is. But this was not mere nervous laughter, this was hysteria. Tears rolled out of his eyes. And he kept laughing. And sobbing. And laughing. And speeding. Damn. How well could he see the road with tears in his eyes? I gripped the handle of my suitcase, cramping my hand, and watched the miserable landscape whizzing by. Were we going to crash and die here on Highway 15? I held my breath.

Just as I had considered and rejected the idea of forcibly taking over control of the speeding car, his laughter and sobbing merged into a long gurgling sigh. ''I never have been able to lie to you,'' he said. His foot eased up on the gas.

I loosened my cramped hand and allowed myself to

breathe. He spoke again in a voice of forced calm. "I want you here because the police suspect me. Because I would too, if I were them. Because you've solved a murder." He glanced over at me, his swollen eyes pleading. "Figure this one out, Kate. If you don't, I don't know who will."

Was it time to tell him that I had only figured out that last murder by a fluke? That I couldn't save him? That he was doomed? I looked over at him and saw the wetness on his face left by his tears. And remembered his heavy foot on the pedal. No time for realism.

"I can try," I said softly. I realized I was trembling. "But only if you help me. You've got to tell me everything. Agreed?"

"Agreed," he said flatly, as if the feeling in his voice had been washed away by his tears.

"How is Bradley Beaumont strange?" I began again.

"He's just not exactly of this world." Craig let loose another sigh. "He walks around talking to himself. And laughing his weird laugh. Fran says he's a writer. Maybe that's it. You'll see when you meet him."

"Who else?"

"Their kid, Paul. He's just a teenager. And their handyman, Avery Haskell. That's all the staff that was there last night. And that's when Suzanne . . ." His voice broke. I tensed, waiting for the Toyota to accelerate again. But Craig didn't tromp the gas. He sucked in a series of deep breaths instead, and drove on in silence.

I glanced at his gaunt face and settled into silence myself. I wouldn't push him anymore. Not while he was driving, anyway.

The silence in the car provided a hospitable environment for self-recrimination. What the hell was I doing down here? Did I really know the man who drove in torment beside me? And what made me think I had even a chance at figuring out who had killed Suzanne? I closed my eyes and began relaxing my still-trembling body, starting with my scalp. Thirty miles later I had reached my ankles, further detours into fear and doubt having slowed my progress considerably, when Craig's voice brought me back to the inside of the Toyota and current reality.

"I'll tell you about the guests," he said. His words raced as fast as the Toyota had earlier. "Besides me and Suzanne''—he faltered and then rushed on—''this couple, Jack and Nikki. He claims to be a rock promoter or something. She's an actress, black and beautiful. There's a man in a wheelchair, Don. He's pretty quiet. Hangs around with the Beaumont's kid sometimes.'' He stopped for a moment to think and then rattled off the rest. ''Then there's Ruth Ziegler. She's a kick. I think she writes pop psychology books. And Terry. I mentioned him before. The one who insisted on a search warrant? Mr. Social Consciousness incarnate.'' He paused. ''Those are all the guests.''

''That's it?'' I asked incredulously. ''No one else? How can the Beaumonts make a living?''

''They just bought the spa. Got a good deal because it's been abandoned for years. They're rebuilding it bit by bit, and renting out the rooms that they've finished as they go. Ought to be a good investment if they handle it right.'' Providing hard information seemed to have done Craig good. Or maybe it was the preceding thirty miles of silence. His tone was conversational now, at ease. ''They've placed a few ads, like the one that I saw in the *Vegetarian Times*. Vegetarian cooking, by the way. You'll appreciate it. And Fran told me they expect more people this weekend. Some kind of weight-loss program.''

''Back to the people who were there last night,'' I said. ''They all claim they didn't know Suzanne?''

''That's what they say,'' he answered thoughtfully. He took a highway exit marked DELORES, then circled back under the freeway in the opposite direction of the signs pointing to that town. We drove along a tree-lined road for a mile or so. ''But you'll be able to ask them yourself. We're here.''

''Here'' was a gap in the trees with a tasteful cream-colored sign proclaiming ''Spa Santé, Hot Springs and Resort'' in brown script. As we drove through the gap I saw scattered stucco buildings of various shapes and sizes. A few sported sparkling white plaster exteriors, but most were brown and cracked with decay. Some were even missing sections of roofs and walls. Those in the worst condition were cordoned off by white nylon rope strung on wooden stakes. Flowers bloomed everywhere. Bursts of color from red geraniums, white alyssum, yellow pansies, richly purple violas and just-planted pink primroses reclaimed the faded beauty of the spa. Packed-earth paths flowed gracefully between the old and new buildings and around the flower beds. The whole compound was encircled by orange trees.

Craig pulled up beside the largest stucco building and parked. "Are you ready to meet people?" he asked.

I looked into his ravaged face and returned the question. "Are *you* ready?"

"Always ready, always willing, darlin'," he replied. An old joke of his. He twisted his face into a parody of his old easy grin. Watching him, I felt the sudden pressure of imminent tears once more. But I shook them off and twisted my own features into an answering smile.

"Lead on, Macduff," I said, misquoting Shakespeare in a show of camaraderie.

We walked up the stairs of the big building and across the large porch with a redwood bench and invitingly placed lounge chairs. Craig held open a glass door and waved me into an attractive lobby decorated in muted pastels. He hurried me past the registration desk. "They'll be in the dining hall. That's where everyone hangs out."

The dining hall was beyond another set of glass doors. I peered through the glass and saw a spacious room with high wood-beamed ceilings and large sunny windows. One long table with room for at least two dozen people dominated the center of the hall. A buffet extended the length of the side wall, and at least thirty smaller tables were scattered throughout the remaining expanse. The buffet and tables were made of dark lacquered wood. Many of the tables were brightened by fresh flower arrangements. A waist-high counter, complete with cash register, stood sentry at the front of the hall, but no one was on duty behind it.

As Craig and I opened the glass doors, the disconcerting sound of uninhibited laughter reached us.

I located the source of the sound. At the end of the long center table an older woman with short, frizzy grey hair was wiggling her finger at a weasel-faced man who looked to be about my age. He was frowning peevishly. Whatever the joke was, I would have bet it was at his expense. A bearded man in a wheelchair was talking softly to a teenage boy at a table by the windows, oblivious to the others in the room. The boy looked up at us, shouted "Mom!" and continued to listen to the bearded man's words.

The swinging doors to the kitchen opened, and a plump

Eurasian woman came bearing down on us, one arm clutching linen napkins, the other outstretched in my direction.

As I watched the five strangers, my skin prickled into goose bumps. Was one of these strangers a murderer?

Or—the thought crept into my mind before I could block it—was the murderer the man who had picked me up at the airport and now stood expectantly by my side?

- Two -

"HELLO, HELLO! I'm Fran Beaumont. Welcome to Spa Santé," bubbled the Eurasian woman musically. She smelled of fresh-cut apples and oranges. She dropped the napkins on a nearby table and clasped my hand in hers briefly. Up close, she wasn't really as plump as she had looked at a distance. It was just her baggy pink sweatshirt which gave that impression, as well as her soft moon-shaped face with features so delicately sketched as to seem an afterthought. "I'll bet you're Craig's wife. Bradley said you would come."

"Ex—" I began, but faltered. I glanced at Craig again. He looked uncomfortable but said nothing. Did he even know our current marital status?

A tremor of uncertainty traveled across Fran's soft face. I sympathized. Just what rules of etiquette govern when greeting the wife, or ex-wife, of a man whose girlfriend has just been murdered in your establishment?

"Just call me Kate," I said, mustering up a smile for her gracious attempt at Southern California hospitality.

"Oh, Kate," she said with a relieved rush of breath. She clasped my hand again. "I'm so glad you're here. We fixed up a room for you, no charge of course." No charge? Why no charge? But there was no opportunity to ask. Fran was rolling now. "And my husband, Bradley, says it will be safe. Really. He says it must have been a maniac, a Night Stalker, some random force of evil." Was this supposed to make me feel better? For the first time I felt real fear seeping into my consciousness. "But, on the other hand, if it was, well . . ." She paused.

"If what was what?" I asked.

She bent forward and whispered. "If the murderer was someone we know." I could see fear in those delicate eyes now. "What if they strike again?"

I shivered. And as I did, something slithered against my leg. Whoa! I jumped backwards and felt a piece of that something squish underneath my descending foot. A hell-born yowl of outrage propelled me forward again.

"Oh, God. I'm so sorry," said Fran, wringing her hands. She bent over and, with obvious effort, picked up an immense black ball of fur. "Roseanne, cut that out," she admonished. "Bradley says we should get rid of her, but . . ." She ended her sentence by burying her face in Roseanne's fur.

From the safety of Fran's arms, Roseanne glared up at me with glowing yellow eyes, as if daring me to tangle with her again.

"Good God," I said, now cold under the sweat that had drenched me when I stepped on her paw. "How much does that cat weigh?"

"Twenty-seven pounds," Fran answered. A blush suffused her round cheeks. "I've tried to put her on a diet, but she chews the bottoms out of her cat food bags and steals scraps and—"

"What an advertisement for a health spa," teased Craig. When Fran didn't smile he amended his comment. "The 'before' shot of course."

I laughed. Fran forced a weak smile. Roseanne stared at me appraisingly. Was I laughing at her? She flexed her claws.

"Kate," Fran whispered again. I looked into her eyes and saw that the fear I had almost forgotten was still there. "Craig says you might be able to figure out this . . ." Couldn't she spit out the word "murder"? "This . . . this thing. Please try. We'll do anything we can to help you. I've got to know."

"I'm not . . ." I began to object. But her eyes were so frightened. I turned and glared at Craig. Had he tried to pass me off as a detective? He quickly averted his eyes. Fran saw the exchange and retreated into hospitality once more.

"But of course you're welcome to stay, no matter what," she said with a tremulous smile. "I didn't mean to push you. Bradley says I suffer from foot-in-mouth disease. Just forget I asked."

Damn. I hated it when people did that to me. How could I gracefully refuse a retracted request?

"I'll be glad to pay for my room," I said. I meant it. I didn't want to be under any obligation to this frightened woman. Or to raise her hopes.

"No, no. We insist, don't we, Roseanne?" she said, gently setting the cat down on a chair with a fond pat. "Would you like to meet some of the other guests?" she added quickly, closing the subject of free accommodations.

I shrugged. I could always insist on paying her later.

As she turned to introduce me to the others, I noticed that all eyes were already upon us. Fran noticed one set of eyes in particular.

"Paul, what are you doing home?" she called to the teenager. "It's only two-thirty."

He mumbled something under his breath, his expression no friendlier than Roseanne's.

"Kids," Fran said with a forced laugh. "Paul, come say hello to Kate. She'll be staying with us for a while."

Paul rose from his seat slowly, nodding a goodbye to the bearded man in the wheelchair. He wasn't a bad-looking boy. Medium height and slender in his jeans and T-shirt. Adidas running shoes with the laces nonchalantly untied. His features were even, with just a touch of acne, under dark shaggy hair. If he had smiled, he might have been handsome. But he didn't. He kept his eyes lowered sullenly as he walked across the room.

He extended his hand to shake mine without making eye contact. "Paul," he muttered with the brief shake. His hand felt hot and dry. Then, "gotta go." He walked toward the glass doors.

"Wait a minute," said Fran. Paul stopped in his tracks. "As long as you're here, you might as well be useful. You can start setting the tables for dinner."

Paul rolled his eyes but complied silently. He picked up the napkins that Fran had set down and stomped to the other end of the room to begin placing them on the tables.

Fran sighed. "He's a good kid, really. Bradley says not to pay him any attention when he acts this way."

I wanted to meet Fran's husband, Bradley. According to Fran, he was a man with all the answers. Maybe he knew who murdered Suzanne. Or—

An insistent whirring sound interrupted my thought. The man in the wheelchair had rolled up. I focused my eyes on his bearded face, avoiding looking at his legs. His sea-blue eyes looked made for laughter. There were even old laugh lines radiating from them. But those lines were overlaid with lines of pain. And his eyes were filled with bitterness. How long had he been in the wheelchair?

I forced a smile and tried to dismiss my pity and fear. I could never get past those first reactions to a wheelchair-bound person. The fear that this could also happen to me, the physical pang of pity, and even the irrational guilt that it wasn't me in the wheelchair. But the man wasn't looking in my direction anyway. He was focused on Craig. I relaxed my face.

"I'm sorry," he said to Craig. His voice was low and gruff. "Wasn't your fault. Anything I can do, just ask."

"Thanks," answered Craig softly, his eyes moistening. This was interesting. Maybe the police suspected Craig, but if Fran and this man were any indication, the Spa Santé crowd didn't seem to share that suspicion.

The man turned his wheelchair in my direction with a short series of clicks and whirs. "Don Logan," he said holding out his hand.

"Kate Jasper," I replied and bent down to take his hand. It was calloused and had a strong grip. In fact, his whole upper body looked solidly muscular under the flannel shirt.

"Craig's sister?" he asked, looking at me with a spark of curiosity in those bitter blue eyes.

I was confused for a moment, then understood. Jasper, the same last name as Craig's. "No, no," I answered. "Craig's wife. I mean, former wife." How many times was I going to be asked that question? Maybe I should have reverted to my maiden name. But it was long, unpronounceable, and unfamiliar after fourteen years. "And Craig's friend," I added in explanation.

"Good," said Don solemnly. "Craig needs a friend right now."

His chair whirred backwards. "Good meeting you," he said and maneuvered past us and out the glass doors.

"Don's fantastic," said Fran after he was out of sight. "He's off to work out. He exercises religiously, every afternoon. Bradley says, with his chair and van and everything,

Don can do almost anything anyone else can." Bradley again. I was getting tired of Bradley. And I hadn't even met the man yet.

"We've fixed up a bunch of the units for the disabled," Fran continued. Her eyes were bright now, flickering with plans. "Wide doorways, ramps, grab-bars, special bathrooms. Our handyman Avery knows all about that stuff. He used to be a hospital aide. And then, when we have a few more special units finished, we're going to place some special ads. And then . . ." The brightness faded from Fran's eyes. "That is, if everything is cleared up."

No wonder she was worried. An unsolved murder could kill Spa Santé's business before it even got going. I wanted to comfort Fran. To tell her the police would clear up the murder. To tell her *I* would clear up the murder. But there was no reason to believe either scenario. I kept my mouth shut. I had already promised too much to Craig. Fran straightened her shoulders abruptly.

"Two-thirty and I haven't even started tonight's buffet," she said. "Craig, introduce Kate to Ruth and Terry, and I'll get back to the kitchen where I belong." With that, she hurried back through the kitchen doors and disappeared.

Craig introduced the frizzy grey-haired woman as Ruth Ziegler. Ruth immediately jumped up from her chair and engulfed me in an intense Leo Buscaglia hug. A bit demonstrative for a stranger, but living in Marin had inured me to this brand of New Age effusiveness. Then she held me at arm's length and surveyed my face as if it were a crystal ball. Her clothing was right for the occasion. A flowing purple caftan. And her face could have been a wise gypsy's, brown and crinkly with a long hooked nose, generous mouth and all-seeing black-button eyes.

"There's a lot of compassion in you, and intelligence," she announced finally. She gave me another quick hug and stepped back. I felt my face flushing. This kind of scrutiny was usually reserved for prospective in-laws.

"Craig needs plenty of support right now," she added. Great. Another member of the Craig Jasper fan club. Didn't any of these people see him as a murder suspect? "He needs to mourn properly. You can help him do that."

At least she wasn't asking me to play detective. But how was I supposed to help Craig mourn properly? Before I could form my thoughts into a coherent question, she had turned on Craig with an even more fervent hug than the one she had given me. I hoped it was what he needed.

The man at the table rose to introduce himself. He was a small slender man, shorter than I was, and probably lighter. He watched Ruth with a look of amusement on his long weasel face. His pinched nostrils quivered over a wispy greying mustache, and his close-set eyes were smiling under wire-rimmed glasses. His clothing was not amused however. His duckbill-cap demanded "Food Not Bombs" over badly cut brown hair, and his T-shirt ordered "CIA Out of Central America." I groaned to myself. Aggressive social consciousness always sparks my own guilt over good causes long ignored, marches unjoined and contribution requests unpaid.

"Terry McPhail," he said and offered his slight hand for shaking.

"Kate," I replied shortly as I pumped his hand. No use confusing him with my surname.

"Ruth thinks a hug can cure everything," he said, with a thumb pointed in her direction. She still had Craig locked in her loving grip.

"And Terry thinks political activism will solve everything," came her retort, muffled by Craig's chest. "But only eventually. And meanwhile, as we wait, we must suffer nobly." She released Craig and held him at arm's length, as she had done with me. "At least a hug is immediate," she concluded.

I began a question for Terry. "Is Ruth your . . . ?" Mother, girlfriend, wife? I figured Terry was about my age. Ruth must have been at least twenty years his senior.

"No," he answered with a chuckle. "I've just met her. We just argue like family."

Ruth motioned us all to join them at the end of the long table. I sank gratefully into a chair. Craig sat next to her, his eyes bleary again.

"The lecture begins," warned Terry as he took his seat.

Ruth reached for Craig's hand and held it. She peered into his eyes. He stared back, mesmerized. I began to fidget, uncomfortable in this role of intimate observer. "Don't deny your grief," she advised him. "You have to pass through the tears, the fears, the anger, the guilt. But there will come an end to the worst of the mourning. If you don't hold back."

"Give sorrow words," Terry added softly. "The grief that does not speak whispers the o'er-fraught heart and bids it break."

Ruth turned to Terry, her eyes wide with astonishment. "Shakespeare?" she asked.

"Macbeth," he confirmed.

"And I thought all you read was the *People's Daily World,*" Ruth said.

Terry's face went pink. He opened his mouth to respond but was cut off by the bark of Craig's laughter. We all turned to stare at him. His head was thrown back and tears glistened in his eyes as he laughed uncontrollably. He quickly subsided into a few muffled snorts as we watched.

"I'm sorry," he said, choking back the last of the snorts. "It's not you—"

"We understand," said Ruth gently. Did we? I wondered.

"Hey, man, it's okay," added Terry. "But let me give you some real advice. Don't let the cops hassle you. Stand up for your rights." Craig's face paled in response. "They'll pull all kinds of shit if they want to hang this one on you."

This was not what Craig needed to hear, true or untrue. Ruth and I sat up to object in unison.

"Terry—" she began.

"Craig—" I said.

"So how are you all getting along?" asked a voice from above us. Fran had returned to our table with a friendly smile and a tray of condiments.

The startled silence lasted only a few seconds.

"Have a seat," offered Terry expansively. Fran sat down, still smiling. "I was just filling Craig in on what he can expect from the local Gestapo."

"I don't think—" I began.

"That's okay," said Craig softly. His face was still white. A muscle was twitching underneath his cheekbone. "I want to know the worst."

"Listen, man," said Terry. He certainly wasn't quoting Shakespeare now. "I read this story in *Mother Jones* about this guy they coerced a confession from. They kept him up for twenty-four hours, fed him phony information, played with his mind and convinced him he had killed a woman in an alcoholic blackout—and he wasn't even drinking at the time. If his family hadn't had the bucks, he would be on death row now, but they hired some attorneys who got the confession suppressed.''

''That isn't the situation here,'' objected Ruth. ''Chief Orlandi isn't like that. He's a fair and decent man.'' That was good to hear.

''All cops are potentially corrupt. It's built into the system. Orlandi and his friends are gone for the moment but they'll be back. Just wait till the local powers-that-be in Delores start pressuring Orlandi to solve this thing. He'll do anything to solve it, including manufacturing a murderer. Start leaning on Craig. Start leaning on witnesses. Just think of the pressure he can put on Fran here. Threaten to shut down her operation for all sorts of code violations—''

An explosion of sobs interrupted his monologue. For a moment I thought Craig had finally broken down completely. But the source of the sobs was Fran, not Craig. Craig just looked white and stunned. Fran had buried her head in her hands as her whole body convulsed with the impact of her loud weeping.

''Terry, stop it!'' ordered Ruth.

Terry complied instantly, snapping his mouth shut in surprise.

Ruth rose from her chair and bent over Fran to give her an all-healing hug. Fran continued to weep, bursting into fragmented wailing phrases with every other sob. ''Oh God . . . So afraid . . . Bradley says.''

The rest of us sat uncomfortably transfixed while Fran cried herself out. Gradually, her sobbing and wailing tapered off. Ruth stepped back, and Fran's soft face emerged pink and puffy, her delicate eyes nearly swollen shut.

''Sorry,'' she breathed.

''No, *I'm* sorry,'' said Terry, eager to redeem himself. ''I didn't think. I just thought that some information—''

''You're forgiven, Terry,'' said Ruth sharply. ''Why don't you quit while you're ahead?''

I began to laugh, comic relief pushing the tension from my head. Fran and Craig joined in. Terry even managed a weak smile. And Ruth beamed at us as if we were students who had learned the lesson correctly. Once the laughter was over, there seemed little left to say.

Fran reached into her pocket and pulled out a key. ''Kate,

why don't you get settled in your room? It's all made up for you."

As I thanked her for the key I was assailed with a physical pang of longing for the privacy of my own room. Away from involuntary hugs, uncontrollable laughter, sobbing, police horror stories and the company of possible murderers. Because there was a good chance that someone I had met here had murdered Suzanne. Or someone I had yet to meet.

I got up to leave and waved a quick goodbye, nice-to-have-met you, to the assembled group before heading gratefully to the glass doors.

"Wait," called Craig as I pushed a door open. "Your suitcase is still in the car."

I turned my head to look at him as the rest of me continued its forward progress. And walked smack into a solid and silent human body.

- Three -

I DIDN'T HAVE to look up to know the body was human—and
male. The giveaway was the smell of testosterone-tinged work
sweat. Not to mention the hair sprouting from the open-
necked denim workshirt an inch away from my face.

"Jesus!" I yelped and jumped back. Someday I would
learn to watch where I was going.

I looked up in time to see the flicker of distaste that crossed
the face of the silent man before me. Too late, I noticed the
silver cross nestled among his chest hairs.

"Sorry," I said.

But the man said nothing. And didn't move at all as I
looked up at him. My skin crawled. Was he mute? He was a
solidly built man. I could attest to that, having just collided
with him. But there was something about him that reminded
me of a ghost. Bleached, that was it. His hair was a red-
brown, but his eyebrows and mustache were blond-edged.
His blue eyes looked watered down. And his freckled skin
looked faded, as if the color should have been richer.

"Excuse me, ma'am," he said finally, his voice low and
toneless.

I jumped again. I had become used to his silence. He
walked slowly past me into the dining hall without another
word.

And past Craig who had come up to join me.

"Making friends everywhere, I see," Craig said.

I ignored the sarcasm. "Who was that?" I asked him.

"Avery Haskell, handyman."

"God, he's spooky. Is he always so quiet?"

"Just ask him about the Lord. He'll talk," said Craig.

"Born again?"

"Very," he answered shortly. No jokes. Unusual for Craig, who usually launched into a monologue worthy of *Saturday Night Live* when faced with even a trace of evangelistic fervor. I looked up and saw exhaustion tightening his features. A pang of guilt reminded me of what he had been through in the last twenty-four hours.

"Just give me the keys and I'll get my suitcase," I said softly.

"No, no," he insisted, giving himself a visible shake. "I'll get it."

Once he had the suitcase out of the car, we walked without speaking down a dirt path, packed hard by decades of visitors' feet, passing one of the roped-off buildings. The thin October sunlight felt good on my shoulders. I looked up and noticed the glowing day for the first time. And looked down at the ground where red and pink geraniums mingled with white daisies along our path. Fran's work, I would have bet. Fran. That reminded me.

"Who'd you tell I was a detective?" I asked sharply.

Craig's cheeks flushed. "I never said you were a detective. I-I just told Fran about how you got involved in a murder before."

"Anyone else?"

"Well . . ." Craig lowered his eyes. "Just Chief Orlandi."

"The policeman who's heading the investigation!" I yelped indignantly. "I can't believe you told him about me!"

"Just wait until you meet Orlandi," Craig muttered, eyes still downcast. "You'll be surprised what falls out of your mouth." He walked a few more steps and added defensively, "Anyway, I didn't tell him you were a suspect or anything. I just told him you helped solve a murder before."

I snorted. Wonderful, I thought. The police are going to love the idea of an amateur getting involved in this. But Craig looked miserable enough. I didn't pursue the thought any further as we trudged along, and we trudged for a long time. We must have covered a half a mile in silence, passing nothing but orange trees and abandoned buildings on the way.

The spa's facilities seemed to have been scattered randomly on its vast acreage. I wondered if this was part of the health plan. If I had to walk half a mile to a meal—and who knows how many more miles to sample the various baths, tubs and pools—I couldn't avoid getting in shape, simply from the exercise. On the other hand, I might have a heart attack.

"How much farther?" I asked as we came around a bend in the dirt path.

"We're almost there," Craig assured me. I was glad he was carrying my suitcase.

We circled a stand of orange trees. Craig pointed at the large gleaming white stucco structure now fully visible.

We came around a bend in the dirt path. Craig pointed at the large gleaming white stucco structure in front of us.

"This is it," he said. "Rose Court. It's built Spanish style, around a courtyard with a rose garden. They're still working on the interiors."

"How come you know all about the building?" I asked.

"My room—our room—was in there, but I . . ." He looked at me, eyes full of fear. "I couldn't stay there after Suzanne died." His voice quavered. "So I paid the difference and had Fran move me to the next building. I . . . I . . ."

"That's okay," I said quickly. Craig probably did need to mourn, maybe to lament loudly and tear his hair, but I just couldn't handle any more emotionalism without some time off.

"I'm next door in the Orange Blossom Building now," he said after a few breaths, his voice a little steadier. "Room five."

"Honey," I began and immediately regretted the endearment. "Craig," I started over. "Why don't you take a nap? It'll do you good."

"Maybe I will," he answered, dropping the suitcase. And then with a weak smile he added, "Thanks, Mom," and turned to leave.

I stood standing in front of Rose Court for a moment, watching Craig shuffle toward the Orange Blossom Building. I heard a bird warble, and smiled. Then I heard a high-pitched cackle reminiscent of the loon's call of distress. I stood very still. I had heard a cackle like that before, but it hadn't been a bird's call; it had been a human's. I had heard it while working in a mental hospital.

I turned quickly to look behind me, but saw only a dirt

path, a few decaying buildings and a lot of flowers. I shivered and picked up my suitcase.

The lobby of Rose Court was painted in decorator pastels. A soft-sculpture cactus stood in one corner, a tasteful listing of room locations in the other. I looked at the number on my key, went up the stairs to the second floor and opened the door to my room.

Good God! Was this one of the interiors they had refurbished? I hoped not. I hoped for Fran's sake that they hadn't put money into this psychedelic-rustic decor. The curtains were saffron-yellow. The peeling wallpaper was paisley. Orange, mustard, russet and black paisley. And the furniture was painted liver-brown with orange leatherette trim. At least the bedspread was a restful salmon shade. But then again, it didn't match the rest of the room. No wonder Fran wasn't charging me.

Suddenly nauseated by a mixture of tension and paisley, I flopped onto the bed and stared up at the white plaster ceiling. My brain instantly began sorting through the day's impressions. And suspects. Fran? Would she kill to protect her investment in Spa Santé? Or to protect her son, Paul? Or her mysterious husband, Bradley? And how about that spooky handyman, Avery? I shivered. He had the requisite personality for a mass murderer in my book. Or Don Logan, confined to a wheelchair? Or Ruth? Maybe she hugged Suzanne to death. Or Terry . . . ?

Suddenly it hit me. Almost everyone had been sympathetic to Craig, but no one had mentioned Suzanne with regret. No one had mentioned her at all. No "such a lovely girl" or "what a tragedy." Why not? Because they didn't know her? But they didn't know Craig either, and they spoke to him as a friend. What did these people think of Suzanne?

The question pulled me up into a sitting position at the end of the bed. I had disliked Suzanne instinctively when I met her. Tall, beautiful, competitive and arrogant, she had not made a good impression on me. But then I could have hardly failed to dislike her. She was the woman Craig had preferred to me. But how about these spa people? Had she offended them? All of them, any of them? Maybe enough to incite murder? Or were they just avoiding her name in deference to Craig's feelings?

Just what had gone on at Spa Santé before Suzanne's death?

I hit the bed with the palm of my hand. No more Ms. Sensitivity. I would force Craig to tell me. I jumped up, ready to charge over to the Orange Blossom Building. But I stopped before I got to the door. How much of a nap could Craig have had in twenty minutes? Damn.

I put the questions on hold. I would give Craig more time to sleep. Then I would interrogate him mercilessly.

I spent the next half-hour on the telephone. I called in to my business, Jest Gifts, and told my warehousewoman, Judy, that I was no longer in my Marin office doing necessary paperwork but in Southern California for an impromptu vacation. After a series of squawks that forced the telephone receiver from my ear, I told her my ex-husband was very ill. Not completely a lie. He was sick with worry. Her squawks grew quieter. Then I promised I'd get everyone their pay checks in time for next week's payday. The squawks ceased entirely. She even sent her get-well wishes to Craig before hanging up.

My phone call to Wayne was more difficult. Right off, I told him I wasn't getting involved with sleuthing. But after my protracted description of Spa Santé's inhabitants and events, he pointed out that I was already into it up to my ears. Then he quietly reminded me that he loved me. No pleas, commands or warnings. Just a quiet reminder.

I hung up the phone thinking of Wayne and how I had learned to love him. I smiled as I pictured his homely, kind face in my mind and considered his parting words. Then a disconcerting train of thought came roaring through.

If Wayne were to die, I would eulogize him: *He was such a good, kind, loving and intelligent man. How can I live without him?* I even felt a momentary clutch of grief imagining the event. But Craig wasn't eulogizing Suzanne any more than the rest of the spa people were! Had he loved Suzanne? He was sobbing a lot, but was he really mourning her death? Or was he just afraid? Everyone reacts to loss differently, I told myself impatiently, not to mention love. But still . . . Craig just wasn't acting like my idea of a man who had lost the woman he loved.

I looked at my watch. My ex-husband had had enough time to sleep. I strode from the paisley room determined to find him.

But Craig didn't answer my knock on his door. I left the

Orange Blossom Building and headed back over to the dining hall. I was almost to the main building when I heard the popping of gravel and Indian-style war whoops.

Looking up, I saw a motorcycle skidding into the gravel parking lot. The curve of the skid pulled the cycle nearly parallel to the ground, but it righted itself before it came to a final stop. Two people jumped off. One laughing driver and one angry passenger. ,

The driver was a smiling red-haired man with a friendly beat-up face. He wasn't dressed for motorcycle-riding. No helmet, no boots. Only a white muscle shirt, cut-off jeans and high-top sneakers. His face wasn't at all handsome. His eyes bulged and his teeth protruded. But his broad smile was attractive. His nose looked like it had been broken a few times. I could see why. "Whooee. Whooee, baby," he was warbling to his companion. "Lighten up and live a little."

He reached to embrace her. She turned from him, her long-legged, dark-skinned body rigid. I could see she was a female and guessed that she was black. Her tank-top and leopard pants did nothing to conceal the perfectly formed body. But I couldn't see her face under her crash helmet. It was a good guess she wasn't smiling, though.

"Grow up!" she shrieked. She turned back to him, lowering her voice into a plea. "You're going to kill yourself if you keep riding like that, Jack."

"Or someone else," came a low voice behind me. My heart jumped in my chest. I turned and saw Avery Haskell standing at my side. He stood watching the pair of riders as if he hadn't said anything to me. Was he trying to be spooky? As if in answer, he turned and walked up the stairs of the main building, stopping briefly to nod at Don Logan, who was watching the whole scene from his wheelchair on the porch.

The redheaded biker lifted the helmet of his companion's head and kissed her fully on the mouth. "You know I'm indestructible, baby. Ain't nothing going to harm me." He brought his cupped hands up to his mouth and blew a jazz riff through them as if they were a trumpet.

She pushed him away, but a smile was creeping over her face. Her beautiful face. She was movie-star beautiful, with large, clear, wide-set eyes under perfectly arched brows, luminous cocoa-colored skin, delicately flared nostrils and a sensual mouth with perfect, gleaming white teeth.

He lifted her off the ground and twirled around like a manic ballet dancer. Her curly black hair ruffled as they moved.

She shrieked, "Put me down! Put me down!" But she was laughing now, like a kid with her daddy. Their ages were right for the roles. She didn't look much more than twenty years old, and he had to be over forty.

He set her down, and they held onto each other, laughing. When he kissed her again I began to feel like the voyeur that I was. At least Avery Haskell had the decency to absent himself before things got sexy.

I lowered my gaze and turned to leave.

"Hey, pretty lady," I heard the red-haired man shout.

I glanced back over my shoulder. He shouted, "Yeah, you!"

The young woman smiled at me and rolled her eyes heavenward as if to say, "He's obnoxious but harmless."

I smiled back. If she didn't mind his calling me "pretty lady," I didn't either.

"You Craig's old lady?" asked the man as he danced toward me, dragging his young friend along. "Fran said you were coming."

"I'm Craig's friend Kate," I said carefully.

"I'm Nikki Martin," said the woman politely. "And this is Jack," she said, pointing at the redhead with an affectionate grimace.

"Baby, you say that like I'm a disease," Jack said, pulling Nikki to him playfully. She rolled her eyes once more.

"I knew Suzanne," I said on a sudden inspiration. These folks might just talk about Suzanne if prompted. They certainly weren't shy.

"Man, Suzanne was some good-looking woman," Jack said, shaking his head sadly, his expression suddenly serious. He looked old and naked without his smile.

"And she sure knew how to throw it in men's faces," added Nikki. Her bitter tone and expression held no affection for the dead woman.

"She was a cock-tease," agreed Jack, a little smile of memory lighting up his face. "Jeez, she even came on to that kid Paul."

"When she wasn't busy hitting on you," Nikki threw in.

"Hey, you know she didn't have a chance with you around, baby." He gave Nikki an extravagant leer. She lowered her eyes coquettishly. "Pissed her off, too."

"Who, Suzanne?" I asked.

"Yeah," he answered. "That lady had to be the belle of the ball, the most beautiful woman in any room. And she just couldn't be. Not when Nikki was around." I looked at Nikki's stunning face and body and saw that he was right. Suzanne had been beautiful, but not that beautiful. I smiled with the thought of how that must have frustrated Suzanne's competitive spirit, before guiltily remembering that Suzanne was now dead.

"Pissed Craig off too," Jack continued.

"What?" I asked, startled.

"Suzanne's cock-teasing. Didn't set well with old Craig at all. He wasn't hip to her games. Didn't realize it was all a tease."

Damn, I thought. The elusive motive.

My thoughts must have shown on my face.

"Hey, man," he said. "It was no big thing. She just got under his skin a little."

"Jack, you talk too much," said Nikki sharply. He certainly did. I just hoped he hadn't talked like this to the police.

"That's all right," I said, attempting a nonchalant smile. But it wasn't all right at all. I was desperately trying to rid my mind of the image of an enraged Craig throttling Suzanne. And in the midst of that image I realized I still didn't know exactly how Suzanne had been killed. There were far too many things that I didn't know.

"It was nice meeting you," Nikki was saying politely while looking over my shoulder. She tugged on Jack's arm, impatient to leave. I turned to follow her glance and saw why. Craig was walking up the path in our direction.

"Hey, man. How ya doin'?" Jack shouted to him.

"Okay," said Craig. "How are you?"

Nikki tugged on Jack's arm again. This time she nearly pulled him off his feet. "I guess I'm moving," said Jack. "The old lady's in a big hurry. Can't wait to get me back to the bedroom." He winked largely and let out a braying laugh.

Craig managed an answering smile. Then Nikki and Jack ran stumbling down the path, wrestling and embracing as they went. I sighed with envy. I wanted to be at home, snug-

gling with my own sweetie. But I wasn't. I was at Spa Santé,
coddling a suspected murderer. I hardened my heart and will,
straightened my shoulders, and turned to Craig.

"I want to know everything," I said, keeping my voice
low and unyielding. He flinched at the tone. "And I want to
know it now."

– Four –

"EVERYTHING?" Craig asked. His eyes were wide with surprise. Or fear.

"Yes, everything," I repeated resolutely. "When did the two of you come to Spa Santé? Who did Suzanne talk to? What did she talk about? How did people respond to her? I want to know every unpleasantness, every angry word, every dirty look. Do you understand?"

He nodded, eyes still wide.

"And I want to know exactly how she died."

A bark of bitter laughter exploded from his lips. "That's all?" he inquired sarcastically.

"No, that's not all," I answered seriously. "I also want to know how you really felt about Suzanne."

Craig abruptly hunched into his shoulders and thrust his head forward. "I was sick to death of her," he hissed. My body recoiled with the violence of his response. But he didn't seem to notice, and continued in a low, intense whisper. "Constantly picking fights, flirting, complaining, nagging. I wanted out, but I didn't know how to tell her. You didn't tell Suzanne anything she didn't want to hear."

He stopped his tirade as suddenly as he had begun, and swiveled his head around to see if there was anyone close enough to hear. There was no one left in the parking lot, only Don Logan still on the porch out of earshot. "Let's find somewhere we can talk," Craig said softly in my ear.

I nodded silently, too stunned by his outburst to speak. Craig marched up one of the dirt paths, his footsteps angry on the packed earth. I plodded along after him, and wondered. What if he had killed Suzanne? It hadn't seemed a real possibility before. But the unexpected intensity of his whispered words had frightened me. Did I just toddle on home now? Forget the whole thing had happened?

Craig slowed his footsteps and turned to me, waiting for me to catch up. "It wasn't always like that with Suzanne," he said as I reached him. His voice had lost its violence. "When I first met her she looked up to me. She listened to my business strategies. Emulated my health regime. She even took up vegetarianism—for a while, anyway. And I began running with her. She called me her 'success mentor.' " His tone went bitter again on the last two words.

We walked along side by side as Craig brooded. "I still don't know why she latched onto me," he burst out. "The challenge of a married man? Or maybe she thought my financial success would rub off on her. To her, I was a winner, and winning was what mattered to Suzanne. I'll tell you, though. All that attention and appreciation was very seductive. Especially since you resented my success."

"Wait a minute," I objected, stopping in my tracks. "I never resented your success. You were the one who was tired of me." Craig stopped, turned and stared at me, openmouthed.

I stared back. And thought of that year when we had continually separated and reconciled and separated again. I looked into his brown puppy-eyes and remembered his seemingly constant criticism of my 'negative attitude,' my downscale clothing and my barely profitable business. The criticism had seemed a bitter cup, especially after the years I had spent as his business manager, babying his computer-software house into the prosperity referred to. Had my stubborn resistance to an upwardly mobile life-style felt like a personal rejection to him? The answer in his eyes was obviously yes.

We all see the same events through a different kaleidoscope. For the first time, I glimpsed his view. And it shook me.

I lowered my eyes, forfeiting the staring match. "Back to Suzanne," I said, in as brisk a tone as I could manage.

Craig lowered his own gaze and we began to walk again, avoiding, by unspoken mutual agreement, the questions of the past.

"Suzanne changed," he said. "When I first met her I saw

this bright, beautiful, committed young woman who thought I knew everything. But after a while, she realized I didn't know everything. And the things I did know weren't enough for her. She wasn't satisfied at work either. Uncle Eli had her doing 'shit-work.' At least that's what she said. Uncle Eli—''

''Who is Uncle Eli?'' I asked. We had reached the end of the dirt path. I gestured toward the stone bench beneath an orange tree.

''He's one of the founding partners of the law firm Suzanne worked for,'' Craig said, taking a seat. ''Rosen, Chang and Ostrow.'' I flinched. *That* Uncle Eli? The lawyer who was responsible for our divorce. Craig continued, oblivious of my reaction. And he's Suzanne's uncle. Eli's watched out for Suzanne ever since her mother died. He even gave her a job in his firm, once she passed the bar exam. But he wanted her to start at the bottom. Uncontested divorces, simple wills, DUI's—''

''What are DUI's?''

''Driving Under the Influence. Actually she liked those. Once in a while she could save someone's license with a little fancy footwork. But what she really wanted to be was a frontline trial attorney—Melvin Belli, but better-looking. Her idea of paradise was being engaged in a loud, messy custody battle or defending a major felon. She wanted to get in there and fight. In court and in life. She loved to argue and she loved to win.''

''She won you from me,'' I said softly, looking over at his tension-ravaged face with unexpected pity.

Craig kept his eyes down. ''I guess that was the game,'' he mumbled. ''Anyway,'' he went on, shaking his head as if to rid himself of disturbing thoughts, ''Suzanne had had it with Uncle Eli. She was talking about striking out on her own. One of her law school buddies had invited her into a partnership in criminal defense work. Lots of drug dealers, lots of bucks—''

''No!'' The shout rang out, cutting off Craig's sentence.

I looked up and saw Fran's son, Paul, running down one of the many dirt paths in our direction. The handyman, Avery Haskell, was close behind him. I jumped to my feet and centered myself in a tai chi posture, ready to protect the boy from Haskell. But Craig laid a restraining hand on mine.

''The kid's just upset,'' Craig said gently. As Paul came

to a sudden stop midway down the path, I saw that Craig was right.

The boy put his hands to his streaming eyes and turned to Haskell. "No!" he shouted once more. "It's not fair. It's all bullshit!" His shrill voice pierced the air. Birds flew up from the trees behind us.

Haskell put a hand on the boy's shoulder, murmuring something inaudible. The boy shook his head violently. Disjointed pieces of what he was saying floated to us through his sobs. "She didn't care . . . I can't . . . not fair." He wrenched his shoulder out from under Haskell's hand, shouting "No!" once more, and raced back the way he had come.

Haskell stood silently for a moment, looking after the boy as he ran. His eyes seemed to glisten with sorrow. Aha, I thought. The spooky handyman does have human feelings. But, just as that thought touched my mind, Haskell lowered those eyes and saw us on the bench. Instantly, the veil came down. His eyes became a zombie's once more. He nodded in our direction politely and walked slowly away.

"Good God," I said. "What was that all about?"

"The joys of adolescence," Craig responded.

I turned to him. "How did you know that Paul was just upset?" I asked.

"That kid's been like this ever since we got here. And it got worse when Suzanne would tease him. He's a troubled kid, to put it mildly. Fran is too obsessed by the spa and her husband, Bradley, to pay much motherly attention to Paul. And Bradley . . ." Craig paused. "Bradley's too obsessed with himself to notice much of anything going on around him. Zo, das iss my diagnosis," he finished in a heavy Freudian accent. "But Ruth could probably give you a better opinion," he added as a serious afterthought.

"What did Suzanne—" I began.

A high-pitched loon's cackle broke into my sentence from somewhere behind us. I jumped up and turned to look. But I saw orange trees and nothing else. Then the cackle erupted again.

"What the hell was that?" I demanded.

"What was what?" Craig returned my question, his eyes wide with incomprehension.

"That laugh," I answered, shivering. "You must have heard it."

"Oh, that," he said lightly. "That's just Bradley. You know, Fran's husband."

"That's Bradley!" I shouted. "Why didn't you tell me he was crazy?"

Craig pulled his head back, startled by the intensity of my words. "That's just how the man laughs," he explained in a voice of forced reason. But then his face grew troubled. "Suzanne thought he was crazy, too."

"Tell me about it," I ordered. Now we were getting somewhere.

"But Suzanne was hypercritical of everyone," Craig continued, ignoring my order. He looked into my eyes; then suddenly he was looking through me again.

"It's hard to explain Suzanne," he said softly. "Her father walked out on her and her mother when Suzanne was thirteen. He went back to Sweden. Then Suzanne's mother proceeded to drink herself to death. When her mom died, Suzanne came up from L.A. to San Francisco. To live with her mother's brother, Uncle Eli. Sometimes I wonder if Suzanne's arguing and criticizing and complaining was really a bid for attention. Or for love. Acting out the adolescence she never had." His eyes came back into focus slowly.

"That's why I couldn't just walk out on her," he said, looking for sympathy in my eyes. "For all the garbage she threw at me, I-I still felt sorry for her. Can you understand that?"

I nodded. I was beginning to feel sorry for her myself. As well as for Craig, mired in ambivalence. But I wasn't there to sympathize.

"Tell me how the people here at the spa felt about her," I demanded.

"She wasn't a big hit," he said sourly. "She flirted with that poor kid Paul, drove him crazy. She made fun of Terry's political idealism, told Bradley Beaumont he was a 'loony' to his face, called Jack on his 'rock-promoter' pose, drove Jack's girlfriend nuts by flirting with him, and generally bitched and moaned to everyone who would listen."

"About what?" I asked.

"About the food. About the inadequate company at the spa—meaning everyone here. About me. About her job. About her uncle. You name it." Craig smiled a very tired, self-mocking smile. "This from the woman who was impressed by my positivism. Needless to say, I wasn't very happy with her either.''

Just how unhappy had he been? I shook the question from my mind and asked a different one. ''So, who did she really get to?''

He rested his chin on his hand and thought for a while before answering. ''No one person more than anyone else,'' he said finally. ''No one that she made mad enough to kill her. Not that I could see.''

But someone must have. Craig saw the look in my eye.

''Don't you think I'd tell you if I knew? If I even had a suspicion?'' he asked bitterly. ''Let's face it. The only other alternative is me.''

''But Bradley—'' I began.

A whirring sound came toward us. I looked up and saw Don Logan in his wheelchair. Damn. Craig and I exchanged frustrated glances. With all the paths that webbed the spa grounds, how come everyone came down this one?

''Where can we talk in private?'' I whispered, once Logan had passed.

''My room, or yours,'' Craig said. His voice was soft and wistful.

''Does your room have paisley wallpaper?'' I asked brusquely.

He shook his head.

''Yours,'' I said.

''Nice room,'' I commented a half-mile later. And it was. Craig's new room was white with subtle peach and aqua accents. A framed poster of Monet's restful ''Poppy Field'' was the only decoration. It even smelled fresher than my room. I sighed with envy.

On the long walk to his room Craig had advised me to get the history of Spa Santé from Fran. According to her, the psychedelic paisley in my room had been installed by the last owners, a cult that had restored most of the spa in 1970 and whose precepts included vegetarianism, spiritual practice and group sex. The usual formula for the early seventies. They had lasted close to three years before going under.

I sat down in a softly upholstered aqua easy chair and sighed once more.

''You could stay here,'' Craig whispered. I looked at him and saw his puppy-dog eyes filled with longing. And pleading. Was he simply yearning for human companionship? Or was he pleading for the old conjugal pleasures?

"You mean we could switch rooms?" I asked, filling my voice with innocence. "I wouldn't mind that."

Hurt replaced the longing in his eyes. "Kate, you know what I—"

I cut him off. "Tell me about the body."

"What?" said Craig, his head bouncing back as if he'd been slapped.

"Suzanne's body. You found it. What did it look like?" Cruel, but effective. All vestiges of pleading were wiped from Craig's face. The lines of tension had returned.

"I suppose you want it from the start," he said.

I nodded. He sighed deeply, like a tired dog.

"Better you than Chief Orlandi again," he muttered. Then he sat down on the end of the bed and took a big breath.

"The last time I saw Suzanne was around eight o'clock last night. Before that, we had eaten dinner in the dining hall. Everyone was there. Suzanne was complaining—same old stuff. If she had wanted health food, we could have stayed home. Where was the room service? And the wallpaper—we had one of the paisley rooms, they're cheaper—why couldn't I put out the money for one of the nicer rooms? She said she was sick of her job. Sick of uncontested divorces, DUI's, adoptions, et cetera. Sick of Uncle Eli. Sick of me."

"So, what did you say?"

Craig flushed. "I told her I was getting sick of her, too." He looked down at his lap. "I may have yelled a little."

Damn. I could imagine what he called yelling "a little." When we were married, things would fall off the walls from the volume of his voice before he even noticed he had raised it. But he had never struck me. He wouldn't have considered it. His violence had been limited to his mouth. It was heartening to remember that.

"Then what?" I asked.

"Then we came back to our room," he answered glumly. "And argued some more."

"About what?"

"Same old stuff. I told her she ought to be nicer, stop antagonizing people. She told me I wasn't the man she had thought I was. I may have told her to . . ." His voice trailed off.

"To what?"

"To go fuck herself," he answered in a small voice. He looked up at me, his eyes begging for understanding.

"Did you yell that too?" I asked.

"I suppose."

Great. Had someone heard him? "So then what happened?"

"She got dressed to go jogging. She had already run her six miles that day, but she wanted to run some more. I offered to go with her. It was dark by then. But she said, 'Don't bother. You can't keep up anyway.' Which was true. I had never developed her speed. Or stamina. She put on her Reeboks and left."

"And?"

"And . . . that was the last time I saw her alive. God, I wish I hadn't yelled at her," he said, his eyes filling with tears. "But she really was impossible. I didn't know . . ." His words trailed off into a sob. He put his head into his hands and wept loudly, tears leaking through his fingers.

I went to the bathroom and found a box of Kleenex. I came back and handed it to Craig. He blew his nose loudly. Then he went on as if he had never stopped.

"So, I got out my *Computerworld* and read for a while. After a couple of hours had passed I began to worry, but I figured she was just staying out to bug me, so I pulled out *Inc* magazine and read it cover to cover. It was almost twelve o'clock by the time I finished it. I wasn't sure whether to be mad or concerned. Suzanne hadn't pulled this particular stunt before.

"I went out to look for her. The moon was almost full, so I could see fairly well. I walked the perimeter of the spa on the path that she usually ran. Nothing there. Then I went up and down all the paths, calling her name—not very loud because I knew I'd feel like an idiot if she was with someone else. The second time I passed this one open-air mud bath, I circled around and looked in the entrance. And I saw her. Her blond hair was shiny in the moonlight.

"I called out 'Suzanne,' and wondered what she was doing there. Then I noticed that there was something wrong with her body. It was face down . . . and crumpled. I moved closer. She looked . . . She looked like a cat had dragged her through gravel. Her shirt and shorts were shredded and dirty. Her legs had little cuts and scrapes all over them. Her neck looked wrong. And she wasn't breathing.

"Then I bent down and touched her arm. Her skin wasn't warm enough."

He stopped speaking and stared into space with glassy eyes. I shivered.

"Craig," I said gently after a few endless moments had passed.

His eyes came slowly into focus.

"Sorry," he said softly and resumed his story. "I guess I panicked after I realized she was dead. I ran and knocked on the doors of the main building. You know the rest."

"The police," I prodded.

"Orlandi," he whispered. He shook his head violently, as if clearing it of bad thoughts. Then he continued. "By the time it was daylight the coroners had taken Suzanne's body away. Then Orlandi questioned me again. It went on forever."

Craig looked up at me with a grey face. "Is that enough?" he asked wearily.

I wanted to say yes, but I had to know one more thing. "What killed Suzanne?" I asked.

He stared at me. "I don't know. Nobody told me. She just looked . . . destroyed, that's all."

Craig stood up abruptly. "Let's get out of here," he said. "Let's walk."

So we left his nice room and went for a walk. Craig led the way up one path, then down another, with furiously pounding footsteps. I had to trot to keep up with him. Finally he stopped.

He pointed to a low circular brick wall, surrounded by yellow tape and crime-scene warning signs.

"This is the mud bath where I found her," he said. "Maybe it will tell you something I can't."

I walked around the brick structure until I saw an opening. I could just see the top of the stairs that led down into the mud. The yellow tape kept me from getting close enough to see anything more. Even so, as I stared down my skin began to crawl. Suzanne had died here.

"Row, row, row your boat, gently down the stream. Merrily, merrily, merrily, merrily. For *death* is but a dream," crooned a voice behind me.

- Five -

FOR ONE FRIGHTENING MOMENT I thought the singing behind me was Craig's—that despair had finally driven him over the brink into madness.

But when I turned to look behind me, I saw another man. He was tall, slender and handsome, his face lit up by large, glowing eyes. The kind of eyes you sometimes see on movie stars. Eyes where the whites show beneath the irises, as if to highlight their radiance. Eyes that can look incredibly erotic. Or insane, depending on the circumstances.

"Or is life a dream? And death merely the awakening?" he asked the air whimsically. No, his eyes did not look erotic.

I didn't answer his inquiry. It didn't seem to be directed at me. Instead, I looked a question at Craig, who had circled around the mud bath after me.

"Bradley Beaumont," Craig mouthed soundlessly, and tapped his head in the age-old gesture indicating insanity. Nice timing. Now he admits Bradley is insane.

"Maybe we aren't even the dreamers, but the dreamed," Bradley commented. He smiled. "Have you ever wondered?" His luminous eyes looked directly into mine with the last question.

"No, I haven't given it a lot of thought," I answered. Years ago, working in the mental hospital, I had acquired the habit of answering such questions honestly.

"That's okay," he assured me. "They only act out my dreams anyway."

"Ah," I said. True, the border between sane and insane

is not always clear. But Bradley's reference to the all-knowing "they" stamped his border pass as far as I was concerned.

Bradley Beaumont bowed slightly, like a proper Japanese businessman, then walked away. As he walked away, he let out his high-pitched cackle.

I fixed my gaze on Craig. "Does he act like that all the time?" I asked.

"Most of the times I've met him," Craig admitted. "Though I've seen him act normal. More than normal. Charming, intelligent, witty. Perceptive, even. He seems to change from day to day."

"You could have told me all this before. Bradley is more than 'a little bit strange,' damn it."

"I don't think he's actually crazy." Craig said defensively. "Not the violent type, anyway."

He had a point. If all crazy people were murderers, there would be a hell of a lot more murders. But still, Fran's husband, Bradley, was a possibility in my book.

"So what did the police think of Bradley?" I asked hopefully.

"How would I know?" Craig whined. "They don't tell me what they think. Remember, Bradley can act pretty together when he feels like it. They probably don't even realize."

"Someone must have told them about his loon routine," I argued. "Ruth Ziegler, if no one else. Isn't she a psychologist or something?" Craig nodded. "She would have to have noticed. And I can't imagine her not telling the police. Or Terry—though maybe not. Informing isn't politically correct. But Jack might have. He's got a big enough mouth." I looked into Craig's worried eyes. "Don't you see? Even if Bradley isn't our murderer, his lunacy has got to squeeze you down a slot on the police suspect list."

"I don't know," he said doubtfully.

Then I remembered. "Didn't you say Suzanne called Bradley a loony to his face?" I asked.

Craig nodded.

"Well," I prodded. "How did he react?"

"He just laughed. One of those strange laughs. Fran was the one who got mad. She told Suzanne she could leave Spa Santé if she felt that way. But then Bradley pulled Fran away and calmed her down. And I persuaded Suzanne to leave it alone, at least for the moment. So it all blew over.''

"Was this last night?" I asked.

"Yes," he answered. His eyes were wide now. "But, Kate, you don't kill over an insult."

"I don't. Maybe you don't. But I won't speak for anyone else," I said. "Why did Suzanne call him a loony anyway?"

"Oh, he was into one of his philosophical raps—his way of coming on to her, I think—and Suzanne wasn't interested."

"A man spurned," I said.

"Maybe," he agreed reluctantly.

"What else?" I asked. "Tell me more about Bradley."

"Well, he really is bright. Fran says he's a brilliant writer. And he's a great cook. Curried vegetable-nut loaf. Brazilian greens and beans. And he makes a tofu-tahini spread that—"

I cut him off. "I don't mean more about his cooking skills." The talk of food had stirred my gastric juices. My last "meal" of vegetable juice and nuts was too long past. My stomach began growling, then pleading.

Craig heard the sound. "I didn't even think to ask if you'd eaten," he said. He looked at me with concern. "You need some food, don't you? Don't worry. Fran will fix you up a snack."

I opened my mouth to object and then thought better of it. Fran. How far would she go to protect the man she loved? It might be interesting to talk to her.

"I'd love a snack," I said.

Once more we walked to the main building that housed the dining hall. We had reached the gravel parking lot when Craig stopped in his tracks. I could feel him go stiff with tension without even touching him. I followed his eyes to the porch.

The man who stood there looked like Santa Claus in disguise. He was white-haired, big-bellied and rosy-cheeked, but he didn't wear a beard. And, instead of the familiar red suit, he wore a short-sleeved dress shirt tucked tightly beneath his belly into sagging, navy blue pants. His small blue eyes glinted with jollity under tufted white eyebrows. Or was it suspicion? I couldn't tell. Whichever it was, he was certainly watching us attentively.

I turned to Craig. His skin tone had gone beyond white

into grey. "Chief Orlandi, Delores Police Department," he whispered.

I looked back at the man on the porch. Santa Orlandi, the police chief. He walked down the stairs to meet us.

"I'll just bet you're Mrs. Jasper," Orlandi said sociably. I nodded my confirmation. I wasn't up to correcting him. "The great detective of the north country, I hear,' he added in a friendly tone, which didn't quite rob his words of their sarcasm.

Damn. I threw a glare in Craig's direction. But it was no use aiming my wrath at him. He was too frightened to notice anyone but the police chief. He stared at Orlandi, mesmerized and unmoving, except for a stray muscle twitching in his cheek.

"Well, ma'am," continued Chief Orlandi, his blue eyes absorbing both Craig and myself. "I could most likely benefit from your vast experience, but I'm a little too busy today." I breathed a sigh of relief. Somehow, I didn't want to talk to this man. My relief was premature. "There's always tomorrow, though," he said. "We'll have a nice little talk then. Just the two of us."

"Nice meeting you, ma'am," he finished, and extended a plump hand for shaking. His grip was surprisingly gentle, and brief. He dropped my hand after one squeeze, and smiled. "I look forward to our talk tomorrow," he added.

Then Orlandi turned to walk away. After he had taken a few steps I heard the tension come whooshing out of Craig's body in one long sigh. Chief Orlandi turned back to us. "And I'll be talking to you again, too, *Mr.* Jasper," he said to Craig. "Soon." Then he walked away, his steps unhurried.

Craig waited until Chief Orlandi had driven out the gates before speaking. Then he let fly.

"I told you he thinks I did it!" he wailed. "He'll keep questioning me and questioning me. He'll never believe me—"

I interrupted him abruptly. "You need some rest." I couldn't take another bout of hysteria.

"What?" he asked, blinking, cheated of the momentum of his tirade.

"Rest," I said, in the tone that one tells a dog to "sit."

"Rest," he repeated. "You're right. I need rest." He spoke slowly and carefully. "Thank you. I'll go lie down now."

As I watched Craig move down the dirt path like a sleep-walker, I found myself longing for Wayne's soothing presence. Would Wayne know how to handle all this? Would it even be appropriate to ask my current lover to support me in supporting my ex-husband? My ex-husband who probably didn't even know his "ex" status? I shook my head and walked up the stairs and across the porch. It was too complicated to even consider.

Ruth Ziegler was the only one left in the dining hall. She sat at one of the tables near the windows, her frizzy grey head bent over a yellow notepad. I could hear her muttering as she wrote, deep in thought. I watched her and wondered. Should I ask her about Bradley? She was a psychologist. Or ask her about Craig, for that matter?

I walked to her table. She looked up at me with an unfocused smile on her wise gypsy face.

"Fran's in the kitchen," she said. "How do you like *Letting Grief Go*?"

"You mean, as a philosophy of life?" I ventured.

"No, no." She laughed a vibrant, uninhibited laugh. "As a title. All this talk of death and loss has given me the idea for my next book. But I like to start with a title. It's important. My first book was *The Things We Do For Love*. My second, *Being Your Own Fairy Godmother*."

"I think I've seen that one," I said. "Next to *Women Who Love Too Much*."

"You see," she bubbled, her black button-eyes gleaming. "You remembered the title."

I nodded, glad to have made her happy. The simplicity of her enjoyment was catching.

"Now I want to write something about the importance of letting go. Of grief, death, the loss of love." She looked down at her yellow pad. "Terry thinks politics will feed the hungry. And maybe they will. But will they heal the broken heart?"

"That's almost a good title," I said.

"*Who Will Heal the Broken Heart*?" She pondered. "Close, very close." She bent her head over her yellow pad and began to write again.

"I'll leave you to it," I said quietly.

She nodded, her eyes glued to her notepad, and reached out her left hand blindly to squeeze mine. "Thank you, my dear," she murmured.

I tiptoed across the hall to the three-quarter swinging

kitchen doors, keeping quiet for the sake of Ruth's concentration. Then I peeked over the top of the doors. Fran was there alone, chopping carrots rhythmically at a large butcher-block worktable in the center of the kitchen. Such a soft woman, I thought. But she wielded her knife with strength enough. Chop, chop, chop. She scooped up the pile and threw it into a giant, simmering stewpot. The spicy aromas that came from the pot made my mouth water. She grabbed a bunch of spinach and went to the sink to wash it.

"May I come in?" I asked.

Fran jumped, spraying water from the wet spinach onto the tiled floor as she did. I watched her eyes go round with fright as she raised her arm defensively in front of her face. Then she recognized me.

"Oh, Kate," she said, her eyes returning to their natural delicate shape once more. "What a start you gave me!" She dropped her arm and took a breath. Whom had she been expecting?

"Sorry," I said. "Shouldn't have snuck up on you that way."

"No," she replied. "It's all my fault. I get so wrapped up in my thoughts, I forget the outside world." She giggled nervously. "Silly of me." She looked up at me expectantly, too polite to ask me directly what the hell I wanted.

"Craig said maybe you could fix me a snack," I explained.

"A snack?" she asked brightly, as if she had forgotten the meaning of the word.

Then, suddenly, she came to life. "Oh, a snack! Of course, I can. Let's see, we've got carrot sticks, celery, cucumber, jicama." She pulled a platter of raw vegetables out of the refrigerator. "And tofu-tahini spread. Orange-mustard dip." She went into the refrigerator again. "How about some sliced melon? Peaches? I don't have any fresh bread, but if you don't mind yesterday's." A brown loaf emerged. "With all this fuss, I didn't bake any this morning, but Avery went into town for some—"

"That's fine," I assured her, before the whole contents of the kitchen ended up on her worktable.

In a matter of a minute she had arranged all of the goodies on a plate for me and gone back to her work. I pulled up a chair, dipped a carrot stick into the orange-mustard dip and crunched.

"Craig tells me Bradley is a master vegetarian chef," I mumbled through a mouthful of sweet and sour carrot.

She looked up from trimming the spinach and beamed a smile at me. "Oh, he is," she said in a breathless tone. "I'll bet he could get a job as a chef anywhere now. And his recipes are really healthful. I'm so glad Craig appreciates them. Not everyone does, you know." She shook her knife to emphasize her displeasure. "Bradley says most American palates are numb from salt and sugar and grease."

I nodded my agreement and spread tofu-tahini on the bread. A bite told me it was great. Maybe Bradley deserved his master chef reputation.

"Of course, he's really a writer." Fran said the word *writer* with the kind of reverence most people reserve for God. "He's working on a novel. A really important one. One that will integrate the great moral philosophies of East and West." She looked up at me, her eyes requesting a response.

"Sounds interesting," I garbled dutifully through my bread.

"Oh, it is. Though some of it's a little beyond me. Writers are different, you know. Some people just can't understand that." Did she mean people like Suzanne? I wondered. "Writers are on a different plane than the rest of us." I nodded before taking a bite of jicama. Bradley was definitely on another plane.

"Bradley's a twin as well as a writer," Fran said, tossing chopped spinach into the simmering pot. "I think being a twin makes you more sensitive." She paused and wiped her hands on a towel. "And his twin died. Ursula was her name. I never met her." Pulling a bag of mushrooms out of the refrigerator, she added, "She committed suicide, when they were eighteen."

"Ursula?" I asked.

"Uh-huh. Bradley says it was like half of him died. Can you imagine? I can't. But I was an only child. My dad was a G.I. Married my mom after the war was over. My mom was Hawaiian, Japanese really, but born in Hawaii, you know." What a faucet Fran was. Turn her on and she just kept talking. Like a lot of people I've met on buses. I bit into the peach and sat back to listen.

"My dad died when I was little. Mom bought this cute motel, the Hawaii Star, and ran it. I helped out there until I left home. So, I know a lot about the hotel business." I watched her chopping the mushrooms. I'll bet she did. If nothing else, she was incredibly efficient.

"When I saw this spa, I knew it was perfect. Mom died last year. Left me enough money to buy Spa Santé and fix it up. And, the best part is, Bradley doesn't have to work a regular job anymore. His bosses never appreciated him anyway. But here, he can cook and help with other chores, and write when he feels like it. And Avery Haskell is a big help. I don't know what we'd do without him."

"How'd you find Haskell?" I asked.

"Oh, that was really neat. We didn't even need to put an ad in the paper. He just showed up a couple of weeks after we bought the spa. Said it looked like we could use a hand." She threw the chopped mushrooms in the pot, then giggled. "Boy, did we ever! This place was a wreck. It was originally built in the twenties, by this German businessman, Otto Keller. He had had arthritis and swore the natural springs here had cured it. So he built the spa."

She pulled another huge pot out of the refrigerator. How could she lift it? It was as big as she was. I moved to help her but she wrestled it onto the stove before I could. Maybe she used her own exercise equipment.

"So, anyway," she continued, not even out of breath, "Otto Keller owned the spa until he died in 1939. It was *the* place to vacation. Lots of celebrities came here. Charlie Chaplin visited. Keller even built a small theater here. We still use it for videos, but its not like it used to be. After Otto died, his relatives weren't interested in running the spa anymore. They didn't need to. They had plenty of money from his other businesses. So it sat here, run-down and neglected, until The Inner Light Foundation bought it."

"The paisley people?" I asked.

"Uh-huh," she answered. She aimed a guilty look at me. "I hope you don't mind the wallpaper."

"No, it's fine." I lied automatically and just as automatically regretted it. It wouldn't be the first time my knee-jerk manners had undone me. I was trying to think of a way to retract the lie, when the swinging doors creaked open behind me.

Avery Haskell strode in silently, carrying two grocery bags. He noted my presence with a curt nod.

"Did you get the bread?" Fran asked him.

"Eight sprouted wheat. Two rye," he answered briefly. He began unloading the bags.

"Have you seen Paul?" Fran asked.

Haskell shrugged, his eyes meeting mine for an instant, then dropping. He folded the empty paper bags carefully.

"How come that kid is never around when I need him?" Fran asked angrily.

Neither Haskell nor I ventured an answer. I wondered why Bradley wasn't there doing his share, and then remembered. He was a "writer." Exempt from ordinary kitchen duty by all appearances.

"Can I help?" I offered.

"No, no. Don't be silly. Guests don't work," said Fran with another giggle. "We're really doing fine. It's just that kid of mine. He makes me so mad. He knows he's supposed to be here giving me a hand."

Time to change the subject. "So," I said, turning to the handyman, "you're Avery Haskell."

He nodded acknowledgment without raising his eyes. This man was no faucet.

"Fran tells me what a big help you are," I offered.

He muttered something that might have been, "Thank you."

"Where are you from?" I tried.

"Lots of places," he said with a shrug.

"Oh, don't be such a sourpuss," teased Fran.

"I've made my amends," said Haskell softly. "And let it go to God."

Fran said nothing in response, just kept working. Maybe the answer made sense to her. She was, after all, married to Bradley Beaumont.

I took my last bite of melon and put my plate in the sink.

"What do I owe you?" I asked Fran.

"Nothing," she answered. "It's on the house."

"Oh no," I said. "I insist. Charge the room and the food to Craig Jasper's account."

– Six –

"CRAIG WOULDN'T mind paying?" asked Fran, a trill of hope in her musical voice. She paused to switch on a blender filled with garbanzo beans before looking at me for assurance.

"Craig won't mind a bit," I promised her over the roar of the blender. Not after I beat him into it, I told myself.

As Fran switched off the garbanzos I heard the tail end of a soft chuckle from Avery Haskell. I turned to him in time to see the flicker of a smile that transformed his face from a zombie into an attractive human being. Then the mask came down again.

Haskell must have a sense of humor, I thought in amazement. Or maybe he just disliked Craig. Not a member of the Craig Jasper fan club?

Fran's cheery voice broke into my ruminations. "You should try out some of the facilities while you're here," she said, pouring lemon juice into the garbanzo mixture. "We have a swimming pool, mineral baths, mud baths. Our mud baths are wonderful. We add peat moss so you don't sink right in. You have to scoop the mud over you . . ." She stopped mid-sentence. A nervous giggle escaped her lips. I saw Suzanne's crumpled body in my mind's eye and shivered.

Fran added some garlic before continuing. "There's a hot tub by the pool," she went on. "And if you'd like a massage, they're available by appointment."

"A massage might be nice," I said slowly. Especially if Craig paid for it. "Who does them?"

"On the weekends, Mary Flynn or Larry Ortega. Weekdays, Bradley does them." I flinched involuntarily and hoped

Fran hadn't noticed. Apparently not. She was still smiling as she added tahini to the blender. "He's certified in shiatsu," she added in a voice rich with adoration.

"Thanks for the offer," I said brightly and then walked quickly to the swinging doors. "And thanks again for the snack. See you later."

Fran gave me a short wave over her shoulder before switching on the blender again. And Haskell nodded to me briefly as the garbanzos whirled into oblivion. I thought I saw another twinkle in those serious eyes. Was he amused by the thought of my being massaged by a maniac? Or my quick evasion? Or by something else altogether?

I walked through the dining room and onto the porch. Why wouldn't Haskell say where he was from? I stood for a moment considering the question as I stared out over the landscaped grounds of Spa Santé, seeing Haskell's brief smile superimposed on the view. And why the zombie act? What was the man hiding?

"Sit down if you'd like," offered a gruff voice to my right. I refocused my eyes and turned toward the voice. Don Logan sat looking up at me from his wheelchair, his blue eyes just visible under the rim of the cowboy hat he now wore. He gestured to the redwood bench at his side in invitation.

"Why, thank you," I said and plopped myself down on the hard bench, delighted at the easy interrogatory opportunity. But what to say? Once I was seated, Logan had taken his eyes from my face, returning his gaze to the view of the spa grounds.

"Nice place here," I ventured.

"Yeah," he agreed.

We surveyed the colorful gardens, time-worn dirt paths and plaster buildings in silence. Should I make small talk? Or just dive in and ask him his opinion on who killed Suzanne?

"Nice plants," I said.

"Uh-huh," he agreed once more.

"Where are you from?" I asked. I hoped he wouldn't give me a one-word answer to that one.

He turned his sea-blue eyes on me slowly. "Sonoma County," he answered. Two words.

"Oh, Sonoma!" I said, filling my voice with all the enthusiasm of finding a long-lost relative. "Just up from Marin, where I live. Beautiful land up there. Nice cows."

His eyes crinkled into a near smile. "Yeah," he agreed.

"So, what do you do up there?" I persisted.

"Used to ranch some of those 'nice cows.' Family ranch. Four generations. Mostly program computers now," he added with a glance down at his nonfunctioning legs. My eyes followed his glance involuntarily.

"I still ride once in a while," he went on. "It's easy, once I'm strapped in the saddle. Can't do all my old rodeo tricks, though." He turned his attention back to the view.

"Oh," I said. I was all out of chitchat. I sat quietly for a little while longer, then rose to leave.

Logan looked up at me as I did. "Kate," he asked in a low tone, "why did you come here?"

"I—Well I—"

"Seems to me," Logan said, ignoring my splutters, "seeing as your husband was down here with another woman, you shouldn't be all that eager to help him out. My wife sure wouldn't have been."

"We're divorced," I explained carefully. "He's not my husband anymore. Just a friend."

Logan stared wordlessly at me, disbelieving. How could I make him understand?

"You're divorced, right?" I began.

"No, my wife's dead," he answered. Damn. How long would it take for me to learn to think before speaking?

"I'm sorry," I said softly.

"Not your fault," he replied, his voice rough. He lowered his eyes.

"Anyway," I hurried on, "Craig and I get along better now that we're not together. I'm not invested in being angry at him anymore. And he's been a good friend to me too. I—"

My explanation was cut short by the sound of running feet and squealing laughter. Nikki Martin came galloping down the path in front of us. Jack was pounding after her, pretending to be a motorcycle. He clutched imaginary handles and made revving noises.

"Varoom, varoom!" he roared. "I'm coming to get you."

This brought renewed squeals of delight from Nikki. Jack revved up again. Varoom! Varoom! Nikki ran a few more steps, then turned back for a peek at Jack. That peek cost her her advantage. Jack leapt forward and caught her. He threw his arms around her waist and pulled her to him. She struggled and he fell to the ground, carrying her down on top of him. Cocoa-brown limbs and beige, freckled ones flailed. Then, in a flurry of movement, Nikki had Jack's arms pinned to the ground above his head.

"Help, help!" he screamed in falsetto voice. "She's got me."

"That's right. Beg for mercy, you fiend," she replied, her voice deep with melodramatic menace.

"Ooh. Mercy! Mercy!" he begged in piteous tones, while ogling her lasciviously.

His words and lecherous expression brought renewed shrieks of laughter from Nikki and an immediate reversal of their positions. Now Jack was on top.

I smiled as I watched them romp. If they didn't mind exhibiting their passion, I wasn't going to deny myself a little voyeuristic pleasure. I remembered Don Logan next to me and turned to see his reaction.

Logan wasn't smiling. His eyes were narrow with disgust. He shook his head.

"Drugs," he grunted.

Drugs? Jack and Nikki? I would have guessed natural exuberance. Maybe a little alcohol. Was Logan right?

I turned back to see Jack plant a big kiss on Nikki's nose. She stopped struggling. Then he licked her face. She shrieked again and gave Jack's chest a violent shove. He tumbled off her, laughing. Then he was up and running again, with Nikki trailing behind him, shaking her fist.

"You'll pay for that, Jack Ireland," she shouted.

I heard a click followed by a whir at my side. Don Logan was heading down the ramp that led off the porch. He doffed his cowboy hat to me at the bottom of the ramp. "Nice talking to you," he said.

I waved goodbye to him with a "see you later" and turned back to see Jack and Nikki disappear around the corner of one of the dilapidated stucco buildings.

Don Logan and I hadn't been the only ones watching the show. Fran's son, Paul, stood mesmerized under one of the orange trees. Once Jack and Nikki were gone, he turned on his heel angrily and ran off, his still-untied shoelaces dragging in the dirt.

Poor kid. The scene had to have churned up his adolescent hormones. It had even given my middle-aged ones a goose.

I shook my head to clear it of those hormones and sat back down on the redwood bench. Ready to think. Had I learned anything yet that might pinpoint Suzanne's murderer? I wished I knew what had killed her. But I didn't. I went back to the suspects. Suzanne had come on to Jack. That had to have made Nikki mad. Or did it have to? I could still see Nikki's perfect face and body in my mind. Nikki was beautiful enough to hold her own against any encroaching woman.

Avery Haskell was secretive, for whatever that was worth. Bradley Beaumont was nuts and Suzanne had scorned him. And Fran's adoration of Bradley seemed almost as unbalanced as Bradley himself. But given all of that, where was the motive for murder?

I heard feet shuffling up the dirt path. Paul Beaumont. The boy scowled as he climbed the porch stairs and entered the building. Plenty of adolescent rage there. And I had felt an unhealthy *frisson* of anger from Don Logan too while he was watching Jack and Nikki. But so what? I smacked my palm on the bench in frustration. If I was Chief Orlandi, I would be measuring Craig for the electric chair, too. He was the only one who had known Suzanne previously. I blinked. Or was he? That's what I had assumed, but . . .

What if one of these people had known Suzanne before Spa Santé? And had borne a grudge? I shifted with excitement on the bench, then deflated. Suzanne would have said something, I told myself. I blinked again. That was another ungrounded assumption. It didn't absolutely follow that she would say something. Not if it would have been worth it to her to keep an earlier relationship a secret. But why?

An ugly thought seeped into my consciousness. Blackmail. From what I knew of Suzanne, blackmail wouldn't necessarily have been beneath her moral standards. I doubted that she would have blackmailed anyone for money. But for power, for advantage? It was possible. But who? What? My mind raced. Maybe the socially conscious Terry McPhail was a secret Republican. Or a CIA agent. How many agent provocateurs were left in these days of political indifference? And there was always Avery Haskell. He was hiding some secret. Had Suzanne known what that secret was?

I got up from my seat impatiently. Tantalizing as it was, none of this conjecture was getting me anywhere. I needed to clear my mind and start over. I walked down a dirt path at random until I found a secluded patch of grass where I could practice my tai chi.

Tai chi is both a "soft" martial art and a moving meditation, as well as an exercise system. The efficiency of addressing all three needs at once was one of the things that kept me practicing the tai chi form year after year. Not to mention the centered balance and coordination the slow and precise practice had brought to my awkward body, and the clarity I knew it could bring to my cluttered mind. I desperately needed that clarity of mind right now.

So I began the form, sinking my weight down through my torso, through my legs, and into the ground beneath my feet. Then the unhurried stepping, turning, shifting, pushing, kicking and releasing until I felt the "chi" energy circulating. By the time I had made the 180-degree turn in preparation for the heel kick, most of the tension of the day had drained from my body, and my mind had cleared.

But that turn brought me face to face with Paul Beaumont. The boy stood staring at me, his eyes oozing hostility. I dropped my leg and arms.

"You really think you're something, don't you?" he said, his voice high and tense. He didn't give me a chance to answer. "Karate bullshit!" he yelled.

Mid-yell he raised his arms and leapt at me. His hands landed on my breasts. In the instant it took my mind to register the shock of his assault, my body spontaneously began tai chi again. I didn't resist Paul's force but instead sank back, absorbing his energy, then returning it. I turned at the waist and brought up my right arm under his arms. The move lifted his hands from my breasts. He slammed his arms back down, but I swept them away with the momentum of my left hand as I turned back. Then I centered myself fully and pushed from that center with my whole body.

My hands connected solidly with his chest and he was suddenly backpedaling wildly. Then he was down on the ground, his eyes wide with surprise.

I was pretty surprised myself. Both by the assault and by my successful defense. Though I shouldn't have been surprised by the assault. My tai chi teacher had warned against the practice of tai chi in public. It invites challenge. And Paul had thought I was doing karate! Damn.

The surprise on Paul's face was gradually turning to fear. Was he afraid of me? Or just now realizing what he had done? Before I could find the words to speak to him, he pulled himself up off the ground and ran. And he ran fast. As I watched him I wondered. Could he have outrun Suzanne Sorenson?

Upon that thought I sank to the ground myself. I was drenched with sweat. What would have happened without my tai chi training? What if he had had a weapon? I tried to shake the "what-ifs" from my mind. But I couldn't forget the intensity of his hatred. And his hands on my breasts. Had Paul merely been challenging me to a fight? His hands straying to grope along the way? I thought of Jack and Nikki's playful sparring. Paul had witnessed it, too. It might have given him the idea.

Or had Paul's leap been the first step of an attempted rape? I shivered as I faced the thought.

I told myself that he was just a kid. But somehow that didn't comfort me. Then I wondered if Suzanne had been sexually assaulted before she was murdered. The hair went up on the back of my neck.

And what the hell was I supposed to do now? Call the police? Tell them a fifteen-year-old boy had copped a feel? Or talk to his parents? His father was in another world, another universe really, and his mother was actively denying any serious family problems. Would either of them even believe me? And what would they do to Paul if they did? Something that would help? Or something that would push him further into violence? My mind was whirling faster and faster. It ached from the activity.

I rose to my feet and straightened my posture. Decisions could be postponed. It was time to take care of myself. I took a deep breath and sank into the tai chi form once more.

Ten minutes later I had finished my tai chi for the day. And I had reached a conclusion. I would talk to Paul Beaumont myself. And I wouldn't speak to the police or his parents, not unless his assault on me was related to Suzanne's murder. I sighed. Some "unless." Now, all I had to do was to figure out who had killed Suzanne. And why.

I searched my mind as I walked to my room. I just didn't

have enough information. But Felix Byrne might be able to get me some, I thought. I speeded up to a trot. Felix was my best friend Barbara's boyfriend, but more important, he was a reporter. One who liked to dig. The things he could find out about people amazed me, even worried me at times. And he owed me. If it hadn't been for me, he wouldn't have met Barbara. And he wouldn't have scooped the Marin murder story that landed him his job as western correspondent for the *Philadelphia Globe*.

I opened my door, shielded my eyes against the glare of the psychedelic wallpaper, and sat down to dial Felix. As the phone rang, I crossed my fingers and hoped he remembered he owed me. It seemed to me he had once mentioned that *I* owed *him* for all the information he had gathered for me in the past.

"You're involved in another one?" was his only comment when I told him why I had called.

"Not me," I said. "Craig. I was nowhere near the place when it happened."

"Likely story," he grumbled. "I suppose you want me to spend the day at the computer, running down all the suspects."

"How's Barbara?" I asked. A subtle reminder.

"Barbara is fine. She told me you'd be calling." It made sense. Barbara was a practicing psychic. Between her and Felix, privacy didn't stand a chance. "I get the story, whatever you find out?" he asked.

"Of course," I assured him. I kept the hesitation out of my voice and told myself the murderer couldn't be Craig.

"As soon as you find out?" he pressed.

"Right," I said. Luckily he hadn't been specific. As far as I was concerned, "as soon as" could mean that minute, that day or that century.

"Okay," he said. His voice deepened with ghoulish anticipation. "Who are the suspects?"

By the time I put down the phone, I realized just how little I did know about the people at Spa Santé. With the exception of Craig and Don Logan, I didn't even know where the guests lived when they weren't on vacation, or where the Beaumonts or Avery Haskell had lived before the spa. I could almost hear Felix shaking his head in disgust when he had elicited the last of my meager information.

I lay back on my bed and wondered. Had one of these people crossed paths with Suzanne Sorenson before Spa Santé? And if so, where?

A sharp rap on my door brought me back up to a sitting position. And back to the fear I thought I had released. I was alone in this room. A room to which every member of the spa staff could probably find a key, including the youngest member of that staff, Paul Beaumont. A Technicolor image of the boy brandishing a knife burst into my mind. I shook the image away, rose to my feet and centered myself.

"Who is it?" I shouted.

- Seven -

"It's Jack the Ripper," the voice announced.

I stared at the locked door until recognition penetrated my fear-soaked mind. The sound of the voice and the poor taste of the joke couldn't belong to anyone else.

"Not funny!" I yelled and flung open the door.

Craig stood on my doorstep looking pale and sheepish.

"I didn't think," he mumbled, hanging his head.

"You didn't think! There's a murderer running around and your idea of a joke is to tell me you're Jack the Ripper!"

"Kate—" he began.

"You scared the hell out of me," I interrupted. I could feel angry blood rushing to my face. "And what if someone else heard you?"

"Kate—" he tried again.

"How do you think that would go down with Chief Orlandi? Do you suppose he would think it was funny?" I yelled. My head was buzzing with adrenalin. "And another thing—"

"All right," Craig said, throwing his hands up in the air. "I'm a bozo, a diddle-brain, an asshole of the highest order. I admit it. I'm sorry."

I closed my mouth for a second. Then I opened it again, but without yelling. "I couldn't have said it better," I conceded. "You are a bozo."

"Feel any better?" asked Craig quietly.

"Yeah," I confessed, smiling with the realization that I did feel better. A lot better.

"Good," he said, a grin spreading over his tired face.

"Me too. Almost seems like old times again, with you yelling at me."

I tensed, ready to object loudly. I hadn't yelled at Craig that often when we were married. It was later, when we were separating, that I had done the yelling. Old times, indeed! Craig must have seen the objection forming in my face. He quickly changed the subject.

"Fran's got the dinner buffet ready," he said. "Are you hungry?"

What the hell. I was hungry and I told him so. Amazing what a few rounds of tai chi, an assault and some yelling can do for your appetite.

As we walked over to the dining hall, I asked if he knew where the various spa guests were from.

"Jack and Nikki are from Los Angeles," he answered. "Hollywood, La-La Land. Cultural center of California according to them. San Francisco is dead. Long live Los Angeles."

"What about Ruth Ziegler?" I asked.

"I think she's from Northern California, the Bay Area," he answered after a little thought. "I can't tell you where I got that impression. She didn't really say. Terry's from the Bay Area, too, I think." He paused. "I'm not sure, though. Why don't you ask them?"

I nodded. We climbed the stairs of the main building. As we passed through the lobby to the dining hall, I thought how familiar this building had become to me in the five hours I had been here. Spa Santé was a second home to me now. The kind that can appear in nightmares for years.

I surveyed the dining hall, hoping to see Paul Beaumont. I wanted to get my woman-to-boy talk over with. But the boy was nowhere to be seen. Nikki and Jack were there, staring romantically into each other's eyes over carrot juice, at one of the tables by the windows. Two couples and a family I hadn't seen before had come in for the meal. Don Logan sat alone. And Ruth and Terry sat at the long communal table in the center of the dining room, engaged, as usual, in spirited conversation. Ruth broke off long enough to wave at me and then turned back to Terry.

But the surprise guest star was Bradley Beaumont, who stood behind the counter at the front of the dining room, doing host duty. He didn't seem crazed any longer. I looked closer. His eyes weren't glowing. That was the difference. Instead, his eyes held the still, empty look of the depressive cycle of manic-depression.

"The buffet tonight or just the salad bar?" he asked, his voice dull.

"The buffet," Craig answered in an over-hearty voice. Was he trying to compensate for Bradley's low spirits?

"The buffet for me too," I said.

"All on Mr. Jasper's bill, along with the rest?" Bradley asked, his eyes on the form in front of him.

"Right," I said and walked to the buffet.

Craig followed me a for a few steps. Then he tugged at my elbow.

"All on my bill?" he asked, his eyes wide.

"I forgot to tell you," I said, grinning. "You're paying for my room and board while I'm here."

"Me?" he asked plaintively.

"Yes, you," I confirmed. He wasn't getting any sympathy from me. He was the one that had asked me to come down here. And with the kind of money he made from his computer software company, he could easily pay the cost of my room at Spa Santé, or a suite at the Hyatt Regency for that matter, and write it off as a minor travel expense. "Any problem with that?" I asked him.

"No, no," he agreed, slumping his shoulders. He sighed a martyred sigh.

"As long as you feel so bad, there's also my airplane ticket," I added. "And expenses—"

"Okay, okay," he capitulated. "I won't complain. I'm happy. See?" He bared his teeth in an attempt at a smile. He managed to looked like a mad dog. "Happy," he reiterated through his teeth.

It was like old times, all right. Only I wasn't feeling nostalgic.

The buffet looked good, though. Good in the sense of "good for you." Great bowls of spinach and garden salad. Platters of raw vegetables. Cauliflower, broccoli, carrots, zucchini, jicama, celery, sprouts and bell pepper. Dips and dressings, with their healthful ingredients proudly posted. Meatless minestrone soup. Low-fat potato-corn chowder. Tubs of brown rice and cooked vegetables. Steaming polenta. Vegetable-nut loaf. Bread and fruit. Not a naughty bit in sight.

I began heaping my plate. If the food I had gobbled up in Fran's kitchen had been a fair sample, this food was going to taste as good as it looked. Craig loaded up, too. I was pleased by the return of his appetite. I gave myself a mental pat on the back. My harassment always did cheer him up. We sat down with Ruth and Terry.

"Thanks for the title," said Ruth, turning her gypsy smile on me. "I have a feeling *Healing the Broken Heart* will sell like . . ." She paused. "Like oat-bran hotcakes."

"Of course it will sell," groused Terry. "More self-indulgent, psychoanalytic bullshit. The newest opiate for the masses."

I flinched, shocked by his blunt appraisal. But it didn't bother Ruth. She laughed.

"Did it ever occur to you that the good fight for social justice is, itself, an opiate for the masses?" she asked, her black button-eyes gleaming mischievously. "Or perhaps an opiate for the elite?"

"Not that old argument," snarled Terry, glaring fiercely through his wire-rimmed glasses. "Who cares whether political activists are unconsciously working out Oedipal complexes? The struggle against poverty, injustice and racism is what matters. Are you going to look for a warp in Martin Luther King's upbringing, or respect what he accomplished? You want to talk about what causes unhappiness? Look at social injustice, not psychology."

"I'm not saying injustice doesn't cause misery," Ruth argued. "It does. But even if all injustice was eradicated, there would still be a lot of unhappy people around. Look at Suzanne. Beautiful, privileged and successful. But happy? What do you think, Craig?" she asked suddenly, turning her eyes on him. "Was she happy?"

Craig dropped the forkful of salad he had aimed at his mouth. His face paled. "No, she wasn't happy," he mumbled.

So much for cheering him up. I just hoped Ruth knew what she was doing.

"Because she couldn't let go," Ruth said softly. "She had to be the best. But she could never believe she was good enough. Who was she trying to impress? Someone from her past, I'd bet."

Craig nodded, his eyes held by Ruth's. The gypsy fortune-teller had him now. "And no one else could ever be good enough. Others were always to blame. But, you know what? There was nothing anyone else could have done for her. She had to come to terms with her life on her own. You couldn't have helped her."

"I couldn't?" asked Craig softly.

"No," said Ruth authoritatively. "Let go of it. It wasn't your fault."

Craig stared at Ruth for a while, then smiled weakly. "Well, I'm certainly glad that's settled, Ollie," he said in a fair Stan Laurel imitation.

Ruth smiled back. "Go ahead, joke," she said. "But think about it."

"Okay, I'll try," promised Craig. Then he pointedly broke eye contact and plunged his fork into his salad once more.

I followed suit and took a bite of polenta.

"Just what does all this have to do with political activism?" Terry asked, his weasel face pinched with irritation.

"Nothing," said Ruth seriously. "Just that. Nothing. Sometimes there's nothing anyone can do." She lowered her eyes. Without the life in those eyes lighting up her face she looked elderly. "My oldest son had everything society could promise, and he died. Killed by accident in a fraternity prank. I could blame myself or blame others. I could hate forever. Or I can let it go and move on with my life. Allow closure. Allow my broken heart to heal."

That was a real conversation stopper. Not to mention an appetite killer. I swallowed hard on my mouthful of bread. But Terry wasn't deterred.

"You could commit yourself to work for legislation to ban fraternities," he pointed out.

Ruth brought her eyes back up. She patted Terry's hand. "If anyone can change the world, you can," she said affectionately. "You're persistent enough."

I went back to my meal with a sigh of relief as Terry and Ruth continued to argue.

The meal was good. But Ruth and Terry's sparring got old fast. I waited until Terry paused for air and asked him where he was from.

"Ah, the private Gestapo begins interrogation," he drawled. His eyes filled with disgust behind his wire rims. I jerked up in my chair, feeling propelled by that disgust.

"My name is Terrance Douglas McPhail," he rattled off, name, rank and serial-number style. "I live in Berkeley, California, where I own and operate Radical Tees." He reached in his pocket and pulled out his wallet. "Here's my driver's license and my social security card. Anything else?"

I stared at the glowering face on Terry's license photo. Here was my opportunity for information-gathering. But his rapid-fire hostility had stunned me into blankness.

"And I didn't kill Suzanne Sorenson," he added truculently.

"What's Radical Tees?" asked Ruth in an easy voice. I shot her a grateful look.

"A screen-printing shop," Terry answered. He reached in his wallet again, this time for a business card. "T-shirts, bumper stickers, posters, caps, jackets, sweats. You've got a message, I'll print it for you." He handed Ruth the card.

I pointed at his "CIA Out of Central America" T-shirt. "Yours?" I asked.

"Guilty as charged," he said, but he was smiling now, the disgust gone from his eyes. "This too," he added pointing proudly at his "Food Not Bombs" cap. "T-shirts, caps and bumper stickers. The literature of the nineties. People don't read pamphlets anymore, much less books—" He broke off and frowned again. "But, that's enough about me. Don't you want to interrogate Ruth?"

I looked over at Ruth nervously. She beamed her gypsy smile at me. "Go ahead, honey," she said encouragingly.

How do you interrogate a woman who calls you "honey"?

"All right, where are you from?" I asked, forcing a "just joking" note into my voice to take away the sting.

"San Anselmo," she replied. Bingo! San Anselmo was in Marin County, my home county. And, more importantly, Suzanne's. Ruth must have seen my eyes light up. "I'm a therapist and a writer," she said gently. "Not a murderer."

If I was polite, I would quit here, I thought as I wriggled uncomfortably in my chair. But I just couldn't. "Did you know Suzanne before you met her here?" I asked.

"No," she answered brusquely. That was an awfully short reply for Ruth. It seemed that I was getting close to the limit of her immense supply of good humor. I looked into her eyes. They weren't beaming anymore. Maybe I had gone beyond close and hit that limit.

"Thanks," I said, keeping my voice cheerfully nonchalant. "Interrogation over."

I could feel the tension lift. Ruth smiled once more. Terry relaxed in his chair. And Craig breathed an audible sigh of relief.

Terry began a new diatribe against police practices, and I sank gratefully back in my own chair. I looked around the dining hall. Avery Haskell had joined Don Logan at his table, but there was still no sign of Paul Beaumont. Was the kid hiding out? Or helping Fran in the kitchen?

I watched Haskell bow his head before eating. "Thank you, Jesus," he said.

"Anyone want something from the kitchen?" I asked.

"No thank you, Jesus," replied Craig loudly.

Haskell's head jerked up. He scowled in Craig's direction. No wonder he wasn't a member of the Craig Jasper fan club.

I glared my own disapproval at Craig. When was he going to learn? He deflated and mumbled, "Jeez, I was just kidding."

"You might feel better if you apologized to Avery," Ruth suggested in a whisper. She sounded just like my second-grade teacher, Miss Johnson.

Suddenly, it was all too much for me. The omniscient Miss Johnson had always made me nervous. And I was tired of Craig's antics. I got up, walked to the kitchen and peered in over the swinging doors. But the kitchen was empty. Not even Fran was there.

"Looking for me?" came her musical voice from behind me. I swung around to face her. Her delicate face was shining with sweat. "I've been setting up our video for the evening, *Solar Cooking for Vegetarians,* in the old theatre. I ran all the way back in case anyone needed anything," she explained.

I surveyed the hall. Bradley had disappeared from his station at the front counter. Paul was still nowhere to be seen. Avery Haskell sat eating quietly, the only other representative of Spa Santé.

"Is your son around?" I asked.

Fran blinked, but answered without asking me why I wanted to know. "I think he's doing homework. But he should be there at the video."

That's how I ended up spending my first evening at Spa Santé watching a video about cooking vegetables and grains with sunshine. A method I hope I will never have to use. Or hear about again. And Paul Beaumont never did show up.

During the first segment of the video—how-to graphics for putting together the insulated solar-box cooker—I tried to make some sense of Suzanne's death. I considered means, motives and opportunities all the way through construction to solar recipes. By the time we got to the ecological benefits to be derived if all good citizens cooked with sunshine only, my thoughts had drifted to Wayne. I let them drift.

Craig was silent as he walked me back from the theatre. I was glad for his company, voiceless as it was. The night air was cool and the spa was quiet. Too quiet. The white nylon ropes surrounding the old deserted buildings gleamed in the moonlight. Ghosts guarding ghosts. I could barely see the path. I sensed my way by the feel of the packed earth under my feet as we walked to Rose Court.

Craig broke his silence at my door.

"Kate, I've thought about us a long time now," he said slowly, his brown eyes serious. "We could make it work if we gave it another try."

I was too stunned to respond, blind-sided by his proposal. He tried on a grin before continuing. "I could stop being such a bozo. How would that be?"

"Don't do this to me," I said. I could hear my own voice rise in pitch as I panicked. I lowered it. "Or to yourself. I'm with Wayne now. You and I are friends. That's what works."

"We're still husband and wife," he said wistfully.

"Not anymore," I answered. "The divorce was final two days ago."

His eyes widened for a moment and then he slumped down into himself. "I didn't know," he mumbled.

"I'm sorry," I said, turning away from him. I didn't want to see his face filled with hurt. I didn't want to talk anymore. I wanted to hide in my room.

"Kate," he said. I turned back to him. An effort at a smile was stretched painfully over his face. "Don't worry. I was just kidding around. You know me, always joking."

He gave my shoulder a quick squeeze. "I'll settle for friendship," he said. Then he was gone, in a clatter of footsteps down the stairs.

I took a big breath and opened the door to my room.

– Eight –

A BLAST OF psychedelic paisley greeted my eyes when I opened the door. But all else was quiet. At least until I went to bed. Then my mind assaulted me.

I stared at the white stucco ceiling, seeing things projected there that I wished would go away. Paul Beaumont's hatred as he leapt at me. The cross on Avery Haskell's hairy chest. Don Logan's crippled legs. My imagination's view of Suzanne's crumpled body. Fran's knife, efficiently slicing vegetables. Bradley's crazy eyes. And Craig's mobile face in attitudes of hurt, shock and anger.

I pulled my tense body out of bed, grabbed an orange leatherette chair and shoved it against the door.

Hours later, I woke up in the heart of a nightmare, sweating, my pulse pounding. A bodiless fanged face, distorted beyond recognition by hatred, had forced me to the edge of a cliff. Its shouts were hoarse and garbled with rage. And I couldn't breathe. My long blond hair was strangling me.

I threw off the tangled covers that were bunched up around my neck and convulsively reached to run my hands through my own short dark curls. Their damp, springy touch reassured me. I jumped from the bed into the shock of cold air.

The orange-trimmed chair was still there against the door. It was nine o'clock in the morning. Apparently no one had entered my room during the night. But the chair had failed to protect me from my own fears. I shivered in the cold, then began to move.

I have a rule. When assailed by overwhelming anxiety, make a list. As an abstemious obsessive-compulsive, list-making is my equivalent of a double scotch. I pulled the chair away from guard duty at the door and pushed it up to the small desk against the wall. Spa Santé writing paper sat on the desk, compliments of the Beaumonts. I pulled out a buff sheet and quickly began making rows and columns.

I labeled the columns SUSPECT, MOTIVE, MEANS and OPPORTUNITY. Then I began filling in the names of the suspects: Bradley Beaumont, Fran Beaumont, Paul—

The shriek of the telephone in the silent room startled my hand into spasms of illegibility. I sprang out of my chair and ran to the bedside stand to grab the receiver on the second shrill ring. Please be Wayne, I implored it.

No such luck. The voice on the phone was Fran's. "Excuse me for disturbing you, Ms. Jasper," she twittered anxiously. "But Chief Orlandi would like to speak to you."

"No problem," I assured her nonchalantly. "Put him on."

There was a silence on the other end of the phone.

"Fran?" I probed.

"Oh. Sorry, Kate. He wants to *really* talk to you. In person, I mean. To . . . to interview you." I had a sinking feeling she had been seeking a euphemism for "interrogate." Damn. What did he want from me?

"Where is he?" I asked gloomily. "Down at the police station?"

"No, no." Fran giggled. Did she think I was joking? "He's in my office. There's a door off the lobby on your left, before you get to the dining hall. He'll interview you there. I mean, if that's okay?" she added hastily.

"Fine," I said. I kept my voice friendly. Poor Fran. Not only was she doing most of the work at Spa Santé, now she was making phone calls for the police. "Is fifteen minutes all right?" I asked.

"Perfect," she said, obviously relieved. "Thank you."

It took me four minutes to shower and dress, two minutes to call in at Jest Gifts, two more minutes to write out a list of questions for the Chief, and six minutes to jog to the main building. I climbed the stairs and came to a stop in the lobby a full minute early. Not bad, I congratulated myself.

A uniformed policeman emerged into the lobby from a door near the registration desk. He was tall and stringy, with an oddly protuberant belly that could have been a recklessly swallowed cantaloupe.

"Mrs. Jasper?" he inquired. I jerked my eyes up from his belly guiltily and nodded.

"The Chief's in here," he said, opening the door and pointing inside with a hitchhiker's thumb. I forced my features into the smile of a conscientious citizen and entered the room.

The room was no bigger than a large hot tub. There were some tall ferns in two corners, but most of the floor space was taken up by a battered grey office desk, behind which Chief Orlandi sat. A photo blowup of Fran, Bradley and a younger and happier Paul Beaumont peered over Orlandi's head. An open box of doughnuts, some styrofoam cups and a thermos of coffee sat in a clearing on the desk, surrounded by stacks of paperwork. It reminded me of my own desk at home. Except for the doughnuts and coffee.

"Pull up a chair," Chief Orlandi said with a grin. "Thought we could have a little talk." The grin transformed his face from Santa Claus's into a crocodile's. I wondered if he thought his grin was reassuring. Or was it a conscious effort at intimidation?

I sat down as ordered, my own smile wavering. The man in the uniform sat down next to me and pulled out a notebook and pen.

"Officer Dempster, here, is going to take a few notes," Orlandi said genially. "If you don't mind." I shook my head vigorously. Not me. I wouldn't mind. I'm a good citizen.

"Like a doughnut?" he asked, his eyes clamping onto mine.

"No," I squeaked. Damn. Needed to get my voice back down to a normal register.

"Coffee?" His eyes remained on mine.

"No thanks," I replied in the deepest voice I could muster. I toyed with the idea of asking him how Fran felt about coffee and doughnuts defiling her health spa, but came back to sanity before actually articulating the question.

"So, Mrs. Jasper," he said, settling his bulk back into his chair, but never releasing my eyes. "What do you think of all the excitement here?"

The best defense is an offense. I looked at my notes and went to my first question.

"Was Suzanne sexually assaulted?" I asked.

His grin disappeared as he sat up in his chair.

"Not that we know of," he answered, his voice not quite so genial. "Why the question?"

"I . . ." I what? I didn't want to tell him about Paul Beaumont. Especially if Suzanne hadn't been assaulted sexually. "I just wondered," I finished lamely.

"Well, I 'just wonder' about a few things too," he drawled. He jutted his head forward. "Like why you're down here, Mrs. Jasper."

"To give Craig some support," I said. It was a conscious effort to keep my voice steady. "Craig is no longer my husband. He's my friend."

Orlandi stared at me, saying nothing. I went on.

"Our marriage was an on-again, off-again affair for a long time. We lived apart more often than we lived together in the last five years. And once we both had other . . . other loves in our lives, we became friends again."

He still look unconvinced.

"Listen, we do each other favors all the time! He took care of my cat when Wayne and I went on vacation. I helped find his mother in-home care so she wouldn't have to go to a nursing home. He found a computer job for my niece. And took me to the doctor when I was too sick to drive. He even gave me a fax machine for my birthday. . . ."

Abruptly, I realized I was babbling. Whatever technique Orlandi had been using, it was working.

"But enough about me," I said, going back to my notes. "Who had the opportunity to kill Suzanne?"

He settled back into his chair, smiling again. Was that a good sign? "Looks like just about everyone had the opportunity to do in Miss Sorenson," he said. His voice was full of geniality once more. "Maybe you've got some information we don't. Anything you'd like to share?"

I shook my head.

"Had you met Suzanne Sorenson?" Orlandi asked.

I nodded. Unfortunately I had. Just a few times. But that had been enough.

"What did you think of her?" he asked. His tone was conversational but his eyes were clamped onto mine again.

I hesitated but decided on the truth. "I didn't like her."

"Why?" he pressed. How to explain? The way she put her arm proprietarily around Craig every time I was near. The sneering way she drawled "a gag-gift business" when I told her what I did. The way she flirted with Wayne, and then made fun of his homely scarred face once he had turned his back. The way Craig fell for her, in spite of all that.

"She was selfish, arrogant, insensitive and two-faced," I said bitterly. Damn. I hadn't meant to use that tone. "And those are her good points," I added lightly.

"And . . ." prodded Orlandi.

"Seriously, those were my impressions. I can't really tell you any more. I didn't know her that well." My excuses sounded inadequate in my own ears, but I had already said too much.

"Your husband knew her that well, though, didn't he?"

"My ex-husband," I corrected.

"Okay. Your 'ex-husband.' How did he feel about Miss Sorenson?" Orlandi's eyes were still on mine.

"We didn't talk that much about her," I said. "I think he was embarrassed." It was true, up to a point. The point being yesterday afternoon, when Craig had exploded into his anti-Suzanne tirade.

"He must have told you about the fight they had, the night she was killed?" said Orlandi in a quiet voice. Could he see into my head? I shook off the idea.

I told myself that he couldn't force me to respond, and looked down at my notes one more time.

"How was Suzanne Sorenson killed?" I asked.

"How do you think she was killed?" Orlandi returned the question, crocodile grin back in place.

"I—"

A knock on the door saved me from having to answer. Officer Dempster opened the door and stuck his head out. I could hear the low rumble of Avery Haskell's voice but not his words.

"What is it, Dempster?" asked Orlandi impatiently.

"The coroner's office is on the phone, sir," Dempster replied, his voice stiff. Had Orlandi hurt his feelings with the impatient tone?

Orlandi rose, came around the desk and gave Dempster a pat on the shoulder.

"Baby-sit her," Orlandi said, with a nod in my direction. "I'll be right back."

I didn't much like the order, but I kept my mouth shut.

Orlandi left the room and Officer Dempster sat back down next to me.

"So," I said conversationally. "Get many murders here in Delores?"

Dempster's eyebrows went up, and he grunted what sounded like a negative. That was all the answer I got.

I sighed and gave up. So much for the small-talk strategy. I pulled out a pen and starting marking up my questions list. A loud yowl distracted me somewhere between "cause of death" and "police records." I looked down. Roseanne was leaning her substantial weight against my leg.

"No food here," I told her, shaking my head. She widened her eyes in disbelief.

Then she tensed her muscles and sprang. The jolt when she landed in my lap stunned me. Twenty-seven pounds of cat does not feel like a cat at all. It feels like a compressed Saint Bernard or maybe a bag of cannon balls. I was wondering if I'd have any bruises, when Roseanne began to claw my thighs. My cat, C.C., must have sent her a telegram. I plucked Roseanne's meaty paw from my pants leg. She dug in again and began to purr. Maybe she was C.C.'s cousin.

"How the hell did she do that?" asked Officer Dempster from my side. His eyes were wide with wonder. "She must weigh thirty pounds."

"You're close," I said, delighted at the potential for conversation. A little cat-talk and then I might find out what the police department knew about Suzanne's death. "She's twenty-seven pounds, according to Fran."

"Jeez, I never saw a cat that big before," he said.

"There was one in the National Enquirer—" I began.

Before I could finish, the door to the office banged open and Chief Orlandi stomped in. His face was contorted in anger. I felt myself shrinking in my seat. Roseanne sprang from my lap. Her push-off was almost as painful as her landing.

"You want to know how Suzanne Sorenson died?" he asked in a voice full of menace.

I nodded. Waves of anger were radiating from his Santa Claus form. Was he putting it on? Was the Delores Police Department so small that he had to play good cop/bad cop all by himself?

"She was choked," he hissed. "And dragged. And bludgeoned. And smothered in mud." A flood of nausea was enveloping me. I couldn't tell if its source was Chief Orlandi's rage or his all too vivid description of Suzanne's death. "Someone sure hated that woman," Orlandi continued. He walked around the desk and slammed into his chair. He clamped his eyes on mine once more. "Was that someone you, Mrs. Jasper?"

My mouth dropped open.

"Me?" I whispered. He couldn't be serious.

"Where were you on Tuesday night?" he snarled.

"Tuesday night?" I repeated stupidly.

"Yes, Tuesday night. And Wednesday morning."

Suddenly my head cleared. "In Marin," I answered angrily. "I wasn't here. I am not a suspect. I was at home, working."

"Prove it," he snapped.

"Ask Southwest Air," I answered shrilly. This was ridiculous. "I left San Francisco a little before noon on Wednesday."

"You could have flown down the night before and flown back early Wednesday morning," he replied.

"What!" I yelped. Then I remembered. "Craig called me early Wednesday morning, at my house in Marin."

"So he claims. He could have been calling your answering machine."

"No! I was in Marin, damn it."

"We'll check, you know." His tone vibrated with menace.

"Then check," I replied testily. I just hoped they could check. But who were they going to ask? My cat? She was the only witness. If only Wayne had spent that night with me. Maybe he could lie? No. I shook off the thought. That would only get me in worse trouble. Had any of my neighbors noticed me? I was so lost in thought that I failed to notice Chief Orlandi's re-transformation.

"Mrs. Jasper," he said, his voice friendly again. I looked up. The crocodile grin had returned. "You really want your husband back, don't you?" he coaxed.

"You must be kidding," I said. "I have a lover. His name is Wayne Caruso. Craig is my friend—"

"Mighty convenient, the way you showed up here," he continued, as if I hadn't spoken.

And so it went. If Chief Orlandi had been playing good

cop/bad cop with me, he had done a damn good job. A half hour and a couple of personality switches back and forth later, he had asked me some new questions and many of the same old ones. Over and over again. Then Officer Dempster had taken my fingerprints and I was dismissed. At least for the time being. I was told to keep myself available for questioning.

By the time I had left the little interrogation room I had begun to wonder if I *had* been in Marin the night of the murder. I stood in the lobby forcing myself to remember Tuesday evening. I had read an Anne Tyler novel, *Breathing Lessons*, late into that night. And the next morning I had received the divorce decree. No, I told myself, there is no way you could have misremembered that.

I shivered with the realization that Chief Orlandi's interrogation had made me unsure of my own memory, my own sanity. Now I knew how brainwashing worked. And now I knew why Chief Orlandi's very presence could turn Craig to stone.

I drew a deep breath and walked slowly out into the sunshine on the porch.

"Hey, wanna beer, pretty lady?"

The sunlight had blinded me for a moment. As my eyes adapted, Jack Ireland's grinning mouth appeared followed by the rest of his face, Cheshire-cat style. He was wearing the same grungy cut-offs as the day before, but nothing else. Except for a turquoise stud in his left ear lobe, that is. It went well with his red hair and freckles. He smiled up at me from the bottom of the stairs, dangling five cans of a six-pack from the empty plastic circle where the first can had been.

"No thanks," I said. But his friendly smile was infectious. My shoulder muscles relaxed, and I smiled back.

Nikki came up the dirt path. God, she was beautiful. But not happy at the moment. Her large eyes were full of concern, maybe anger. The flare of her nostrils was exaggerated as she marched toward Jack.

"Jack, where'd you get that beer?" she asked softly. She lay her brown hand on his freckled shoulder.

"Downtown Delores," he said, turning briefly in her direction. He kept his eyes down. "I've only had one." He turned back to me. "Sure you wouldn't like one? You look pretty fuckin' blitzed."

I shook my head. Was my state of mind that obvious? Probably. I had sweated through my turtleneck and corduroys. And I had probably tugged my hair in all directions. I usually did when I was nervous. I reached up and tried to comb it back into place with my fingers.

"Jack, you promised," Nikki said.

Jack turned to her. "I love you, baby," he replied, quietly. "But I gotta have a beer once in a while." He held the six-pack out away from his body with one hand and pulled her to him with the other.

She pushed him off. "Come on, honey," she said, putting out her hand. "This is one of the things we came here to get away from."

He hesitated, then handed the cans to her. She rewarded him with a gentle kiss on his forehead.

"Unbelievable, what the old lady will do to get a beer," he boomed out. He winked largely at me, then turned back to Nikki. "You coulda just asked for one," he told her. "You didn't have to steal the whole six-pack."

Nikki said, "Ah Jack, cut it out." But she was smiling now. Looking at him with love in her beautiful eyes. Actually, it was getting closer to lust.

Every time I was around these two I felt like I was intruding. There was more smoldering passion in Nikki's last look then in the whole of *Gone With the Wind*. I wondered if her magic would work on film. If it would, Nikki's career as actress was assured. I decided to leave them to it.

"See you two later," I mumbled and started down the stairs.

"I didn't mean to interrupt," Nikki objected. She looked up at my face. "You do look pale. Have you had any breakfast?"

"Breakfast had me," I replied. "Breakfast being Chief Orlandi."

"Oh, you poor thing!" said Nikki at the same time as Jack asked, "You sure you don't want a beer?"

I laughed. "I take it you've experienced his interview technique."

Jack rolled his eyes and said, "Fuckin' right, I have." Then he screwed up his face in a fair imitation of Chief Orlandi's contorted rage, and bellowed, "Drugs, Mr. Ireland.

This murder has drugs written all over it. And you are a drug-user, aren't you?''

"Oh, no! Not me, Mr. Policeman! Not little ole me!" Nikki contributed in a falsetto, clutching her hands over her heart. I giggled. Jack guffawed.

Then Nikki stretched her lovely dark face into Orlandi's crocodile grin. It was too good an imitation. I began sweating all over again. She said in a deep bass, "Miss Sorenson was beautiful, wasn't she, Miss Martin? Did you think she was more beautiful than you?" She contorted her face further, into anger, and jutted it forward. "Is that why you killed her?"

"Whooee!" said Jack, clapping. "You've got him! Is she a dynamite actress or what?"

I clapped too. Nikki clutched invisible skirts and curtsied. "For my next performance—" she began.

"Your next performance may be sooner than you think," came Chief Orlandi's unamused voice from the top of the stairs.

"Busted!" whispered Jack.

- Nine -

CHIEF ORLANDI LOOMED above us on the porch at the top of the stairs. His face was unreadable in the bright sunlight. No grin. No rage. Nothing at all in those Santa-blue eyes. Officer Dempster stood behind him, hands clasped behind his back, cantaloupe belly quivering. His face was easier to read. His eyes were watering with the effort not to laugh. At least Officer Dempster appreciated Nikki's imitation of his chief.

Meanwhile, Nikki, Jack and I huddled together, still as stone, unified by guilt. Three children caught by the principal while smoking in the schoolyard. Worse. Three children caught by Ayatollah Khomeini while reading *The Satanic Verses*.

After an eternity of staring, Chief Orlandi inched his way down the stairs, watching us the entire time. He stood a few grueling minutes longer at the foot of the stairs, his eyes glued on us. Then he deliberately withdrew his gaze, flashed his crocodile grin once more, and walked briskly away to his car. Officer Dempster followed in his wake. We let out a collective sigh of relief as they drove off.

"Holy shit," murmured Jack.

"Talk about acting ability," said Nikki. "That guy is wasted on the Delores Police Department."

"What do you think the sentence is for making fun of a police chief?" I wondered aloud.

"Zero to life. It depends whether he can pin a murder rap on you, too," Nikki answered solemnly.

Damn. That was disturbing thought. Had we tweaked the tail of a very large and predatory tiger? I felt sick again.

"Hey, you two!" Jack said. "Lighten up." He cupped his hands to his mouth and blew out a short jazz riff which ended in a Bronx cheer. "We're alive! Free! The Chief had his fun. Now, let's have ours!"

He grabbed Nikki's free hand and twirled her under his arm. The six-pack of beer she held in her other hand trailed out behind her. A smile crept over her face as they danced. This was where I had come in.

"I'll see you guys later," I mumbled.

"No, wait," Nikki said, waving the six-pack. "I still need to get rid of these. Why don't you and Jack go to breakfast? I'll meet you there."

"Sounds good," I agreed. It was eleven o'clock. Maybe breakfast, call it "brunch," would make me feel better. And even if Nikki and Jack were "bad company," as my mother would say, they were good company compared with the rest of the spa folk. Which wasn't saying a whole lot.

Jack squired me into the dining hall, keeping up a steady stream of mildly lecherous patter as we went. The patter should have offended me. But coming from Jack, it just didn't. I was still trying to figure out how he got away with it, as we approached the front counter.

Fran looked out at me over the counter. "I hope Chief Orlandi didn't give you a hard time," she said. "I . . . I have to cooperate with him. I mean, a murder! I can't just let that go. Bradley says we should resist Orlandi, that he's got the 'soul of a lobster.' But we're doing business in Delores, and if the murder doesn't get cleared up . . ." She trailed off, misery distorting her delicate features.

"Everything's fine," I said firmly. "Of course you have to cooperate."

"Hey, Orlandi is part of the entertainment," Jack chimed in. He blew a "ta-da!" through his cupped hands. "Hail to the Chief! Watch him smile! Watch him glower! Watch him turn men into mouses, women into . . ."

"Spouses," I suggested.

Fran giggled.

"Don't you worry, Mama-san," Jack went on. "What goes around comes around." I didn't know just what that was supposed to mean in the context of Orlandi's murder investigation, but it made Fran smile. Jack reached across the counter and patted her shoulder. "You've got a dynamite place here. Nothing Chief Orlandi can do is gonna hurt it."

As I piled my plate high with home-baked bread, fruit and scrambled tofu, I watched Jack dancing his way around the buffet table. I felt a surge of affection for him. For all of his clowning, he had been kind to Fran. He wasn't rewarding himself with food, though. He was hardly putting anything on his plate. A piece of honeydew and a slice of bread do not a brunch make. He saw me looking at his meager meal.

"The rest of my breakfast is out under a tarp in one of those construction areas," he whispered in my ear. The whiff of beer that hit my nostrils told me what he meant. One can from a six-pack hadn't produced that brewery bouquet. Poor Nikki. Loving this sweet drunk had to be crazy-making. He must have noticed I wasn't returning his smile.

"Hey, you wouldn't tell Nikki, would you?" he asked, his smile fading.

Damn. I wished he hadn't told me. I didn't care if he drank. But I thought of Nikki, out pouring away five cans of beer somewhere, thinking that was all there was. Then I took a grip on myself and gave my brain a hard shake. It wasn't my problem.

"No, I won't tell her," I replied curtly.

"It's just a little beer, man," he said as he followed me to the table.

"Let's talk about something else, all right?" I offered, and sat down.

"Like murder suspects," he said, a Cheshire-cat smile taking over his face.

My face smiled back involuntarily. Drunk or not, the man had charm. "All right," I agreed. "Tell me about some murder suspects."

"Hey, Suzanne liked to pull everyone's chain. I mean, she did it as automatically as other people smile and shake hands."

"Like who?" I pressed.

"Shit, she'd tease Bradley, then put him down. She wouldn't give Don Logan the time of day, like his being in that chair put him beneath her notice. And Terry . . ." Jack shook his head and laughed. I looked at him encouragingly and shoveled a forkful of scrambled tofu into my mouth.

"Kinda funny, really," he said. "Mean, but funny. That

lady had a mean tongue on her. But she was just giving back what she got with Terry.'' I kept eating and nodding encouragingly. Get to the point, I urged him silently. Obligingly, he continued his story.

"Old Terry is telling her what a sell-out she is for going into law for the money. You know, why wasn't she doing 'people's law' instead of divorces and wills and that shit? How he dropped out of law school because it was 'about people like you.' Well, she turned around, looked him in the eye and said, 'Flunked out, huh?' He turned redder than . . ." Jack groped for the comparison.

"Red dye, number three," I mumbled through my banana-applesauce bread.

He chortled appreciatively. "Red dye, number three. You got a tongue on you too, pretty lady," he said.

"So, what did Terry do?" I asked.

"He cursed her. Whooee! Said some nasty things. Got redder and redder. But he never denied it. Suzanne says, 'Looks like I was right,' and walks away." At this point in his story, Jack let out a whoop and roared with laughter. "She really got him. You shoulda seen his face."

"Then?" I prodded.

"Then, nothing, I guess. He went back and sat down next to old mother hen Ruth. But the looks he shot Suzanne across the room. Whooee! If looks could kill!"

I smiled a large encouraging smile and asked, "Who else?"

He bent over the table and whispered, "There's that Zombie for Jesus who works here." I chuckled at the description. Emboldened, he raised his voice again. "I'd hate to be locked in a room with him for very long. He hated Suzanne the minute he laid eyes on her. And then there's—"

"Jack, be quiet," came Nikki's voice from behind us. I hadn't even heard her walk up.

I turned, and saw that she was glaring down at Jack. She paused for a quick smile in my direction. "Excuse me," she said. "I need to knock some sense into his head."

I shrugged my shoulders guiltily. I had been the one to pump him. Nikki lowered her head to Jack's level and looked him in the eyes. He attempted a smile.

"This is no game, Jack Ireland. You're going to get someone in trouble if you keep running off at the mouth like this," she said. There was no playfulness in her voice now.

Jack looked subdued. "Listen, baby," he said softly. "I've got to play all this shit like a game. It'd eat me alive, otherwise."

She bent down and kissed him on the forehead. "I know, honey," she whispered. "But keep it in the family, okay?"

Jack nodded solemnly, then winked at me as soon as Nikki turned to go to the buffet. I suppressed a giggle and bent my head over my food. I've learned not to encourage the naughtiness of children. It makes their mothers angry.

I was dutifully avoiding Jack's eyes and stuffing fruit into my mouth when I heard the clatter of running footsteps. I turned around and saw Craig rushing in our direction.

"Thank God you're okay!" he shouted. With one last stride, he threw his arms around me. I wriggled out of his embrace.

"Where were you?" he yelped. His eyes were frantic. "I looked all over for you. I called your room—"

"Whoa," I said. "Calm down. I'm a free woman. What is all this?"

"I was worried. I thought you'd been killed too, I . . ." He was beginning to hyperventilate.

Damn.

I stood up quickly. "Sit down and breathe," I ordered and shoved him into the vacant chair.

He slumped into it and pressed his face into his hands. I massaged his shoulders and listened as his breathing evened out.

"Hey, man. It's okay," said Jack. "Orlandi was just giving Kate the old third degree for a while."

Craig's head popped out of his hands. His eyes were wide as he twisted around to look at me behind his chair. I sat down across from him so he wouldn't have to strain his neck.

"Oh, God. He doesn't suspect you, does he?" Craig asked.

"He suspects everyone," I answered. Craig didn't look reassured. I looked at Jack for backup.

"Hey, he accused me of murdering the lady 'cause he thinks I'm a dope addict," Jack said. "And Nikki 'cause of jealousy."

"Are you still running your mouth?" Nikki snapped. She had definitely returned from the buffet. She slammed her plate on the table. A strawberry rolled off. Craig and I watched it roll.

"Baby!" implored Jack. "I was just telling Kate's old man here how Orlandi sweated us. He's probably sweated everyone here. Maybe we should all get together and talk about it. Let it all hang out. Then—"

"That's a great idea," said Nikki through clenched teeth. She certainly had a flair for drama. Her lovely face was fierce now. "Except for one little thing."

I squirmed in my chair nervously. I had a feeling I knew what was coming as Nikki continued: "Someone really killed that woman. And Orlandi's doing what he knows how to do to find out who that someone is. Now, I'm pretty sure Kate didn't have anything to do with it. But one of the rest us did." She settled her eyes on Craig as she spoke. "One of those people you want to get together with is a murderer."

There didn't seem to be much point in sticking around to socialize after that. I nibbled at the remains of my brunch just long enough to indicate that I hadn't taken offense. I hadn't. Nikki had some common sense to go along with her flair for the dramatic. Then I led Craig from the dining room, cheered him up the best I could, and went to my paisley room to call Wayne.

But Wayne wasn't home. All I got to talk to was his answering machine. I whispered, "Wish you were here" and hung up before I got sloppy. Then I called Felix.

"This wasn't easy" were Felix's first words to me on the telephone. "With the information you gave me I'm not even sure I got the right people. Do you know how many people there are in California with the same names?" he grumbled.

"But you got a lot of juicy information?" I prodded.

"Yeah," he said, pride swelling the word. "And, Kate. What you know, I know. Right?"

"You get the story," I agreed.

"Suzanne Sorenson," Felix began. "Not a nice person, according to the secretary at Rosen, Chang and Ostrow. If she had been killed up here you would have had lots of suspects. She went for the win, kissed ass on anyone who could help her career, treated everyone else like dirt. Elias Rosen, the senior partner, is her uncle. And here's an interesting bit . . ." Felix paused for effect.

"What?" I snapped. I hated it when he did that.

"Rosen inherits." Another pause. "Suzanne made a will in his favor last year."

"Now, that is interesting," I said slowly. I stared at the orange and black swirls in the wallpaper and pondered. Why would someone as young as Suzanne make a will? "Did she have anything to leave?" I asked.

"Not very likely, according to the secretary. Suzanne dressed, lived and drove for success. On credit. Silk blouses, a fancy condo, and a new BMW. Her salary barely covered it. No major assets. She rented the condo. And leased the car."

"How do you find this stuff out?" I asked. Felix always amazed me.

"Suzanne kept her personal finances on the company computer." I could hear the smile in Felix's voice. "Took the secretary about five minute to figure out Suzanne's password."

"Success?" I guessed.

"You got it," Felix said, surprised. Then he chuckled. "Are you taking psychic lessons from Barbara these days?"

"It was an easy guess. Suzanne worshipped success," I explained briefly. I picked up the phone and walked to the saffron-curtained window. "But why a will, then?" I asked Felix. "No assets. No one that close to her. It doesn't make sense."

"Rumor has it she did it to spite her father. He deserted her and her mother."

"Yeah, Craig told me some of that," I said, opening the curtains. "Tell me the rest."

I sat down on my bed and stared out the window as Felix continued his lecture on Suzanne Sorenson. There were a few rose bushes in Rose Court, but the clear blue sky was even more attractive. More relaxing. I lay down on the bed and let the details of Suzanne's life wash over me.

Then Felix started in on the suspects. When he got to Avery Haskell, he whispered dramatically, "The man's got a police record," and paused. I sat back up.

"Okay, give," I said. "What's the record for?"

"Assault. On his wife, now his ex-wife. Six years ago. Haskell joined A.A. and got probation."

No wonder the man didn't like to talk about the past. "Anything else on him?" I asked.

"Not much. Vietnam vet. Worked as an orderly at the local V.A. hospital at the time of the assault."

The wheels in my mind began to turn. "You want to hear about Don Logan?" Felix teased. I wondered if he tortured Barbara like this.

"Yes, I want to hear about Don Logan," I snapped.

"Actually, it's a pretty sad story," Felix said, the teasing gone from his voice. "A couple years ago the Logans were coming back from vacation. Coming across the Golden Gate Bridge. Logan's wife was driving. A drunk driver coming the other way lost control, came over the double line and crashed into them. Wife and kid were killed. Logan was crippled."

"Jesus," I said. Then my heart started pounding. Was this the connection? "Who hit them?" I asked. "Suzanne?"

"Nope. A man by the name of Keene. He was killed too."

Damn. I got up from the bed and began pacing. Felix continued the rundown.

"Jack Ireland's got a record, too," Felix said. Then, predictably, he paused. I growled menacingly. He hurried on before I could reach through the phone line to throttle him. "Once for reckless driving. Once for possession of marijuana. His brother's the famous one. Ever hear of Trax?"

My brain scanned. "Some kind of rock group?" I guessed.

"Bingo. Tommy Ire, the lead singer is Jack Ireland's big brother. Tommy shortened his name. Anyway, Jack is a roadie for Trax."

"How about Terry McPhail?" I asked. With his attitude, he had to have been arrested in a protest.

"Would Terry be fifty-eight or thirty-nine?" Felix responded.

"Thirty-nine."

"No record on the younger Terrance McPhail," Felix said. I was disappointed in Terry. With his views, he should have racked up at least one honorable arrest in his lifetime. "Now, the elder Terrance McPhail is more interesting," Felix continued. "Owns a Chevy dealership in south San Francisco, and a couple more down the peninsula. Five-star credit rating. Lots of bucks."

I looked out the window again as Felix rattled off information.

"Bradley Beaumont's made a couple of trips to the psycho

ward. Committed by his parents, no less. He lived with them until he married Francisca.''

"Has he ever been published?'' I asked.

"Nope. Now Ruth Ziegler, on the other hand, is a best-selling author. Psychology for the masses. Her husband was a psychologist, too. Died a few years back.''

I looked across Rose Court to the two buildings on the other side. I wondered idly if their white stucco exteriors camouflaged more psychedelic-rustic interiors.

"Nikki Martin,'' Felix grumbled. "There are seven Nicole Martins in this state. Most of them are under the age of ten. But only one actress with that name. No police record on her. She's been in some local plays, a few bit parts in movies. . . .''

There was an orange tree between the two buildings across the courtyard. A figure stood by the tree, looking up in the direction of my window. It was Paul Beaumont. My heart did a back-flip.

"She models for mail-order clothing catalogues—''

"Felix,'' I interrupted. "I've got to go!''

"What?'' he sputtered.

"I've got to go,'' I repeated firmly. "I'll call you back.''

I dropped the phone on Felix's sputters, my attention consumed by the need to confront the figure across the courtyard. Despite my attempts to reassure myself that Paul Beaumont was only a confused kid, my heart was racing. I had to confront him. To face my own fear.

I strolled to my door nonchalantly. I didn't think Paul could see me, but I wasn't taking any chances. Once I had closed the door behind me, I raced down the stairs in time with my rapid heartbeat.

Outside the building, I blinked for a moment in the sunlight and oriented myself. I could cross the courtyard, in which case Paul would probably see me coming, or I could take the dirt path which circled the perimeter of the Rose Court complex. I chose the path.

Paul was sitting cross-legged underneath the orange tree by the time I had run the perimeter. He was still facing across the courtyard toward my building. I got my breath under control and walked up behind him quietly.

"Paul,'' I began. He jerked his head around. His eyes

filled with panic when he saw me. "I want to talk to you," I said firmly.

He turned his head away from me and mumbled, "I don't have to."

I circled in front of him. "Do you want me to take this to the police?" I asked. He dropped his head, refusing to look at me.

"No," he muttered into his lap.

"Well?" I prodded.

He looked up at me with teary eyes. "I'm s-sorry. I never did anything like that before. I know it was stupid."

I dropped to the ground across from him, relieved by his answer.

"Promise me you'll never do anything like it again," I proposed softly, peering into his distressed eyes.

"I . . . I promise," he replied, hurrying through the last word to get it over with. Then he dropped his head again.

I sat across from him, wondering if he would keep his promise. Wondering if there was a better way to handle him.

"Have you told my mom?" he asked, his voice shrill with worry.

"No," I said.

"Will you?" he pressed, handing me the lever I needed.

"Not if you keep your promise."

Paul nodded impatiently. "Don't worry," he said. "I'll keep it." He jumped to his feet.

I rose with him, not finished yet.

"Paul," I said softly. "Tell me how you felt about Suzanne."

"SHE WAS A WHORE!" he erupted.

- Ten -

I STEPPED BACK involuntarily, rocked by the force of Paul Beaumont's outburst. The word "whore" echoed in the charged air.

"Paul—" I began. But he whirled away from me before I could finish. It was just as well. I didn't know what to say. I glimpsed a shimmer of renewed tears in his eyes as he looked at me one more time. Then he ran.

I tensed to run after him without thinking.

"I'd let the boy go if I were you," said someone at my side.

I jerked my head around and saw Don Logan staring up at me from beneath his cowboy hat. I had been so involved in Paul that I hadn't heard the whir of Logan's wheelchair. I turned back in time to see Paul disappear behind a stand of orange trees.

Defeated, I dropped to a sitting position on the ground. It was too late to chase Paul now.

"Why should I let him go?" I asked Logan angrily.

"What were you going to do if you caught him?" he asked in return. He looked down at me with a trace of a smile in his bitter eyes.

"I hadn't thought that far," I admitted. "But that is one troubled kid."

"He's not a killer," Logan assured me calmly, as if I had asked the question aloud.

"What makes you so sure?" I asked, my anger returning. Would it change his assessment if I told him how Paul had assaulted me?

"You just saw his M.O.," he answered, still calm. "Explode and run. He doesn't have the staying power to finish mowing a lawn, much less kill someone."

"Or the strength," I muttered, thinking of Chief Orlandi's description of Suzanne's death. I could imagine Paul flailing out at Suzanne, hitting her hard enough to kill in a moment of anger. But choking her, then dragging, bludgeoning and smothering her? I couldn't fit Paul into that picture. On the other hand, I couldn't fit anyone into that picture.

"It's all bravado," Don Logan said. "Paul's a very frightened boy. Maybe it's his parents' fault for ignoring him. Maybe it's not. I sure as hell don't know." He paused and shook his head. "I never got that far with my own boy."

I jerked my eyes up to look into his. But his eyes were unfocused, lost somewhere. His boy. The child who had died in the auto accident. I shivered. Any death is sad, but a child's death seems so unjust, so out of order.

"I'm sorry," I said.

"I am too," Logan agreed with a grim smile. He whirred and clicked his wheelchair, turning around to leave. "Nice talking to you," he said.

I waved goodbye as he wheeled away.

I trudged unhappily back to my room and threw myself on the bed to stare at the white ceiling. I thought of children dying. Don Logan's boy. Bradley Beaumont's sister. And Ruth Ziegler's son, lost because of a fraternity prank. Then I thought of Paul Beaumont, angry and suffering.

I jerked myself up off the bed, trying to shake the feeling of depression that Spa Santé itself seemed to exude. For a health spa, Spa Santé had a very unhealthy aura. Was the place a magnet for violence and suffering?

I began to pace the room. Were there ghosts in these decaying buildings? Spirits of disillusioned hippies in the orange and black paisley wallpaper? I giggled at the thought, shaking off a chunk of the depression as I did. Every place has its share of underlying tragedy, I assured myself. Maybe it was simply Suzanne's death which had churned all the misery to the surface.

Talking to myself wasn't enough. I wanted an antidote to the misery. I wanted Wayne. I picked up the telephone and dialed his number. And got his answering machine once more. I wanted to cry when I heard it.

"I love you," I whispered as his announcement ran, and hung up the phone without leaving a message.

It was then that I remembered Felix. My confrontation with Paul had driven him from my mind. But now I remembered dropping the phone on Felix's sputters. Damn. I began my apologies mentally as I hurriedly dialed his number.

But the voice that answered the telephone didn't belong to Felix. It belonged to my friend, and Felix's significant other, Barbara Chu.

"Hello, Kate," she answered the phone. Barbara is a self-proclaimed practicing psychic. I have never been able to tell whether she is really psychic or just very intuitive. Maybe it's the same thing.

"All right," I said. "I'm impressed. How'd you know it would be me?"

"I knew you'd call Felix back," she said. Then she whispered. "He's sulking."

I sighed. "Tell him I'm sorry," I said.

She yelled out, "Kate says she's sorry," and returned to the phone. "Listen, kiddo," she said in a low voice, "I don't want to worry you, but whenever I send my spirit down to visit you at that spa, I get really bad vibes."

My heart constricted. Barbara didn't offer such observations lightly. "What kind of bad vibes?" I asked.

"Wait a sec," she said. I could see her in my mind's eye, sitting quietly to ground herself. Then her voice came over the line. "Hate—hate—hate," she hissed.

"Stop that," I squawked. My arms were covered with goose bumps.

"Sorry, kiddo," she apologized. Mercifully, she had returned to her normal voice. "I didn't mean to scare you. But there is a malevolent spirit near you. Watch yourself."

"What malevolent spirit?" I demanded. "Who is it?"

"I can't tell who. But someone is filled with hatred."

Great. No new information. I didn't need Barbara to tell me that hatred was involved. I had heard Suzanne's death described. And now my stomach was churning with fear.

"You'll be okay," added Barbara, responding to my unspoken thoughts. "Just be careful."

"Thank you for sharing," I joked, but I couldn't keep the bitter fear out of my tone.

She chuckled, then grew serious again. "Kate, please. Watch out. This is a nasty one."

My goose bumps came back. "All right," I answered shortly. I didn't want to hear any more warnings.

"Good." She paused. "I'll keep a third eye out for you, kiddo. Do what I can. But you take care. Now, hold on while I get Felix for you."

I could hear Barbara cajoling Felix into talking to me as I waited on the line. I stared at black paisley squiggles as the phone charges mounted. I worked on calming my churning stomach and wondered if "psychic friend" might be an oxymoron in some cases.

Then the receiver was picked up again. "So what the hell happened?" demanded Felix peevishly. I assumed this was his way of asking why I hung up on him.

"I saw someone I needed to talk to," I explained lamely. I looked out the window across Rose Court again. But Paul was gone. The orange tree stood alone.

"Who?" asked Felix.

"Just a kid," I said. There was an unforgiving silence on the other end of the line. "I thought he might have seen something," I lied. "And I hadn't been able to get near enough to talk to him before." At least I finished with the truth.

"You're a lunatic," said Felix. But his voice was friendlier. "So did he see anything?"

"Uh, no," I answered.

"Are you being straight with me?" he asked.

"Felix, I'll tell you everything when I figure out who killed Suzanne," I offered. I shouldn't have reverted to honesty.

"Aha!" he shouted. "You are holding back. What?"

"Nothing important," I said. "So, did you come across anything about Ruth Ziegler's son in your research?" I asked, to change the subject.

"Yes," he said.

"Well?"

"I'll share what I know when you share what you know," he answered.

The conversation descended further into puerility from that point on. By the time Felix had hung up, I was reduced to sticking my tongue out at the silent receiver.

Fully discouraged, I took off my shoes and curled up under

the salmon bedspread. Wayne wasn't there when I needed him. Barbara was playing Cassandra. I knew she was trying to help, but I didn't need any more fear, thank you. And Felix was no longer speaking to me. So much for friends.

A thudding on my door punctuated my last thought. Barbara's warnings reverberated in my mind.

"Who is it?" I called out.

"Not Jack the Ripper," came Craig's voice, as if through a megaphone. "I repeat. This is not Jack the Ripper."

I opened the door to him happily. Craig was indeed a friend. I had almost forgotten.

"Anyone for tennis?" asked Craig, waving an invisible tennis racket. His tone was light, but the stiff smile on his gaunt face hadn't erased the ravages of recent events.

"Seriously," he said, letting the smile go. "How about a swim. I could use one. And I could use some company too."

"I didn't pack a suit," I objected. I wasn't sure I wanted to go swimming. It might be dangerous at Spa Santé.

"I bet Fran will lend you one," he said.

I thought about the offer for all of fifteen seconds. I had spent too much time mulling over murder, misery and violence. If I pretended I was merely on vacation and forgot it all for a while, maybe something would come to me. This was my version of the unwatched pot theory.

"You're on," I agreed.

Craig's face brightened. That felt good to me. I realized just how tired I was of arguing.

Craig sat on the orange leatherette chair while I put my shoes on. He told me about the yoga movie scheduled for the evening.

As we walked to the dining hall I responded in kind, telling him about the fourth wedding of an old friend (maybe this one would take), a good movie I had seen and a new recipe for black bean soup. Anything but murder.

We had almost reached the main building when we saw a beige Volkswagen bug pull into the parking lot. Two elderly women emerged. Their age and sex were all they appeared to have in common.

The driver was a rock of a woman, a study in earth. Her large, solid backside was packed into heavy blue jeans. Her shoulders were large, and hunched forward under her flannel shirt like a bulldog's. Her jowly face brought to mind a bulldog's too, except for the piercing blue eyes. She shoved a bobby pin into the uncompromising grey braid that was wrapped around her head, and in a low voice said something to her companion, which I couldn't hear.

Her companion chirped something back, equally inaudible. She was air to the first woman's earth. She looked like a geriatric schoolgirl, her frail body clothed in periwinkle blue culottes, white knee-socks and a white sweatshirt with a red and black logo. Thin white hair wisped out from her head and played in the breeze. Her eyes were hidden under thick glasses, but her hands fluttered expressively as she chirped. I wondered what they were discussing with such animation.

The earth woman walked to the main building with long, determined strides. Her companion took two hopping steps to each stride to keep up, all the while fluttering her hands and speaking words I could not make out. They moved up the stairs and disappeared through the doors.

I looked at Craig curiously. "Do you know those two?" I asked.

He shook his head. "Never saw them before."

I sped up my pace a little. We went through the doors into the dining room just in time to hear Fran say to the two women, "Why, that's Kate Jasper, right there. Coming in the door." She pointed in my direction and the two women turned to look.

The bulldog woman frowned. It didn't improve her looks. Her companion goggled at me through her thick glasses. I walked up close enough to read the PBS *Mystery!* logo on her sweatshirt and held out my hand for shaking. I assumed introductions were in order.

I assumed wrongly. Neither of them took my hand. They moved swiftly past me, their steps still out of style. I turned to watch them go and caught a quick double backward glance. It was instantly retracted. Then they pushed through the glass doors and out the lobby.

"Who were those two?" I asked Fran.

"Edna Grimshaw and Arletta Ainsley," she replied cheerfully. "People in Delores call them the twins. They've been here forever. Miss Grimshaw was a nurse for the old doctor here. Miss Ainsley used to be a librarian. They come here to eat sometimes. But today they just wanted to ask . . . .'' Fran's words drifted off.

"They asked you to point me out," I finished for her.

Her eyes widened, and she nodded.

"Why?" I asked. Fran's eyes widened further.

"I don't know," she admitted, her voice rising in pitch. "I'm sorry. I've done it again. I shouldn't have told them, but I thought—"

"It's all right," I cut her off. But it wasn't really. What did the twins want from me? I glanced the question at Craig. He shrugged and turned to Fran.

"I told Kate I bet you'd have a swimsuit for her," he said, his voice a hearty invitation to a new subject.

Fran stared at him for a moment, her eyes blank, lost in anxiety. Finally, her belated response came. "Oh, swimsuits. Of course. There ought to be some extras in the changing rooms at the pool. Just take your pick."

"Fran," I asked carefully, not wanting to upset her further, "did the twins ever ask anything about Suzanne?"

"No," she breathed. "Do you think—?"

"No, I don't," I answered emphatically.

Craig and I made chitchat with Fran until she was smiling again. Then Craig led me through the grounds of the spa toward the swimming pool. Unfortunately the dirt path he chose led past the outdoor mud bath where Suzanne had received her final facial. My stomach tightened as the yellow tape came into view. It made even the pretense of a carefree vacation spirit difficult. Then I heard footsteps behind us.

I turned quickly in the direction of the footsteps and found myself looking into the startled faces of the twins.

"Hey," I shouted. "What . . . ?"

Before I could say more, they bolted down a branching path. Craig put a restraining hand on my arm just as I had decided to give chase.

"Wait," he said. "You'll give them heart attacks."

I pushed his arm away. "Goddammit!" I shouted. "How am I supposed to find out anything if people keep running away and no one will let me chase them?" Mid-sentence, I realized that Craig had no idea of the incidents my complaint encompassed. I hadn't told him about Paul.

He stepped back, shocked. "I'm sorry, Kate. But they're old ladies. What could they have to do with anything?"

I pondered that question silently as we continued on to the pool. It was large, empty and sparkling blue in the sunlight. A paradise of a pool in any other place. At Spa Santé its very perfection managed to look sinister to my eyes.

I changed into the promised swimsuit quickly, a navy blue no-frills racing suit. As I pulled it up over my cellulite, I thought about the twins. Could they have murdered Suzanne for some unknown motive? Edna looked strong enough. But where was the hatred? Goose bumps reappeared on my arms as I remembered Barbara's words. I shook the thoughts away. The only reason I was even considering them was because of their interest in me. But, dammit, what was their interest in me?

I stuck my head out the changing-room door and scanned the horizon. No one was anywhere in sight, except for Craig.

"Race ya!" he shouted and dived into the pool before I even got out of the changing room. What a competitive s.o.b. No wonder he and Suzanne had been drawn to each other.

I jumped into the deep end, sinking into the shock of cold and delicious isolation, grateful for the silence. Then I popped to the surface, inhaled and began a fast crawl to the other side. I pulled at the water with my hands and tried to rid my mind of fear. It was easier here, with my face in the water, the only sound my own breathing and the water around me.

I reached the other end of the pool, grabbed the edge, turned and pushed off. I asked myself what I had learned. Nothing, came the answer. As I turned my head to the side to breathe, I saw the blur of Craig whipping past me. I kept on swimming.

After a few laps I began to feel warm and relaxed. I swam in rhythm and let my thoughts float to Wayne. The water's friendly nudging made me think of Wayne's touch. So gentle for such a fierce-looking man. My body moved sensuously in the water, remembering the last time we had made love. I reached the end of the pool and lifted my hand up to its edge. But the edge of the pool felt wrong.

I blinked the water out of my eyes and saw why. My hand had landed on a shoe. A hiking boot actually. My heart hiccupped in my chest.

I shielded my eyes against the glare of the sun and let them travel up the elongated jean-clad legs, past the chest and then to face that looked down at me. I expected Edna, the bulldo twin. But the face surprised me. It was Avery Haskell's. It wore no expression.

I jerked my hand back from his shoe.

"Sorry," I murmured. His face remained blank.

I turned to look for Craig. But he was underwater. Or gone. My heart began to thud. How much hatred was hidden behind Haskell's blank face?

I floated my feet to the pool floor and stood up cautiously. Then I heard Craig break the surface of the water behind me, panting. The fear drained from my body, leaving me cold and shivering.

"May I speak to you in private, Mrs. Jasper?" Haskell asked quietly.

"What for?" demanded Craig, his tone hostile.

"It's private," answered Haskell, his voice as devoid of expression as his face.

Craig looked a question at me.

"It's all right," I told him, pointing to a group of lawn chairs nearby. My heart-pounding fear seemed foolish now. "Avery and I can talk over there while you swim."

I ascended the pool stairs with all the dignity a thirty-nine-year-old woman in a no-frills bathing suit can muster. Avery Haskell handed me a fluffy white towel. I accepted it gratefully and began toweling myself dry as we walked to the chairs.

I sat down. Haskell remained standing. A good move. The plastic webbing of the lawn chair bit into my thighs.

"Well?" I prodded him.

He cleared his throat. I saw a trace of emotion in his eyes. It took me a second to identify it. The flush of his skin gave me a clue. It was embarrassment.

"I want to thank you for the way you've dealt with Paul," he finally mumbled. For that moment Avery Haskell looked like a teenager himself, gawky and shy. Then he seemed to straighten himself internally.

"Paul told me what he did," Haskell said, his tone now firm. "Can't excuse him, but he promised he won't ever do it again. He'll keep that promise."

felt a release inside of me. The release of the burden of nsibility. "Thank you for telling me," I said.

nodded acknowledgment of my thanks. "Anyway, I

thought you'd want to know,'' he said brusquely. ''Good-bye.''

He turned and marched away before I could say anything in return.

Avery Haskell, all-around handyman. Part-time carpenter, part-time gardener, part-time cook and part-time substitute parent.

I didn't have the heart to do any more swimming after Haskell left. It suddenly seemed a very risky pastime. So easy to push down on someone's shoulders . . . I didn't even want to think about it.

I yoo-hooed Craig out of the water and told him I was going.

''What was the big secret?'' he asked.

''None of your business,'' I answered.

''Come on, Kate,'' he cajoled. ''This is me. Tell me what you talked about.''

''Nope,'' I said.

''Suit yourself,'' he retorted peevishly and dived back into the pool.

I sighed as I went to change my clothes. Two friends alienated in one day over one secret. Was it worth it?

I was still wondering as I walked back to Rose Court from the swimming pool. Then I heard footsteps. Barbara's words of caution came back to me.

I paused to center myself, then whirled around to face whoever was following me.

- Eleven -

ONCE AGAIN I looked into the startled faces of the twins. This time I glimpsed what might have inspired their nickname. Despite their widely differing physical features—Edna's jowly and bulldog-like, Arletta's frail and bespectacled—both faces wore identical slack-jawed expressions: classic cartoon surprise.

"All right. Stop right there," I said, injecting a note of menace into my words. "Why are you following me?"

Arletta came alive first. She closed her jaw, smiled and turned to her friend. "I told you she was a real detective," she chirped.

"Hmph," grunted Edna. Her acute blue eyes were busy studying me.

"Look—" I began.

"Edna's the name," the bulldog twin interrupted gruffly. She thrust her beefy hand out for shaking.

I stepped forward and shook it warily.

"This is Arletta," she announced with a thumb pointed in the chirper's direction. Arletta smiled and gave me a two-fingered wave. "Arletta's got some damn-fool idea that you're like the lady on *Murder She Wrote*—"

"I love mysteries," interrupted Arletta. Her voice was high ~~a~~ trembling. Whether from age or excitement, I couldn't "And when I found out that there was a real unsolved ~~ry~~ here in Delores—"

~~A~~friend grunted disparagingly and shook her head.

~~a~~ turned to her. "Now, don't you go spoiling this

for me, Edna. We talked it out. We're old as Noah's dogs—
nothing to do—nothing to lose.''

"That's a fact," agreed Edna. "Anyone who wants to
murder us is just saving Old Man Time the trouble."

"Anyway," continued Arletta, "we'd love to assist you"—
she looked from side to side and lowered her voice before
finishing—"in your detections."

I was stunned. "Who told you I was a detective?" I finally
asked.

"My nephew Vic," Edna replied. "Kid always was a
joker."

Now I was completely confused. I looked into Edna's blue
eyes for the answer. Who did those eyes remind me of?

"Oh, dear," chirped Arletta. "You don't know who Vic
is, do you?"

I shook my head.

"Vic Orlandi," she informed me. "The police chief."
Now I recognized the eyes.

"Chief Orlandi told you I was a detective?" I couldn't
believe it. Why would he do that?

Arletta nodded enthusiastically. Her thick glasses bobbled
on the bridge of her nose.

"Arletta wanted to follow him around—take notes—help
out," Edna explained. "Being it's a real mystery and all. But
Vic said it was against police department policy—as if he
ever gave a damn about policy before—I can't stand it when
he gets cocky like that. Anyway, he told us you were a real
detective. Said you'd appreciate the help."

It was clear to me now. These two old women were Orlandi's revenge for my laughing at him. I wondered what he
planned for Jack and Nikki. Then I smiled. This game could
go two ways.

"So how's the Chief doing on his end?" I asked.

"Oh, dear." said Arletta, shaking her head. "I don't think
he's doing very well. He was awfully grouchy when we talked
to him last."

"But he won't let go," said Edna, her family loyalty kicking in. "He's tenacious, if nothing else."

"Did he mention who he suspects?" I inquired nonchalantly.

"To us?" Edna growled bitterly. "Forget it. He thinks

we're a couple of old ladies." I squirmed guiltily, since that
was how I thought of them, too.

"He wouldn't even let Edna see the body," Arletta
squeaked indignantly. "As if she would be squeamish. Why,
Edna was a nurse for forty-five years."

"Couldn't stop me from calling the coroner's, though,"
chuckled Edna. Her jowly face stretched into an attractive
grin. "Told them I was calling for Chief Orlandi. Strange
kinds of marks on the body."

"What kind of marks?" I asked eagerly. Orlandi, I thought,
you blew it when you sent me these women.

"Marks around her neck like she was strangled with a cord
of some kind. All the cuts, abrasions and such on her legs
and arms. Looked like she was dragged . . ." Edna paused.
"Maybe I shouldn't have said 'strange.' It's just the variety
of marks that's so surprising. Blows to the back of the head.
Probably with a large rock. And for all of that, it was the
smothering in the mud that killed her."

No, Edna wasn't squeamish. But I was. I felt a little sick.

"Murder on the Orient Express?" mused Arletta. She
smiled, thinking about it. I guess she wasn't squeamish either. "Maybe there was more than one murderer. Maybe each
one used a different weapon on the victim!" She turned to
me, bursting with enthusiasm. "What do you think, Ms. Jasper?"

"Call me Kate," I said absently. I was busy running her
scenario in my head. A family murder? Pictures formed before my eyes. I could see Fran whipping a twisted scarf around
Suzanne's neck and tightening it. Meanwhile, Paul's bashing
Suzanne on the head with a rock. Then Bradley drags her to
the mud bath, where they all push her under. I felt queasy
again. Then I shook my head. It just didn't wash. Even if
they were all psychopaths, I couldn't believe that the Beaumonts were capable of the kind of cooperation necessary to
commit a team-effort murder.

But how about a loving couple committing the crime? Jack
cuts a piece of cord from a curtain pull? He chokes Suzanne?
Then Nikki—

"Kate?" prodded Edna. "Are you still with us?" She
waved a beefy hand in front of my face.

"Shhh!" whispered Arletta. "Her little grey cells are
working."

"Hmph," Edna grunted.

As the twins' faces came back into focus I remembered how they had followed me earlier that day. "Why did you run when I tried to talk to you the first time?" I asked.

"You were working on a suspect," answered Arletta.

A suspect? Then I realized she meant Craig. It was time to come clean.

"Listen, you guys," I said. "That was my ex-husband. I'm not really a detective."

"Don't worry, dear," trilled Arletta. "You don't have to explain." She reached out and patted my hand, then whispered, "We wouldn't dream of blowing your cover."

"But really, I—"

She put her finger to her lips. "Not another word," she said, "Just remember, we'll be nearby if you need any assistance."

She exchanged a meaningful look with Edna. Then they turned and left, Arletta still taking two steps to her friend's one.

"Uh, thanks," I said to their retreating backs.

Arletta threw me a two-fingered wave over her shoulder and they continued on.

I walked back to my room quickly, feeling too exposed to stroll alone on the spa grounds. I trotted up the stairs and barricaded myself inside my paisley cell.

As I turned the lock on the door, a realization hit me. Two willing sources of information had offered me their assistance and I had let them walk off without asking the right questions. Damn. I dropped onto the orange leatherette chair, overwhelmed by all the questions I could have asked. Should have asked.

The twins lived in Delores. And Delores was a small town. The twins probably knew the Beaumonts. If not well, at least better than I did. Wasn't it Arletta who was the librarian? She might be friendly with Paul's teacher or his school friends or Paul himself. And Edna was a retired nurse. She might fraternize with Bradley's doctor, or a fellow nurse from the doctor's office. She might even be able to find out Bradley's clinical diagnosis.

And there was still the possibility that the murderer had come from outside the spa, perhaps from the town of Delores. If there was a local psychopath in town, the twins probably knew about him too. Or her.

And they could pump Orlandi. . . . That train of thought was derailed by another alarming one. What if the twins had been sent by Orlandi to pump me?

I began to pace. I hadn't bothered to question their story. I had even filled most of it in with my own imagination. Orlandi's revenge or Orlandi's cunning? Beyond my tendency to attribute the elderly with honorable intentions, there was no real reason to believe the twins had necessarily told the truth. I reached one psychedelic wall and turned to pace the other way.

All right, so they might have lied. So what? I didn't have any guilty secrets to share. And I still might be able to get information from them. I would endeavor to keep my mouth shut and ask questions only.

I finished my trip to the other wall and pulled another sheet of Spa Santé writing paper from the neat stack on the desk. I took this to my bed, along with the tray the water glasses had sat on. I used the tray as a writing table, propped myself up on pillows and began my list of questions for the twins. First question. How did I contact them? Damn. I couldn't believe I hadn't asked.

The directory assistance operator had a phone number for Arletta Ainsley and one for Edna Grimshaw. The same one. I dialed the number but there was no answer. Just for consistency's sake I dialed Wayne's number once more. There was no answer there either.

Sighing, I returned to my list.

By six o'clock I had filled both sides of two sheets of writing paper with questions. I had done a little work on my suspect list too, adding the hypothetical Delores psychopath and Edna and Arletta to the ranks. I hadn't reached any logical conclusions as to whodunit, however. All my intuition had to tell me was that I was hungry. And afraid. Barbara's warnings had settled into my unconscious.

I waited a little while longer before setting out for dinner, hoping for Craig's knock on the door. An escort to the dining hall might have been nice in my jittery state, but no knock came. Finally, I walked over by myself, listening for footsteps all the way along the old dirt path.

I was glad to see Bradley at the front counter. But then, I

would have been glad to see any human being, along with the comforting sound of other voices nearby. I looked up at the blackboard behind the counter. The movie title for the night was *Yoga, What's It All About?*. The evening buffet included Brazilian black beans and greens and curried tofu-nut loaf. Those were Bradley's specialities, according to Craig.

"Are you tonight's cook?" I asked him.

"Mais oui!" he replied with an expansive bow. Ah. The charming side emerges.

"Would you like to know the secret?" he whispered. His eyes were glowing.

I forced myself to smile and nod. This guy was spookier in his charming incarnation than in the others.

He bent forward, locking his luminous eyes onto mine.

"Bananas," he said in a low voice.

I stared at him, trying to make sense of the word. Was this an effort at self-diagnosis?

"The magic ingredient in my beans and greens," he explained. "Bananas."

"Oh!" I let out a snort of relieved laughter.

He joined in, his laughter high and disjointed.

"I'll have the buffet, then," I said.

"Mr. Jasper's bill?" he asked.

I nodded and scurried to the buffet as Bradley broke into another bout of discordant laughter.

How crazy was the man? Was he merely acting? Bradley reminded me of a woman I'd known a few years back. She was an artist and had enjoyed pretending to be crazier than she really was. On the other hand, her enjoyment of the role hadn't changed the underlying fact of her basic madness. I shrugged away the thought and surveyed the dining hall.

The hall was filled with people. Some were recognizable to me. Others were newcomers. I saw the twins seated at a corner table across the room. I smiled in their direction, but they ignored me. Protecting my cover, no doubt. Terry McPhail was topping off his plate at the buffet. Once he had finished, he went to the table where Don Logan sat.

"Mind if I join you?" I heard Terry ask.

Don shook his head and grunted an invitation to sit down. There was no accompanying warmth in his voice or his eyes, however.

Terry sat, then nodded at Logan's legs. "Vietnam?" he asked.

"No," responded Logan curtly.

So much for conversation at that table. I averted my eyes and ears, and concentrated on filling my own plate high with brown rice, vegetables and a healthy serving of both the Brazilian beans and the tofu-nut loaf. I hoped Bradley's cooking was better than his state of mental health.

I sat down alone at one of the smaller tables and dipped into the Brazilian beans and greens. Delicious. The banana complemented the garlic- and vinegar-flavored beans and greens perfectly. As I took a bite of tofu-nut loaf I heard the noisy arrival of Jack Ireland.

"Just one good gig—" he was saying.

"Two buffets," Nikki said to Bradley. Bradley nodded.

Jack continued, not seeming to notice the interruption. He waved his hands in the air excitedly. "That's all it'll take. If I can get them a gig, it'll all start happening. I can feel it. They're gonna be dynamite. With Mad Dog on drums, Colin doing vocals and bass—"

"Honey," said Nikki gently as she shepherded him to the buffet. "They might be taking you for a ride. Did you front them any money?"

"They gotta have equipment," he answered sullenly.

Nikki stopped in her tracks. "How much?" she asked. Her hands were on her hips now, in the classic pose of disapproving motherhood.

"What does it matter?" he answered impatiently, shuffling his feet. "They're for real. They're good. Why are you giving me shit on this?"

"Oh, honey," Nikki said. "You don't have to be a rock promoter." She put her arms around him. "A roadie's good enough for me."

He shook off her embrace, dancing around like a prize-fighter in his agitation. "Shit! You don't get it. I am a rock promoter! You didn't know me when I put Trax together. My brother and my best buddy and these other assholes. Without me they would have never gotten together. Now they're flyin', man." He slowed down his dancing feet and finished softly. "And I'm a fuckin' roadie."

"That's okay," said Nikki. She put her arms around him. This time he didn't shake her off. She looked him in the eye and said, "I love you exactly as you are," before kissing him on the mouth.

He returned her kiss with passion, then held her out away from his body. "Suzanne called me a phony. Do you think I'm a phony?" he asked.

"No," she answered. "I think you're the man I love." She gave him a gentle punch to the shoulder. "Now, cut out all this foolishness and let's eat."

He lurched back as if she had walloped him. "Whooee, you're a mean woman," he said, grabbing his shoulder. "Guess I'll have to do what you say." He gave her a mock leer and said hopefully, "The chains again?"

Nikki giggled. They sparred playfully as they began filling up their plates at the buffet. I sighed with relief.

"The lovebirds at it again?" asked a familiar voice.

I looked up and saw Craig's smiling face. He looked more relaxed now. Maybe the swim had done him good. I smiled back.

He bent down and whispered. "Do you know you're being watched?" He tipped his head to point across the room.

I turned to look, just in time to see the twins studiously avoiding my glance. I turned back to Craig. "Get some food and I'll tell you about them," I whispered back. "But you've got to keep what I tell you under your hat."

"Bond's the name," he replied with a wink. "Secrecy's the game."

It was a good and pleasant meal, an interval of peace and relaxation. I told Craig all about the twins. He promised to keep his lips sealed. Pretty soon we were talking about old times. Nostalgia can be dangerous.

"Kate, we were always so good together," began Craig.

Time to change the subject, I thought. But I didn't have to.

Two tables over, Jack Ireland jumped up out of his seat and blew a short blues riff through his cupped hands. Heads turned toward him. He didn't seem to notice.

"You're right, as always, baby," he sang to Nikki. He blew a few more notes, then cried, "Enough of this shit!" He pulled Nikki from her seat. "Let's get high and fly," he sang.

"Oh, Jack," Nikki answered sadly. She shook her head.

"Come on, baby," he cajoled. "It'll be copacetic. Do a

little ecstasy—or maybe a toot or two—and then ride the Harley into the desert." He grinned at her. "It's such a trip flying high down the highway. They even named it for getting high. The *high*way. Get it?" He threw his head back and laughed. When he didn't get a response from Nikki, he cupped his hand gently under her chin and pulled her face up to his. "How about it, baby?" he asked softly.

"No, Jack," she said, shaking her head violently. "We came here so you'd get clean."

"Come on, baby," he pleaded.

"Did you bring drugs along with you?" she asked. I shifted in my chair uncomfortably. Wasn't she afraid of being overheard?

Jack shuffled his feet guiltily.

"Jack, answer me!" Nikki said. Apparently she didn't care if anyone was listening. Her tone was no longer gentle. And it was loud. "Where's your stash? Where's the coke? Where's the ecstasy?"

"Forget it," he answered. He threw himself back into his chair. "I'll go by myself."

But Nikki wasn't going to drop it. "You don't need any more drugs," she said. "You're already drunk! You think I'm stupid. I know you've got your beer hidden out there somewhere." Her beautiful eyes were glossy with tears. "Jack, this vacation was for you. To get you clean."

"I know, baby," he mumbled. He reached out a hand and stroked her arm gently. She sat down at the table and put her head in her hands.

"Hey, baby," said Jack softly. "It was just a couple of beers. No big deal. Gives me a little buzz is all."

Nikki lifted her head. Her makeup was dissolving under her tears. "How many is a couple?" she asked. "Twelve? Twenty?"

"I need it," Jack said quietly.

"You need to quit," Nikki answered. "Be real!"

"You think I'm a phony, too," said Jack sadly. He didn't look far from tears himself.

"I think you're an alcoholic," corrected Nikki.

Jack dropped his head.

"Jack?" prodded Nikki gently.

He lifted his head to speak but I missed his words. Just as

he opened his mouth, Ruth Ziegler swept into the room shouting, "I've sold *Healing the Broken Heart!*"

In Ruth's rush to our table she blocked my view of Jack and Nikki.

"I just wanted to thank you for your help with my title," she said. She bent over to hug me. I peered over her shoulder at Jack and Nikki as she engulfed me. But it was no use. I couldn't hear what Jack was saying over Ruth's spate of words.

"My agent says they love the idea. They love the title. They've already made a six-figure offer on the advance!" She clapped her hands together in delight. "And my agent says she can get them to go even higher."

"That's wonderful," I said.

"It is wonderful." She sighed dreamily. Then she scanned the dining hall until she spotted Terry.

"Terry," she shouted. "Did you hear?"

"How could I help it?" he answered as he walked toward us. "You're getting money. The final objective of psychology." His smile took the sting from the words.

Ruth chuckled. "I should have known you could find the grey lining in the silver cloud. But live a little. Congratulate me."

"Congratulations," he said. He gave her a quick hug. "Now all you have to do is write it."

Ruth tucked her hand in the crook of Terry's arm and they walked off together. As her excited babble retreated, I could hear Jack's voice once more.

"Okay," he said. "I'll watch the fuckin' yoga movie. But then I'm out of here. With or without you!"

Nikki offered no reply. They continued with their meal in an uncharacteristic silence, heads bowed over their respective plates.

Damn.

I turned back to Craig. There was a hint of amusement on his tired face. "You could go sit with them," he suggested in a whisper. "Then you could hear everything they say."

"That obvious?" I asked.

"That obvious," he confirmed. "But you should have been watching the old ladies—"

"The twins," I corrected.

"Okay, the twins," he agreed. "The skinny one's eyes almost popped through her glasses when Nikki mentioned drugs.'' He glanced across the room in their direction. "Don't look now, but I think they're at work."

My head whipped around before I could stop myself. Edna was shaking Ruth's hand. From the snatches of conversation I could hear, she seemed to be congratulating Ruth on her book sale. Arletta had moved in on Terry. She looked up at his face, a flirtatious tilt to her head. I could hear her giggle at whatever he was saying.

I turned back to Craig. "Let's hear it for the detective's assistants," I proposed, and raised my glass of organic apple juice.

The after-dinner yoga movie was better than *Solar Cooking for Vegetarians*, but not by much. I told myself I'd stick with tai chi as I walked back to Rose Court from the old theatre. I was alone on the dirt path. Craig had offered to escort me, but the longing look in his brown puppy-eyes had signaled danger to me. I didn't want to reject any more romantic proposals. I didn't want to witness any more hurt in those eyes. So I rejected his offer to walk me home. Now, I listened to my unnaturally loud footsteps echo in the dark and wished I had taken him up on his offer. I stepped up my pace to a near-jog.

By the time I reached Rose Court, my pulse was stampeding and I was out of breath. I was busy blaming Barbara and her spirit guides for my jittery nerves when I saw the dark figure silhouetted in the doorway.

- Twelve -

SHOULD I RUN? Even in the dark I could tell the figure in the doorway was menacingly tall and muscular. At least it couldn't be Paul Beaumont. Paul was small and slender, the guy in the doorway was huge. He looked as big as my sweetie, Wayne.

I centered myself and stepped cautiously forward until I was close enough to see the face that went with the body. It was a scarred and pitted face, dominated by an enormous cauliflower nose and brows so low I could barely glimpse the sorrowful brown eyes peering out. Hot damn! The guy wasn't just as big as Wayne. He *was* Wayne!

"I'm sorry," Wayne growled softly. "Couldn't stay away. Kid at the desk told me which building you were in."

The leap I made into his arms would have probably knocked over a smaller man. But Wayne just moved with it and lifted me into the air. Then he pulled me to his chest. I put my arms around his neck and held tight, my feet dangling above the ground.

"It's okay?" he inquired, his low voice muffled by my hair.

"Okay?" I echoed.

He put me back on the ground and bent his head down to look me in the eye. "Okay that I came here," he explained. "Didn't want to patronize you. I know you can take care of yourself. But I was so worried—"

"It's all right," I said. "Everything is all right now."

I peered under his eyebrows. His eyes still looked doubtful. The incongruity continually amazed me. Here was a man with a law degree. A former bodyguard with a blackbelt in karate who managed several businesses. And he had yet to learn to be pushy. I grabbed his head by its curly brown hair, pulled him to me and kissed his homely face all over until my lips were numb. If that didn't reassure him, nothing would.

It seemed to reassure him. He was smiling when I pulled my lips away.

"You don't know how glad I am to see you," I said. "I must have called your answering machine a million times." All right. So I exaggerated. All in a good cause. "Where were you, anyway?" I asked.

"Getting business taken care of," he answered, "so I could fly down. Know I should have called. But I was afraid you'd tell me to stay home."

He was right. I probably would have told him to stay home. I scrutinized Wayne's shy, scarred face and found myself glad for the pinch of cunning in his soberly thoughtful nature. The miasma of Spa Santé began to lift. I pointed at Wayne's suitcase and gave his arm a squeeze.

"Feel like coming up to my room, big boy?" I said in my best Mae West voice.

Wayne's answer was to pick me up and kiss my lips until they were numb again. Wayne didn't talk a lot. But he was still a great communicator. Once he put me back down, we climbed the staircase together.

My foot was suspended over the last stair when I stopped short. "Who's feeding the cat?" I asked. Had he forgotten my poor cat, C.C.?

"Felix," Wayne answered.

I chuckled. Poor Felix.

"Felix is not happy," Wayne added. He looked at me inquiringly. "Says you're not sharing. Thinks you know who the murderer is."

"I don't have a clue," I said. I took the last stair, and strode down the hall. "And you know what? Right now, I really don't care."

With that I opened my door, flipped on the light and waved Wayne into my room.

Wayne entered the room and stopped dead. For a heart-clutching moment I thought he must have seen a danger I didn't. Then I remembered. It was his first view of the saffron curtains and phantasmagoric paisley wallpaper that covered my room. I kept quiet as he walked over to the wall to study the psychedelic squiggles. Once he had finished, he turned to me, his face deadpan.

"Groovy, man," he pronounced carefully. "Make love not war?"

It sounded good to me.

It felt good too.

We were still at it the next morning, when Craig knocked on the door. Guiltily, I pulled the covers up over my head and Wayne's, suffering simultaneously the fear of discovery and the pleasure of forbidden love usually reserved for teen-agers.

"Kate?" Craig called. "Are you up?"

I buried my face in the tangle of hair on Wayne's chest, ostrich-style. Craig knocked again. Poor Craig. Part of me wanted to cry for his loneliness, for my own betrayal of his renewed romantic longings. But another part of me had the irrational urge to laugh. I began to shake with the tickle of incipient giggles. I felt the tickle spread to Wayne's body, vibrating his long torso with ever-increasing tremors.

"Kate?" called Craig again.

Wayne pulled me up the full length of his torso slowly until our faces met. Then he stifled both of our giggles with a long, silent kiss. I listened to Craig's footsteps receding as Wayne's gentle hands drew me back into passion. Then I forgot to be guilty for a while.

But I made up for it an hour later. The guilt came back the minute Craig knocked on my door again. No matter that Craig and I were divorced and that Craig knew about Wayne. No matter that I was only at Spa Santé to help Craig in the first place. No matter that Wayne and I were fully dressed now. Despite all that, I knew that Wayne's presence in my room was going to be one more hurt for the already battered Craig. Damn.

"Kate?" Craig called once again.

I took a breath and opened the door.

"Look, Ma," Craig said, displaying his hands, palms up. "No panic. I didn't even go and look for you when you didn't answer your door. I had breakfast instead. I'm a new man."

He was looking better; the tension of the last days seemed to have receded from his face.

Not for long. I saw his body stiffen as he looked past me and spotted Wayne. Craig's eyes widened instantly with hurt. By the time he had them back to normal size the old tension had returned, tightening his face into a smiling skeleton's once more.

"You've met Wayne, of course," I said. Thank God for social conventions in times of stress.

Wayne moved forward dutifully, his hand extended.

Craig shook it with unsuitable heartiness. "Just get in?" he inquired hopefully.

"Last night," Wayne answered softly. I recognized the undertone of pity in his soft words. I hoped Craig couldn't hear it.

The artificial smile tightened another click on Craig's strained face. We stood in an uncomfortable silence for a few moments. I tried but failed to think of something neutral to talk about. Craig regained his sociability first.

"You've got to try Fran's breakfast buffet while you're here," he said with a good show of bonhomie. "Great vegetarian cooking. You'll love it."

Wayne nodded politely. I wondered if Craig remembered that Wayne wasn't a vegetarian. Was this his way of baiting Wayne? There was no clue in his frantically smiling face.

"I think I'll go for a drive, myself," Craig rattled on. "Lots of interesting sights around here. I'll walk with you to the dining hall if you'd like. It's next to the parking lot."

"Sounds good to me," said Wayne. He looked in my direction for affirmation.

"Great!" I said, in an effort to match Craig's geniality. I led the way out the door.

Once Craig, Wayne and I had exhausted the subject of sightseeing in Southern California, we let the strained conversation die in peace and trod the dirt path silently. When the main building came into view it was all I could do to keep from running to it to accelerate our parting.

"I'll see you two later," Craig announced with false cheeriness as we reached the end of the path. Then again, maybe it wasn't false. Maybe he was just as heartened by the prospect of our parting as I was.

"See you then," Wayne and I chimed in together. Craig

strode off to the parking lot with one last wave in our direction.

Wayne and I shared a sigh of relief and started up the stairs of the main building.

We were almost to the doors when we heard Craig's shout.

"Kate!" he cried. Then more urgently, "Help! Somebody help!"

Wayne was down the stairs and into the parking lot before Craig's last "help" hit the air. I clattered down a few seconds after him, fueled by adrenaline.

I sprinted through the gravel parking lot toward the sparse row of cars at the front. Wayne stood there bent over Craig in the space between two parked cars. Craig was on his knees, clutching his stomach. Had he been hit? I heard the sound of retching, and ran on. Just before I reached them, my attention was diverted by a motorcycle lying on its side a few feet in front of Craig. There were two freckled legs sticking out from underneath it.

I veered toward the overturned motorcycle. An accident? Was the rider still alive? Then I saw Jack Ireland's head, peering out from under the other end of the bike. His protuberant eyes stared up at the sky, as if surprised at what had happened to the top of his head. "A bloody pulp." The words popped unbidden into my brain. I had heard them so often. But I had never seen the reality they conveyed. Not until now. My stomach spasmed.

He has to be dead, a detached voice in my head informed me. No way a man can live with his brains splashed out on the ground. The air around me shimmered and undulated. I had to sit down. I dropped to the gravel with a spine-wrenching plop, glad I had no breakfast to lose.

Wayne was suddenly there in front of me. He knelt down to put his hands on my shoulders. But I could still see Jack underneath his arm. Jack's head hadn't been pulverized by a fall from his motorcycle. This was no accident. Then I noticed the mark around Jack's neck, a distinct groove that had bitten into the flesh. And I remembered what Edna had said about the mark around Suzanne's neck.

"No accident," I whispered aloud and dropped my head into my hands. Barbara was right. There was hatred here.

But who? Why? Even in shock, the questions began to form. I lifted my head to Wayne. His eyes had filled with

tears underneath those heavy brows. His reaction to shock. I
tugged at his arm and he plopped down next to me. I put my
arm around his shoulder. He gave my thigh a gentle squeeze
of thanks.

I looked in Craig's direction. He was still paper-white. But
he was sitting up now, apparently finished with vomiting. He
stared down at his own lap, unseeing.

"When did you see Jack last?" The voice that asked the
question was, amazingly, my own. And it was steady.

Craig didn't answer right away. He lifted his head. His eyes
were glassy as they stared out in front of him. "After the
yoga movie," he said finally in a dead voice. "Once you had
gone, Terry and Ruth drifted off. Then I offered to help Fran
carry the VCR and monitor back to the main building. Jack
and Nikki were arguing again when Fran and I left."

"Was there anyone else there?" I asked.

"No," he said. A little feeling had crept into his voice.

"And that was the last you saw of him?"

"Yes!" His voice was shrill now and shaking. "Oh God.
I found his body! They'll think it was me for sure. First
Suzanne, now Jack!"

Wayne and I exchanged worried glances. Craig might be
right. But we had to call the police.

Wayne and I helped Craig up and walked him back to the
main building. As we climbed the stairs, Craig began to sob.
Wayne patted his shoulder awkwardly. We found Fran in the
lobby, behind the registration desk.

"We've got fresh blueberry muffins today and tofu ranche-
ros . . ." she began cheerfully. Then her eyes focused on us.
Whatever she saw there told her it was bad news.

"What's wrong? What's happened?" she asked shrilly.
Then she pointed at Wayne in fear. "Who is he? What's he
done?"

I winced and turned to Wayne quickly. His homely face
didn't reflect any hurt. But then, it didn't reflect anything. It
had turned to stone. Damn. With that battered, malformed
face and looming body, he was the physical archetype of a
mass-murderer. I grabbed his hand and squeezed gently in
an attempt to anesthetize the hurt. This wasn't the first time
he had been misjudged by his appearance.

"This is my friend Wayne," I said firmly to Fran.

She stepped back. "Oh, I'm so sorry. I . . . I'm just on

edge since—'' She broke off, probably seeking a euphemism. She attempted a hospitable smile.

Should I tell her there had been a new murder at Spa Santé?

"There's been another accident," I said, opting for euphemism myself. "I need to call Chief Orlandi."

Fran's jaw dropped open. Then she began to wail. "No! Oh, please, no! Not another one!"

I couldn't handle any more hysterics. I left Wayne and Craig to keep her company and found the phone in her office myself. My call to the Delores Police Department was instantly routed through to Chief Orlandi. Thank God for small town police departments. The Chief didn't waste any words, mine or his, once he understood what I was telling him. He cut me off with the admonition to stay put, touch nothing and shut up. He would be there within minutes, he assured me. I hung up and rested my head on Fran's desk for a moment. It was so nice and quiet there. I didn't want to leave.

But I did. I forced myself from my chair and tracked the sound of hysteria into the dining hall. A small crowd was gathering there around Fran. She sat at one of the small tables, sobbing and wailing noisily. Roseanne leapt into her lap and let out a yowl of sympathy. Or was it simply a yowl of hunger?

Craig and Wayne had taken chairs across from Fran. Wayne's homely face was still set in stone. He sat erect and silent. Craig slumped in his chair, his handsome face blank with shock.

Ruth Ziegler had stationed herself at Fran's side. She began stroking Fran's shoulder and murmuring sweet psychotherapeutic nothings in her ear as Don Logan wheeled up. Then Avery Haskell came striding from the kitchen, his hands still white with flour, an expression of concern momentarily replacing his zombie mask. Terry trotted in just as I heard the sirens. I asked myself who was missing.

"Nikki," I answered myself. My stomach clenched with sadness. "Poor Nikki." I realized I had spoken aloud.

"What about Nikki?" asked Terry.

"Oh, God," moaned Craig. He hit the table with his fist and moaned again. Roseanne hissed.

"What's going on?" prodded Terry insistently.

"Has something happened to Nikki?" asked Ruth, her hand frozen on Fran's shoulder.

"Be quiet and let Kate answer," advised Logan from his wheelchair.

Faces were turned in my direction expectantly. Even Fran had stopped wailing to hear my answer. I drew a deep breath. "I can't say anything—" I began.

"Damn right, you can't say anything!" roared a voice from behind me. Chief Orlandi had arrived.

I turned around in relief, glad for once to see his glowering red face. Officer Dempster was behind him, his hand fluttering nervously to and from his holstered gun. And behind Officer Dempster was a young black-haired woman in uniform. Her large dark eyes were wide with excitement. At least someone was enjoying this.

"You!" Orlandi boomed, his finger pointed at me. "Show me the body." His eyes scanned the room for reactions to his words.

Fran was the first to react, throwing herself into a renewed fit of sobs and wails. Roseanne jumped from her lap and marched imperiously into the kitchen. I wished I had that option.

Avery Haskell straightened his shoulders as his zombie mask clicked back into place. Ruth's eyes and mouth opened wide in a curiously youthful expression of surprised innocence, while Don Logan's face aged with a deep frown. Terry merely arched his eyebrows over his wire-rimmed glasses, saying nothing—for the moment.

Orlandi never took his eyes from the faces around him as he shouted over Fran's sobs. "The rest of you sit down! Do not talk among yourselves! Officer Guerrero will be here to make sure no one leaves!" The black-haired officer stepped forward eagerly, scrutinizing the batch of suspects.

Avery and Ruth sat down at a nearby table. Ruth was uncharacteristically silent. Terry, however, now responded in a manner true to his character.

"Body?" he asked shrilly, still standing. "Has there been another murder?"

"Sit down!" Orlandi roared.

"We have a right—" Terry began.

"One more word and Officer Dempster will remove you," Orlandi warned. Terry opened his mouth.

Officer Dempster stepped forward. His hand was on the butt of his gun. Orlandi glowered at Terry.

"Okay," said Terry, throwing up his hands. "Okay." He sat down next to Ruth.

Officer Dempster relaxed. I guess "okay" didn't count as a word. The Chief's eyes lighted on Wayne. "You the boyfriend?" he asked. Wayne nodded.

"You!" Orlandi pointed at Dempster. "Find the ones that are missing." He looked around. "Bradley Beaumont. And the kid—"

"He's at school," Fran mumbled through her sobs.

"Forget the kid for now," Orlandi said. "But find the girlfriend. Black woman. Nikki Martin."

He paused for a moment watching the faces around him. Then he turned to me. "Let's go," he said and wheeled around to lead me outside.

"I don't really want to see the body again," I mumbled as I followed Orlandi down the stairs.

"What? A little mashed flesh bothers you?" he asked. His crocodile grin had returned. "You, the great detective?"

I wasn't glad to see him anymore.

As we walked across the parking lot I saw yet another uniformed police officer standing in front of the space where Jack's body lay. Maybe Delores wasn't as small a town as I thought.

Orlandi took me about four feet from the space between the cars and pointed. The renewed sight of those freckled legs sticking out from underneath the motorcycle brought the sting of tears to my eyes. Jack had been a vital man. Always in motion. Dancing, joking, blowing his imaginary trumpet. And so sadly flawed. I thought again of Nikki.

"Does the body look the same as when you left it?" Orlandi's gruff voice interrupted my thoughts. The body? That was Jack Ireland under there, I thought angrily.

"Yes," I answered aloud. I lowered my eyes so I didn't have to see Jack anymore.

"Did you touch the body?" Orlandi asked.

"No," I answered. The shorter I kept my answers, the sooner I could leave. Or so I hoped.

"How about Mr. Jasper or your boyfriend?" There was a hint of a sneer in the way the Chief pronounced "boyfriend." I looked up to see if the sneer was in his eyes. It wasn't. His eyes were deadly serious.

"No," I answered again.

"Show me how close you got," Orlandi ordered.

Reluctantly, I lifted my foot to step closer to Jack's body. Orlandi grabbed my shoulder gently. The gentleness surprised me.

"Just point," he ordered.

I pointed.

And so it went for fifteen minutes more until Orlandi's final question.

"Just one more thing," he said, his crocodile grin back in place. "Which one of you lost your breakfast?"

"Craig," I said quietly, refusing to return his smile.

As Chief Orlandi and I climbed the stairs together, my legs began to tremble. I wondered if I'd make it all the way up. I did. But by the time we reached the dining hall, the trembling had spread to my arms and hands. Even my face.

Chief Orlandi put his hand on my shoulder and guided me past the cluster of suspects in the center of the room to one of the far tables by the window. "Have a seat," he ordered.

I shook my head. No way. I wasn't going to isolate myself from the others. I jerked my shoulder away from his hand and marched my trembling body back across the room to a seat next to Wayne, smack in the midst of the suspects.

Chief Orlandi followed me, shrugging his shoulders. Then he made an elaborate maitre d' bow, indicating the chair I had already chosen. I dropped into the seat gratefully. I felt Wayne's comforting hand settle onto my thigh and sighed. I didn't dare turn to face him. I was too near to tears. A glimpse of his kind face and they would spill over.

Orlandi bent over me and issued one last order. "You'll answer the rest of my questions later," he growled. Then he stomped over to Officer Guerrero for a whispered consultation. More questions? What more could he possibly have to ask me?

A shrill hoot of laughter punctured my thought. I looked up, startled. Officer Dempster had apparently retrieved Bradley. He sat next to Fran, grinning. The hair went up on the back of my trembling neck. Was Bradley the murderer? The question no longer seemed academic.

I began to scan the faces around me once more. Most, like Craig's, were blank with shock. Only Bradley was smiling. Avery Haskell's head was bent low over clasped hands. His lips moved silently. Praying? Terry squirmed in his chair.

I risked a look at Wayne next to me, and was rewarded by a soulful gaze, only partially obscured by his overhanging brows. I pulled my chair closer to him, so our thighs touched. Tears stung my eyes once more.

"What's happened?" The shout ricocheted off the walls of the dining hall. Nikki had entered the doorway, Officer Dempster steering her by one elbow. She looked at us for information, her face grey with anxiety. When no one answered her cry, she turned to Orlandi.

"What's happened?" she shouted again, her voice growing shriller with repetition.

He strode toward her, arm out in front of him, palm forward, as if to ward off her question.

"Where's Jack?" she screamed.

– Thirteen –

NIKKI'S SCREAM GALVANIZED Chief Orlandi. With one more long running stride he landed in front of her, both arms outstretched now, palms raised in the universal gesture for "Stop."

"Calm down, Miss Martin," he said in a low, reasonable voice. He lowered his arms slowly. "Let's go and talk in the office."

Grey-faced, her eyes round with incipient hysteria, Nikki gawked at him, stunned for the moment by his composure. He motioned her toward the door. She didn't move. "No," she said softly. "Tell me now. Tell me what's happened."

Orlandi sighed, then asked his own question. "When did you last see Mr. Ireland?" he whispered.

"Last night," she replied. "He never came back to the room." The shrill tone had crept into her voice again gradually. She searched Orlandi's eyes. "Is he okay?" she demanded, her voice shriller still and louder.

Orlandi said nothing.

"God damn you! Tell me he's okay!" she screamed. She reached toward his shoulders, as if to shake the statement out of him.

Orlandi stepped back, avoiding her hands. He nodded at Officer Dempster. Each of them took one of Nikki's arms, and together they led her out through the glass doors of the dining hall and into Fran's office.

"NO!" We heard Nikki's howl all the way in the dining room.

I turned to Wayne and saw the moist compassion in his

eyes. That was all it took. All the tears I had been holding
back since I saw Jack's body came spilling out. I cried for
Jack. He would have no chance to redeem himself now. No
chance to cut the big deal, the one that would have made him
a genuine rock promoter. Then I cried for Nikki, left behind,
her last words to Jack spoken in anger.

Wayne put his arm around me. I buried my face in his
shoulder and cried for Craig, frightened and lonely. Blindly,
I reached out across Wayne's lap to touch Craig's hand. Craig
met the touch with a spasmodic squeeze. I even shed a tear
for Suzanne. She'd been selfish, but her life had been a sad
one.

As my tears subsided, my mind began to clear. The torrent
had washed away the dulling film of shock. Suddenly alert, I
came to one happy conclusion. Craig hadn't killed Suzanne.
I hadn't really been certain until that moment of lucidity. I
gazed over at him, trying without words to tell him I knew
he was innocent now. He cocked his head as if trying to
receive the message, then frowned in frustration. So much
for telepathy.

Suzanne and Jack had been killed by the same person. The
marks on the body proved that. At least they proved it to me.
And Craig hadn't killed Jack. His reaction to seeing Jack's
body had been genuine. Maybe you can fake tears, but vomit?
The resident cynic in my brain reminded me about the old
fingers-down-the-throat routine. I told it to shut up. Fake
vomit or no, I'd have bet my life Craig hadn't known Jack
was dead until he stumbled over his body.

I began rapidly scanning faces once more. And I wasn't
the only one. Ruth's black button-eyes were bright with interest as she studied Bradley. Don Logan watched Bradley
too. And Bradley, in turn, was busy grinning at Don Logan.
Hard to tell what that meant. Meanwhile, Terry had his eye
on Avery Haskell. Avery was still silently praying. Fran was
squinting at Wayne. At Wayne! The accusation couldn't have
been made more clearly if she had spoken it aloud.

I did some deep breathing and told myself that Fran's oc-
ular opinions could not be held against her. Then I went on
with my eyeball poll. Wayne was scrutinizing Bradley as well.
And Craig's eyes were fastened on Wayne. But the look on
Craig's face seemed to be less one of accusation than one of

bewildered hurt. Hurt that I would choose Wayne over him? Craig caught my gaze and looked away guiltily.

I tabulated the votes for murderer. Three in favor of Bradley. One for Avery Haskell. A possible vote for Don Logan, though I wasn't sure that a grin counted. And one or two for Wayne. Bradley was the clear winner. But we were missing a couple of candidates: Nikki Martin and Paul Beaumont. And Bradley's superior P.R. effort had to be taken into account.

Bradley let out a high-pitched cackle as if to underscore my point. The suspects were getting restless.

Avery Haskell drowned out the tail end of Bradley's cackle by giving voice to his heretofore silent prayer. "Oh my God, I trust in thee. Let me not be ashamed. Let not mine enemies triumph over me," he intoned.

Officer Guerrero jerked her head in his direction, startled by the psalm. Then she simply averted her eyes, giving tacit permission for this form of speech.

Terry decided to test the no talking rule. He began muttering in a low voice. I caught "constitutional rights" and "police brutality" but nothing else. Officer Guerrero glared at him but remained silent.

"Yea, let none that wait on thee be ashamed," Haskell intoned. He opened his eyes and swept us with his gaze as he went on. "Let them be ashamed which transgress without cause."

Don Logan shook his head irritably and wheeled himself over to the window. Bradley let out another loon's call.

"Lead me in thy truth, Oh Lord. And teach me—" Avery chanted.

"That's enough!" snapped Officer Guerrero. "I know you guys are bored. But you heard the Chief. No talking."

Her words were too little, too late. The spell was broken. The revolution had begun.

"It's ten o'clock," pleaded Fran. "I've got to start working on lunch. Can't I go to the kitchen? It's right through those swinging doors."

"Well . . ." said Officer Guerrero, considering. She ran her hand through her black hair nervously. Then she looked hopefully out the glass doors. But there was no help in sight. The decision was hers.

"Maybe we can bring some of the food out here and

work,'' suggested Avery Haskell. It was amazing how reasonable he sounded when he wasn't quoting the Bible. "Chop up vegetables. That kind of thing.''

Officer Guerrero looked back and forth between Avery and Fran's faces. Checking for conspiracy?

"Okay,'' she finally agreed. "Bring what you need out here. But only one of you at a time. And remember, I'm watching you.''

Guerrero stationed herself by the swinging doors, alternating glances between Fran in the kitchen and the rest of us in the dining hall. Her head bobbed back and forth like a spectator at a tennis match.

Fran made several trips, loading up the long communal table with bags of vegetables and fruits, tubs of tofu, jars of condiments and spices, and bowls of mysterious substances. Then she brought out the knives and other utensils. Guerrero eyed the knives suspiciously but made no objection.

"I'll chop something,'' I offered. Anything was better than sitting quietly watching suspects suspect other suspects.

"Me too,'' growled Wayne.

"I'd love to help,'' Craig chimed in, not to be outdone.

Minutes later we were all seated at the communal table, working quietly at our assigned tasks, like nuns and monks who had taken vows of silence. I felt at peace, carefully sculpting carrot sticks and radish roses. Taking the time for perfection. A life of contemplation was looking pretty good. Then Orlandi came back with Nikki.

I heard her low moaning before I saw her. My body constricted with pity at the sound and my hand slipped, ruining the perfection of my radish rose. I looked up in time to see Orlandi leading Nikki through the glass doors. Her wide-set eyes were now swollen and red, her luminous skin turned to ash. Her perfect body was bent from the middle as if she had been punched in the stomach.

Ruth rushed forward, arms outstretched to Nikki. Officer Guerrero moved quickly to block her path. Ruth came to an abrupt halt, her black gypsy eyes sizzling.

"You are denying Miss Martin the comfort and support she needs to survive this emotional injury,'' Ruth whispered urgently. Her low voice was imbued with both righteousness and menace.

Officer Guerrero shrank back into her uniform as if afraid

of the gypsy curse implicit in Ruth's dark look. But she held her ground. Ruth turned her glare on the Chief.

"Well?" she demanded. "You're in charge here. Are you going to deny Miss Martin aid? Do you want to be responsible for the consequences?"

Chief Orlandi glared back at Ruth for a moment, blue eyes battling black ones. Then he flashed his crocodile grin.

"Go ahead," he said genially, "take care of her." Then his voice hardened again. "But don't discuss the case," he ordered.

Officer Guerrero stepped aside, relief evident on her face. The Chief motioned her to join him outside the glass doors for a consultation.

Ruth took the last few steps to Nikki at a jog. She opened her arms wide and Nikki went to her like a child to her mother. As Ruth embraced her, the young woman let out a piercing cry of grief.

"That's good," murmured Ruth, stroking her hair. "Let it out." She led Nikki to a nearby chair and eased her into it, never once removing her comforting arms. She kept one arm around Nikki even as she reached out to pull a chair forward for herself. Nikki wept through it all.

As I listened to her weep, my heart went out to her. But my brain held back, reminding me that Nikki Martin was an actress. But why would Nikki have killed both Jack and Suzanne? I could imagine her killing Jack in a fit of anger. And maybe having killed Suzanne in a fit of jealousy. But both of them?

That was the crux. Who had the motive to kill both Jack *and* Suzanne? I turned to Wayne, slicing zucchini next to me, thinking the question at him. If only we could talk, even without words. But his eyes were focused on his ever widening batch of zucchini rounds. I picked up a carrot and sliced.

Had Jack known who killed Suzanne? He would have spoken out if he had. Unless . . . My gaze passed over my untidy heap of carrot sticks to Nikki weeping in Ruth's arms. Unless he had reason to protect the killer. All right. Given that Nikki had killed Suzanne, could she have counted on Jack continuing to shield her if they split up? No. She would have had to kill him. Still—I shook my head impatiently, then grabbed another carrot. I was on the wrong track. Nikki had loved Jack too much to kill him. At least I hoped so.

Maybe the killer had only mistakenly believed that Jack knew his, or her, identity. My skin tingled as I considered. Jack babbling on unaware, the killer unsure of what the outspoken redhead really knew. But why wait two days to silence him? I went back to slicing.

I stacked my carrots sticks in a neat log-like pile and pondered. Maybe Jack didn't know anything about the murderer. Maybe he and Suzanne were killed for the same reason. Something they had in common. I looked over at Craig, who sat cubing boiled potatoes with the precision of a robot. Both Jack and Suzanne had argued with their lovers before death. Was our murderer a reverse Cupid, untangling unhappy lovers the quickest way possible?

What else did Jack and Suzanne have in common? They were reluctant visitors at the spa. I doubted either was vegetarian. But then I doubted that many of us here in the dining hall were strict vegetarians. Nikki had probably brought Jack because there was no alcohol on the premises. A cheap alternative to The Betty Ford Clinic. And I guessed that Don Logan was here because the spa was organized for wheelchair accessibility. Most cattle ranchers weren't vegetarian.

I looked over at Bradley. He now stared into space, his luminous eyes flickering through movies only he could see, letting out a piercing giggle every few frames. Now, there was a shining example of the strict vegetarian. Damn. Made me want to bite a cow.

Or something. My stomach growled. I was hungry. I picked up a carrot stick and chomped. Some brunch. I looked longingly at the buffet, hoping that someone else would be insensitive enough to mention that they were hungry and start a line. I sniffed. Could I smell cinnamon?

I was fantasizing fresh cinnamon-applesauce bread when Chief Orlandi stomped back into the room. Officer Guerrero strode in behind him.

"You!" he shouted, pointing at Craig. "You're next. Follow me."

Craig looked at Orlandi and turned as white as the tower of potatoes he had cubed. He laid the knife down carefully and stood up. His hands were trembling.

The carrot I was chewing seemed suddenly dry in my

mouth. I swallowed hard and got it down. I wasn't hungry anymore. I threw an encouraging smile in Craig's direction. But he wasn't looking at me. His eyes were locked onto Chief Orlandi's face, mesmerized.

Chief Orlandi gestured for Craig to precede him. Craig stepped out in front, back straight but trembling. A brave prisoner to the gallows. They exited the glass doors in procession.

"He was a good man," Nikki pronounced into the silence left behind, her voice thickened from silk to velvet by her tears. For an instant I thought she meant Craig. Then she went on. "Jack never hurt anyone."

"Good," said Ruth softly. She stroked Nikki's hair, encouraging her to continue.

Officer Guerrero's head twitched in their direction. Did this count as discussing the case?

"He was an innocent. A child. He expected the best of people," Nikki continued. She looked at Ruth with round eyes that pleaded for understanding.

"Yes," said Ruth, nodding. "Yes."

"He wanted people to be happy. That's all. That's why he clowned around. He was totally generous. He'd give dollar bills to panhandlers. You know what I mean?"

"Of course," answered Ruth, her voice as warm and comforting as a heated blanket.

"And he was talented. But he gave it all away." Nikki dropped her gaze to her lap. Then the wail came. "I'm so sorry!" she sobbed.

"Tell him," said Ruth quietly. "Tell Jack you're sorry. He'll listen."

Nikki looked trustingly at Ruth, her eyes filled with wonder and tears. "Will he?" she asked.

"He's too good a man to turn away," Ruth assured her.

Nikki closed her eyes. "I'm sorry Jack," she whispered. "I always loved you, no matter what I said." Then she wept softly. Ruth put her arms around her, rocking her slowly.

"He heard you," Ruth said after a time. "And he forgives you."

Nikki's quiet weeping blossomed into heaving sobs once more. She wasn't alone in her grief. Through blurry eyes I saw Wayne lay down his knife and shove his zucchini rounds to the side to avoid showering them with tears. Fran didn't bother. She wept copiously into her previously salt-free hummus.

Terry had pulled off his glasses to wipe his eyes. He knuckled them angrily as if ashamed of their wetness. Don Logan turned away, affecting disinterest, but I detected a tremor in his massive shoulders. Reality had even broken through to Bradley Beaumont. He was no longer grinning. His face looked sane now, full of gentle concern. And Ruth had given way to her own sadness. Her work done, she sobbed along with Nikki now.

Avery Haskell recited softly: "Yea, though I walk through the valley of the shadow of death, I will fear no evil. For thou art with me. Thy rod and they staff, they comfort me. . . ." Everyone offers comfort in his own way.

And the tears were not limited to civilians. Officer Guerrero glared through hers, sniffing them away spasmodically. Finally, she pulled out a large white handkerchief and blew her nose. She knocked her hand awkwardly against her gun butt as she shoved her hankie back in her pocket.

Not a dry eye in the house, I thought. Damn. Was Nikki just acting? The question wouldn't go away. Was the questioning my own defense against grief? Pretend this was only a movie, and I could walk away without scars?

The crash of a chair pushed back violently interrupted my self-examination. I looked up to see Nikki on her feet in front of the toppled chair. Her reddened eyes surveyed the crowd intently. Officer Guerrero stepped forward quickly, suddenly alert.

"One of you probably killed Jack," Nikki said. Her voice was cold and hard. Only its underlying quiver betrayed the remnant of sadness.

The room that had seemed quiet before now went entirely still. No prayers, no sobs, no muttering.

"Whoever you are," she proclaimed, "I hope you suffer for your guilt. I hope it torments you. I hope there is a hell—"

"That's enough," Officer Guerrero rapped out. This was clearly discussing the case as far as she was concerned. She grabbed Nikki's arm and led her to a chair on the other side of the room. Nikki allowed herself to be led without protest. Maybe she had said all she needed to.

Ruth got up to follow Nikki, but Guerrero snapped at her,

telling her to go back to her seat. Ruth sank back in her chair, frustration and relief mingled on her open face. She looked exhausted. Her therapeutic ministrations to Nikki seemed to have worn her out.

Avery Haskell was not worn out, though—only inspired. "For a fire is kindled in mine anger, and shall burn into the lowest hell, and shall consume the earth with her increase, and set on fire the foundations of the mountains," he orated, his voice rising in volume and confidence.

Officer Guerrero shot him a look of warning. Haskell stared past her and continued: "The sword without, and terror within, shall destroy both the young man and the virgin—"

"Enough!" shouted Officer Guerrero. I resisted the urge to support her with a loud "amen." I doubted she would appreciate it.

Haskell turned his empty face to Guerrero's angry one for a moment. Guerrero won the face-off. Haskell dropped his head and began to move his lips silently once more.

I went back to my radish roses, sculpting carefully. I wanted out of this room very badly. Badly enough to hope Orlandi would take me next for interrogation. The dining hall needed a psychic fumigation.

But Orlandi didn't take me next. He took Don Logan. Craig never returned to the dining hall, apparently free to go after the interview. Lucky guy. Then Orlandi interviewed Fran. She walked straight to the kitchen when she returned. Bradley was led away next. Then Avery Haskell. Avery returned, but only to repossess our chopped vegetables and knives. Damn. Then they took Terry. Then Ruth. And Nikki left the hall when Ruth did.

By twelve o'clock only Wayne and I were left under Officer Guerrero's halfhearted surveillance. I ran my eyes over Wayne's face. He looked sad and tired, but he returned my gaze with a faint smile. Poor guy. Was he still glad he had come? At least there was no way he could be suspected of this murder. I hoped.

I curled my lips in what I hoped would be interpreted as an apologetic grin. He formed his lips into a silent kiss, which he blew to me from his fingertips. I shuffled my chair in his direction, without getting up. That must have been within the rules. Officer Guerrero ignored me.

Once I had shuffled close enough, I reached out to touch

his hand. He grabbed my fingers and held them. What a warm and gentle hand his was. I sighed. Then I leaned forward for a face-to-face kiss.

"Sorry to interrupt you, *Mrs*. Jasper," came a voice from behind me. The words were polite, but the tone definitely said "gotcha," not "sorry."

I turned my head and was met with the white flash of Chief Orlandi's crocodile grin. My turn. Damn.

We walked silently to Fran's office. Orlandi's grin was long gone by the time we got there. His blue eyes looked bleary. He dropped heavily into his chair and closed those eyes. I nodded at Officer Dempster, siting in the corner under a tall fern.

"Did your ex-husband discuss Jack Ireland with you, Mrs. Jasper?" Orlandi asked in a dull voice. His eyes remained closed. Officer Dempster wrote something in his notebook. He looked exhausted, too.

"No," I lied. It wasn't a complete lie. At this point I couldn't remember what Craig had said about Jack. Nothing murderous. Anyway, I rationalized, a simple "no" made things easier for Dempster to write down.

"Do you have any reason to believe Mr. Jasper killed Jack Ireland?" Orlandi droned on.

"No."

I realized this interview was going to be easy. Chief Orlandi was as tired as I was.

"Have you remembered any other details concerning the discovery of the body since I last spoke to you?"

Easy. "No."

A few more "no" questions and Chief Orlandi seemed to wake up. He opened his eyes and leaned forward, pinning me to my chair with his bright blue gaze.

"Who do *you* think did it?" he asked.

- Fourteen -

THERE WAS NO smile on Chief Orlandi's face when he asked me who I thought Jack Ireland's killer was. Orlandi was serious. And, since he was asking my opinion, he was probably desperate too. Damn.

I squirmed in my chair, wishing I could give him the answer. Wishing that he had the answer already.

"Whoever killed Jack was the same person who killed Suzanne," I offered finally. That was all I knew.

Orlandi dropped his eyes in disappointment and nodded slowly. "Looks like it," he agreed. He leaned back in his chair and his eyelids closed again.

"When was Jack killed?" I asked quietly, not really expecting an answer.

"Probably last night some time," Orlandi said dully. He sighed. I sat up in my chair, amazed by his openness. Did this mean he didn't suspect me anymore? Or just that he was too tired to care?

"How are the alibis for last night?" I asked conversationally, pushing my luck.

"What alibis!" Orlandi exploded. He sat up in his chair and glowered at me. "The only one who has anything even resembling an alibi is Avery Haskell. Spent the evening at an A.A. meeting in San Diego. You know how many people go to those things?"

I shook my head in case the question wasn't rhetorical.

"Over a hundred people at this one," he told me. "And you can bet none of them would say anything even if they had seen him. Anonymity!" He spit the last word out.

"I have an alibi, don't I?" I asked meekly.

"You and your boyfriend? Some alibi!" The Chief focused his eyes on me briefly, curling his lips in a half-smile that never fully blossomed. He leaned back in his chair and closed his eyes once more. Another sigh. "And what about the time you spent walking across the spa grounds alone?" he asked. "Where's your alibi for then?"

"Oh," I said. It was my turn to sigh. I had hoped he would say I wasn't really a suspect.

I waited for more questions, but the Chief just sat motionless, eyes still closed. Was he asleep? I looked at Officer Dempster for guidance. But Dempster just shrugged his shoulders.

"Sorry I couldn't be of more help," I said softly.

"Aw, forget it," Orlandi replied. He waved his hand at me without opening his eyes. "Get out of here."

He didn't have to ask me twice. I got to my feet quickly, nearly toppling my chair in my eagerness. As I reached to right it, Orlandi spoke:

"Keep yourself available for questioning, Mrs. Jasper," he said. His tone was hard and mean.

"Huh?" I mumbled, turning back to him. I wasn't sure if he meant now or later.

Finally, he opened his eyes. And the crocodile smile bloomed. "Don't leave town," he translated gleefully. At least he was happy again. For the moment.

"Got it," I said and skedaddled.

I trotted over to the dining hall. Wayne was sitting quietly where I had left him, his heavy brows furrowed over invisible eyes. I wondered what he was thinking. Officer Guerrero had finally taken a seat. She jumped back to her feet when I pushed the glass door open.

"Wayne," I said quickly. "I'll be out on the porch."

If this was forbidden speech, I hadn't given Officer Guerrero enough time to object. She didn't seem to care anyway. She said nothing and returned to her seat.

Wayne lifted his eyes to me and saluted. I could see worry in those eyes now that they were visible. I resisted the urge to hug him. I was sure Orlandi would appear like a bad genie if I did. So I waved goodbye and left.

I crossed the lobby and stepped out into the midday sunshine. I blinked for a moment, blinded. Then the spa came back into focus. The stucco buildings and colorful landscaping shimmered in the light invitingly. I had forgotten the physical beauty of Spa Santé. I breathed in the clean air gratefully and deeply. If I could have gulped down extra portions, I would have. Freedom feels good. Even the illusion of freedom feels good.

But my eyes betrayed me. They moved involuntarily from the soothing beauty in front of me to the activity in the parking lot on the side of the building. I walked across the porch slowly, irresistibly drawn to look at the spot where Jack's body had been. Or might still be. But I couldn't see the space over the cars. I could tell the location would be invisible from the parking lot as well. There were wooden police barriers in front of the gap between the cars, and yellow tape encircling the whole area now. I breathed a sigh of relief, wondering why I had even wanted to look.

People in and out of uniform buzzed around the yellow tape. Busy bees taking notes, taking measurements, taking pictures.

A blue Toyota rolled into the far end of the lot and stopped. Two men got out. The smaller man looked familiar, even at a distance. He trotted over to the crime scene, where he was waved away by one of the worker bees. He shrugged and returned to join the larger man again. Together, they walked toward the main building.

The larger man was tall and skinny. He looked about sixty or so, with a good-natured face given character by grizzled grey eyebrows over Coke-bottle glasses and a long nose. He was tall enough to block the smaller man from my sight as they walked.

When they reached the stairs, the smaller man came into view. No wonder his lean, small-boned body had looked familiar. It was Felix, sometimes friend and all-the-time reporter. Damn.

"Howdy hi, Kate," he greeted me as they came up the stairs. He wiggled his shaggy mustache in a smile. "This is Eli Rosen," he said, pointing at the lanky man by his side. Then he watched my eyes.

Eli Rosen? I knew that name. I looked at the lanky man climbing up the stairs, hand extended to be shaken. Then I remembered. Suzanne's Uncle Eli.

"Kate Jasper," I said as I shook Eli Rosen's hand. Now

his grizzled eyebrows rose in recognition. They ought to. He had acted as Craig's attorney in our divorce.

"I am pleased to meet you," Uncle Eli said. He had the careful pronunciation of someone to whom English is a second language. And the graciousness not to mention our connection. "Your friend Felix and I met on the airplane."

"Hey, Kate," said Felix eagerly, nodding at the parking lot. "What's with the police? New evidence?"

I ignored Felix's question. I had a question of my own for Uncle Eli. "Did Felix tell you he was a reporter?" I asked. Felix may have been my friend, but grilling an unsuspecting, probably grieving, relative was too much.

Eli raised his eyebrows again, this time in surprise. "No, he did not." The stare he turned on Felix was no longer good-natured. "So, this is the reason behind the many questions about Suzanne. A reporter."

Felix's face reddened. He flashed me a dirty look, then turned back to Eli. "Just doing my job," he muttered.

"Ah, yes," said Uncle Eli. "I too have made enemies doing my job well."

Felix rubbed his chin, considering the last comment. Did this mean he had made an enemy of Eli Rosen? Felix looked the question at me. I shrugged my shoulders. Eli's face was bland once more, giving away nothing. Time to change the subject?

Felix pointed at the parking lot again. "So what's up?" he asked.

I didn't want to talk about it. Especially in front of Uncle Eli. Let someone else tell him that his niece's murder was merely the first of two. Or more. My stomach tightened. Then another question occurred to me.

"Who the hell is feeding C.C.?" I asked Felix. "C.C.'s my cat," I explained for Uncle Eli's benefit. Eli nodded wisely.

"I gave her to Barbara," Felix answered peevishly. "I wouldn't let her starve, you know."

I shook my head, wondering if this series of abandonments would make C.C. neurotic. More neurotic, I corrected myself.

"So," Felix said, pointing for a third time at the parking lot. "What—"

"Who's feeding C.C.?" came Wayne's concerned voice from behind me.

I turned and reached for Wayne, as Felix muttered "Barbara," in exasperation.

Public or not, I needed a hug. Wayne crouched down and embraced me solidly. I held on to him, my face pressed tightly against his chest. Trying to hide from the memory of finding Jack's body. Trying to blot out the whole morning of sadness and distrust. Trying to erase the murky aura of Spa Santé itself.

"Jeez, you guys," said Felix. "How long has it been since you saw each other? Five minutes?"

I held on for a moment longer of safety.

"Give it a break," said Felix.

We gave it a break.

Coming out of the clinch, I saw Uncle Eli's good-humored face beaming at us. At least he enjoyed the spectacle. I introduced Eli to Wayne by name only. I didn't mention that Eli was Suzanne's uncle. Or Craig's lawyer.

Then the four of us stood on the porch awkwardly, not making conversation. Too many subjects were taboo. Suzanne's murder. Jack's murder. Divorce. The nosiness of reporters. The abdication of cat-care.

"You have reservations?" asked Wayne finally.

Eli nodded. "In the Orange Blossom Building," he said.

"I've got Rose Court," said Felix.

"Ah, Rose Court," I said wickedly. "You'll love the decor."

I peeked at Wayne. His face was deadpan, but I knew that paisley wallpaper had crossed his mind and that he was chuckling inside.

I was suppressing my own urge to giggle when I heard clattering footsteps from behind. I turned to see Fran scurrying in our direction.

"Oh, Kate," she said breathlessly. "I'm glad I caught you and your . . ." She darted a quick glance at Wayne. He still made her nervous.

"My friend," I finished for her.

"The lunch buffet is almost ready, in spite of all the . . . the fuss," she twittered on. "I wasn't sure people would realize. I called some of the guests. But I couldn't get Don.

Or Terry. And Nikki's line was busy. If you see them will you tell them—''

She stopped midstream and stared at Eli and Felix. Had she only now noticed them? Not unless she was blind. Or completely rattled.

''Eli Rosen and Felix Byrne, your new guests,'' I said, making the introductions brief. I was tired of being social director. And now that Fran had mentioned the buffet, I was hungry.

''Oh, dear,'' she said, goggling at Eli. She twisted her hands together. ''I'm not sure if your rooms are ready. I'm so sorry. But if you'd like to eat first—''

''I would be pleased to sample your luncheon buffet,'' interrupted Uncle Eli. But he interrupted her so graciously that Fran didn't know she had been cut off.

She looked up at him with a genuine smile on her face. ''Well, aren't you a nice man,'' she said.

''Let's go find the others,'' I said impatiently to Wayne. ''And tell them that lunch is on.''

Wayne nodded.

We didn't have to look far for Ruth. She was climbing the stairs, her face gloomy. When she reached the top stair, however, the gloom lifted.

''Eli Rosen?'' she said, squinting smiling eyes at him. ''Is that you?''

Eli fastened his eyes on her and beamed. ''Ruth Ziegler! It has been years. Are you vacationing here?''

Ruth nodded eagerly. ''And you?'' she asked.

''I have just arrived,'' Eli said. His features clouded momentarily. Remembering Suzanne? Remembering why he was here? But he went on. ''Is your husband with you?'' he asked.

''No,'' Ruth replied. Pink colored her cheeks. ''He passed away three years ago.''

''Ah,'' Eli said. ''I must offer my sympathy.'' But he didn't look sad. He looked pleased. ''Emma too is gone. It's been a little over one year.''

Ruth's black button-eyes sparkled like wet marbles as she gazed at him. Was she smitten? Eli offered her his arm.

''May I buy you lunch?'' he asked.

Ruth placed her hand on his arm with a high-pitched giggle. If I hadn't heard it myself I wouldn't have believed it possible. She *was* smitten! They walked into the lobby together. Fran trailed after them.

I turned to Wayne. He had a big goofy smile on his face as he watched them go. I was glad to see it.

"Was the first woman Fran Beaumont?" asked Felix. Damn. I had almost forgotten Felix.

"That was Fran," I agreed. "Your host."

"And murder suspect," he whispered. I looked at the eager smile on his face and sighed.

"Can't we just forget murder for a little while?" I asked.

"No way—" he began. And then he stopped short.

Fran had raced out the door again, dangling a key in front of her. "Mr. Byrne," she called. "Your room *is* ready. Here's the key. If you'll just sign the register."

"Wait for me, you guys," Felix shouted over his shoulder as he followed her into the building.

Wayne and I were finally alone on the porch.

"Are you all right?" I asked at the same time that Wayne said, "You're okay, aren't you?"

We both laughed, but then Wayne's face grew serious again. "Now where were we?" I asked in mock innocence, my finger under my chin. "It seems to me your arms were around me—"

Wayne scooped me up for another hug, this time lifting me off the ground. I held on, legs dangling. I could just see over his shoulder. Unfortunately, what I could see over his shoulder was Craig shuffling up the path to the dining hall. Craig looked up at us as he came to the stairs. He winced. Damn.

"Put me down," I whispered to Wayne.

Wayne sighed deeply and set me back on my feet. I turned to face Craig.

"Lunch is almost ready," I told him, forcing a cheerful note into my voice.

Craig stretched a tired smile across his face in response. He climbed the stairs like an old man.

"Craig," I said softly. "You're off the hook. Whoever murdered Jack murdered Suzanne. Orlandi has got to realize it wasn't you."

"Does he?" asked Craig, his voice brittle with exhaustion. "What if I murdered Jack because he saw me kill Suzanne?"

"No," I said, ignoring the way my pulse was racing. "It doesn't wash."

"It's the current theory," he responded. Then he sighed. Spa Santé, the Spa of Sighs.

"What's the current theory?" asked Felix, walking up behind me. He held his room key in his hand.

"Never mind," I said quickly. "Say hello to Craig. Then Wayne and I will walk you to your room." This was not a good time to leave Felix to interrogate Craig. The current theory might become the current headline.

"So, Craig—" began Felix.

I grabbed Felix's arm and began walking. He pulled back, stopping me in my tracks. "Don't you want to meet some more suspects?" I whispered in his ear.

His mustache twitched with anticipation.

"Suspects?" he breathed.

"Let's go," I said.

Wayne walked around to Felix's other side and we marched him down the stairs. On the last step, Felix turned and shot Craig one more hungry look, but only Craig's backside was visible as it disappeared through the doorway.

Halfway down the dirt pathway to Rose Court, we saw Don Logan. He sat in his wheelchair, face blank as he watched our approach.

"Mr. Logan," I said with false heartiness. "Fran says to tell you the lunch buffet is on."

"Thanks," he replied brusquely.

Felix nudged me, none too gently.

"This is my friend Wayne," I said. "My friend Felix Byrne. And," I finished with a smile in Logan's direction, "this is Don Logan." One suspect introduction down.

Felix put out his hand. Logan shook it without enthusiasm. Then he whirred and clicked his wheelchair around to face me.

"You have a lot of *friends*, don't you?" he said in a low, insinuating voice.

I could feel my face go red. Had I been insulted? Before I got a chance to ask, Logan whirred away down the dirt path.

"Whoa," said Felix, watching him go. "He's not too friendly."

"Maybe he's publicity shy," Wayne commented.

I gazed at Wayne's thoughtful face absently and wondered.

Had Logan overheard me telling Eli Rosen that Felix was a reporter? Or was he just tired of people intruding on his solitude? Or did he think that "friend" was a code word for "lover" and therefore he should take offense at my having three? I shook my head. It wasn't worth worrying about. Especially when compared to two murders.

Wayne seemed to share my thought. He began walking up the dirt path again in silence. Felix and I followed.

"So when am I going to meet the rest of them?" Felix asked.

"After we show you your room," I answered. I winked at Wayne, hoping to lighten his mood.

Felix's room was across the hall from mine. When he turned his key and opened the door, Wayne and I peered in around him. Sure enough, the decor of this room matched my own. Peeling psychedelic paisley wallpaper in shades of orange and black. Saffron yellow curtains. Liver brown furniture with orange trim. Felix didn't even rate a salmon bedspread. His was bright orange.

"Far out," Felix murmured. A blissful smile appeared on his face as he strolled into the room.

"You like it?" I asked incredulously, following him in.

"I love it!" he answered, stroking the wallpaper. "I crashed in a place that looked just like this in 1970."

I turned to look at Wayne. He shrugged his shoulders. Then he laughed. The laughter was worth the paisley decor. As I joined in, the miasma of Spa Santé thinned a little.

"Far out," Felix repeated. He bounced on his orange bed, oblivious of our amusement. Then he stood up with a look of determination. "Let's go meet some more suspects," he declared.

We decided to check out the pool for anyone who had not heard Fran's lunch announcement. But after that, we would go straight to the dining hall. I was lightheaded from hunger. Actually, from hunger and shock. And fear. But the hunger I could deal with. And Felix wanted to go back to the dining hall so I could introduce him to more "suspects."

Terry McPhail was energetically backstroking across the swimming pool when we arrived. I waved at him and he climbed out, ranting and dripping.

"Fuckin' cops," he said. "Did you see the way they threatened me? You heard them, right? You're witnesses?"

"To what?" I asked.

"Orlandi!" he shouted, waving his wet arms angrily. I felt a spray of water land on my face. "Telling Dempster to remove me. And then Dempster, with his hand on his gun!"

"Oh, yeah," I said. Now I remembered. It had been tense there for a while.

Felix nudged me and whispered in my ear. "Introduce me to the hothead."

"Terry, this is Felix," I said briefly, pointing appropriately.

Terry nodded at Felix, but was not deterred from his screed. "And Nikki. Telling her she has to stay here at the spa. After what she's been through!"

Damn. I had been trying so hard to forget about Nikki. And Jack. I blinked my eyes furiously, afraid I was going to start crying again.

Wayne shook his head sadly.

"I told Nikki to call her attorney," said Terry. "And to call him quick before the cops leaned all over her again."

That sounded like good advice to me.

"Leaned all over her for what?" asked Felix.

"For killing Jack," Terry answered, as if it was obvious.

"Wait a minute," said Felix, shaking his head. "It was a woman that was killed. Suzanne Sorenson."

"No, no," Terry snapped. He waved his hands in the air again. "That was the first murder. I'm talking about Jack Ireland." Terry pointed his bony white finger first at Wayne, then at me. "Early this morning. They found his body."

- Fifteen -

"YOU FOUND A body and you didn't tell me?" asked Felix. His eyes were round with hurt. The hurt phase was mercifully brief. Anger was next.

He narrowed his eyes and stepped six inches from my face. "Another murder and you kept it from me!" he shouted.

I stepped back from the onslaught. Wayne moved in front of me instantly.

"Be cool, Felix," Wayne warned in a low voice.

Felix peered up at Wayne. Hurt entered his eyes once more. "But—" he began.

Terry McPhail had been watching us in confusion. Now a look of comprehension crossed his face. "What are you, some kind of narc?" he asked Felix. He didn't bother to mask the hostility in his voice.

"Huh?" replied Felix, turning to him in bewilderment.

"An undercover cop. I should have guessed." Terry shook his head in disgust. "And I suppose Kate reports to you."

"He's not a cop," I said.

"FBI? CIA? What?" demanded Terry.

"He's a reporter," I answered. I glanced at Felix's hurt face, remembered his past kindnesses and added softly, "A friend too."

Felix blushed when I said "friend." Maybe he was remembering *my* past kindnesses. "Sorry, Kate," he apologized.

Terry, however, was not to be placated. "A reporter," he said. "Shit." Then he turned and jumped back in the pool.

It was hard to tell if he thought a reporter was worse or better than a cop.

"Terry," I shouted. If his head was under water, so be it. "Fran's got a lunch buffet ready."

That duty done, I turned and led the silent march back to the dining hall.

Felix broke the silence once the swimming pool was out of sight.

"Why didn't you tell me about Ireland's murder?" he asked. This time his tone was reasonable, gently inquiring.

"Because I was too shook up," I explained. I turned to face him. "Have you ever stumbled over a dead body?" I asked.

"I've seen some," he said slowly. Understanding softened his eyes for a moment. "Must have been terrible."

I nodded, glad he understood.

"What did it look like, exactly?" he asked slyly.

"Felix!" I yelped.

"Just kidding," said Felix. I smiled in spite of myself. Can't blame a guy for trying.

We walked a few more steps. I looked over at Wayne. He was smiling too.

To Felix, the smiles were a green light.

"Seriously, Kate," he said. "Did it look like the same M.O. as Suzanne's murder?"

"Yes," I answered curtly.

"Come on, Kate," Felix begged, his mustache twitching eagerly. "Give."

I sighed one more, mammoth sigh. Then I gave. The whole story of the morning's events. We kept walking while I rattled off the story as fast as I could move my mouth, not allowing Felix an edgewise moment to interrupt. I wanted this story over with in time for lunch.

By the time the main building came into view, I had finished my monologue with a description of my last interrogation by Chief Orlandi.

"That's all?" asked Felix.

"Isn't that enough?" I responded.

Felix ignored me. He was thinking as he walked. He gazed upwards into nothingness, lost in some inner scenario. If there had been a brick wall in front of him, he would have walked into it. Unfortunately, there was no brick wall.

"So it was Craig who actually found Jack Ireland's body first?" he asked softly, eyes still unseeing.

I nodded.

"And Suzanne's too?" He stroked his chin.

I nodded again. Damn. Maybe I shouldn't have told him about Craig.

He brought his eyes back to earth abruptly as we came to the stairs of the main building. Then he lifted them to my face. "Who do you think did it?" he asked.

"I told you," I snapped. "I don't know. I don't even have a guess."

We had started up the stairs when I heard the sound of footsteps on the path behind us. I turned and saw the twins, Arletta and Edna. They both averted their glances, as if suddenly interested in the landscape.

"Who are they?" asked Felix, nudging my ribs. I shrugged my shoulders.

I wasn't going to tell. I preferred the twins' tailing me to Felix's questions. I only wished they had been the ones to discover Jack's body. Arletta and Edna would have handled the discovery better.

As we walked up the stairs and through the lobby, I told Wayne and Felix about the great vegetarian buffet the Beaumonts put on. Neither one seemed impressed. In the middle of my description of scrambled tofu, Felix went so far as to stick his finger down his throat as if to vomit. Wayne plopped a hand over his mouth to muffle his snicker, but I heard it anyway. Boys!

Bradley was at the front counter in the dining hall. He watched our approach with luminous eyes, a smile fluttering on his lips. Felix nudged me. He didn't even have to ask who Bradley was. I had become conditioned, not to mention bruised, by Felix's inquiring nudges.

"Bradley Beaumont," I whispered. Then I ducked around to Wayne's other side. Let Felix nudge Wayne for information.

"Ah, Ms. Jasper," Bradley greeted me. "Your essence multiplies each time I see you." He giggled at his own sally. I wasn't sure what the joke was. Was he referring to Wayne and Felix? I smiled as if I understood.

"Three buffets," I said.

"All on Mr. Jasper's bill?" asked Bradley, cocking an eyebrow.

Damn. I hadn't thought this out. Craig certainly owed nothing to Felix. But to Wayne? And what about the room? I was here for Craig, and Wayne was here to help me be here for Craig. But did that mean Craig was paying Wayne to sleep with me? Was there an ethicist in the house?

"On me," growled Wayne, cutting short my ethical struggle. I felt oddly disappointed. It was so much easier to obsess about a minor moral issue than to consider the more critical, and brutal, facts of murder.

Bradley looked disappointed, too, as he took the cash from Wayne. Had Wayne ruined his joke? Felix, however, looked smug, having snagged a free lunch, even if it was vegetarian.

I heard the sound of Fran's office door opening into the lobby behind us, then the low rumble of male voices emerging. Chief Orlandi and two grim-faced men walked out.

"You're giving it your best shot," said one of the men to Chief Orlandi. "That's all you can do," added the other man.

The Chief shook his head, looking very tired. "Well, anyway," he said, "thanks for the assist. I can sure use it."

The two men left through the front doors. The Chief stood with bent head and drooping shoulders as he watched them go. Poor guy—

Felix's elbow was in my ribs again. He must have followed me around Wayne.

"Who's that?" he whispered.

"The big guy is Chief Orlandi," I told him, keeping my voice down. "I don't know who the other two were."

"Lakeside County sheriffs," he whispered.

I turned to him, impressed. "How'd you figure that out?" I asked. Maybe he was assimilating some of Barbara's psychic powers.

"It said 'Lakeside County Sheriff's Department' on their car," he answered. So much for psychic powers.

After a long sigh, Chief Orlandi turned back to Fran's office. But as he did, the twins came marching through the front doors. Orlandi saw them, groaned and retreated to the office, slamming the door behind him.

Edna flung open the office door and strode in, undeterred. Arletta fluttered in behind her. Felix's eyes were bulging with curiosity. He tiptoed up to the closed door to better hear the rumbles and twitters that filtered through.

I turned to Wayne. "Ready for a vegetarian feast?" I asked, pumping enthusiasm into my voice.

He nodded his head glumly. I led the way into the dining hall, quickly surveying the diners. Uncle Eli sat next to Craig at the communal table. And Ruth sat across from Eli, her face sparkling with pleasure. Don Logan sat by himself at the window.

I turned my eyes to the buffet. I was ready for food. Fasting has never appealed to me for either spiritual or health purposes. I tend to see angels after a day without food, angel food cake after two days. At half a day, I was shaky and my head ached. My vision was beginning to waver, too, but I could still see the buffet.

Right off, I noticed the carrot sticks I had sculpted, two kinds of bread (probably leftover from breakfast), hummus, vegetable soup, steamed corn-on-the-cob and new potatoes. My mouth watered. I picked up a cube of marinated tofu and popped it into my mouth. It was tangy and sweet at the same time. I grabbed a piece of oatmeal-raisin bread and bit a chunk out of it. Heaven. Thus fortified, I took a plate and began piling it high.

"Isn't this great?" I mumbled to Wayne through another bite of oatmeal-raisin bread. "All you can eat."

Wayne was poking at the tofu cubes with a fork, as if searching for meat. His eyebrows were lowered so far I couldn't see his eyes at all.

"Great," he murmured. He tasted a tofu cube experimentally, and shuddered. He prodded a cob of corn suspiciously. I repressed the urge to remind him that vegetarian corn tasted just like ordinary corn.

"Couldn't hear much," came Felix's voice from behind me. "Sounds like the police chief is pissed at the two old ladies, though."

"Fine," I said curtly. "Let's just eat."

Felix picked up a plate and came over to my side.

"That guy Bradley," he whispered. "Watching me the whole time. He kept giggling. It was really weird."

I had had enough of Bradley Beaumont. Enough of Felix Byrne, for that matter. "Eat," I ordered.

"Isn't there anyone normal in this place?" Felix asked.

I quelled him with a glare, but the question reverberated in my aching head. I took another bite of bread. Were the inhabitants of Spa Santé all off balance? Or was it just the murders that made everyone behave that way?

Felix's gaze lit on Craig and he began filling his plate helter-skelter. A potato, a slice of melon, a dollop of hummus, a handful of carrot sticks, all the time peering at Craig. Once his plate was full, he hoofed it over to the communal table to take a seat next to Craig.

"Oh-oh," I said, nudging Wayne.

Wayne turned my way, and I nodded at Felix.

I peeked under Wayne's eyebrows and saw a flicker of annoyance as he gazed at Craig. Guilt pressed on my chest. I took another bite of bread. How did Wayne feel about protecting Craig? Helping my ex-husband? I had seen genuine sympathy on Wayne's face when Craig found Jack's body, but the sympathy of the moment had probably worn off. Maybe I was asking too much of Wayne.

Whatever he felt, Wayne finished filling his plate quickly and led the way over to the communal table, where he took a seat next to Felix. I pulled out a chair next to Ruth, across from Craig.

"She did not bear easily her mother's death or forget her father's abandonment," Eli was saying. I slurped vegetable soup and listened. "I tried to make it up to her but she was . . . she was difficult." Eli smiled wanly. Ruth reached across the table and patted his hand.

"Such a waste," said Eli, shaking his head sadly, "her short life spent mostly in anger." Ruth shook her head with him, her eyes knowing.

Eli rested his eyes on Ruth's face, drinking in her understanding.

"Suzanne was an excellent attorney. Her work reflected well upon our law firm," he continued. "I only wish she had been a happier person."

Next to Eli, Craig hung his head. Ruth gave a quick nod in Craig's direction. Eli caught the signal and turned to him.

"Craig, do not blame yourself," Eli said gently. "It was not your fault. You were a good influence on my Suzanne. She was happy with you, happier than she had been before you."

Craig's head popped up. "Really?" he asked, his voice full of the need to believe Eli's words.

"Really," Eli confirmed. His eyes were moist beneath his Coke-bottle glasses. He laid a gnarled hand on Craig's shoulder. "You gave her great joy."

Craig straightened his shoulders under Eli's hand.

"This is too much sadness for someone of your age," Eli said to him.

Ruth nodded. "Too much sadness for anyone of any age," she said. She focused her intense eyes on Craig's. "But death is a fact of life. You'll always remember. But, in your own way, in your own time, you *will* feel better."

Craig regarded her hopefully, cocking his head to better absorb her words. "When my son died," Ruth continued, "and when my husband died, I thought I would never heal, but I did. The trick is not to get stuck. To move through the pain, the sorrow, the rage." Now she turned her eyes back to Eli. "To move on with life."

"To move on with life," Uncle Eli repeated thoughtfully. "You are a very wise woman, Ruth."

The table was silent as Eli and Ruth stared into each other's eyes, as if each was seeing the life they wished to move toward in the other. We all basked in the warmth of their mutual enchantment. All except Felix.

Felix took the silence as an opportunity to speak to Craig. In a low, sympathetic voice he said, "It must have been really terrible for you to find those bodies."

Craig slumped back in his chair. His face lost the little color it had gained. "You don't know how terrible—" he began.

"I think now is not the time to speak, my young friend," Eli interrupted. He put his hand on Craig's shoulder once more, this time in warning.

Craig turned to Eli, startled by the interruption.

"This man is a reporter," Eli explained.

"Oh, I know that," said Craig. "I know Felix. He wouldn't use anything I say. . . ." Craig's sentence petered out. He turned back to look at Felix.

Felix blushed. I wondered how he could do a good job as an investigative reporter when he blushed all the time. Maybe he only blushed when he felt guilty. And maybe he only felt guilty when he pumped his own friends.

"Never mind," said Felix. He turned his face away from Craig. "I was just curious."

"Why *are* you down here?" asked Craig, sudden apprehension tightening his face and his voice.

"For the story," Felix admitted shrilly. "I'm a reporter, for God's sake." He paused to glare past Craig at Uncle Eli. "A better question might be why Suzanne's uncle and only heir is here."

Everyone's eyes moved to Eli's face. Why was he here? I hadn't thought to wonder.

Uncle Eli bowed his head to Felix, then replied. "I must discover what happened to my niece," he said, his voice deep and grave. "I accepted the responsibility for her care. That responsibility did not end with her death."

It was a hell of a good answer. I felt like applauding, but took another bite of corn instead. Ruth's eyes shone with admiration as she watched Eli.

I heard footsteps and looked up from my corn to see Terry McPhail approaching with his own plate heaped high. He scrutinized Ruth's face as he stepped up to the table, then sat down next to her and examined the object of her admiration with a critical air.

"Who are you?" he asked Eli finally. His tone was not polite.

"This is Eli Rosen, Terry McPhail," Ruth said, introducing them. The tone of her voice told Terry he should be honored to meet Eli. "Eli is Suzanne's uncle," she added.

"Oh," Terry said, still eyeing him suspiciously. "What do you do?"

"I am an attorney," Eli answered, unperturbed by this second cross-examination.

Terry's face wrinkled in disgust, but before he had a chance to verbalize his disgust, Ruth spoke.

"Be nice," she said, shaking an admonitory finger at him.

Terry deflated visibly as the breath he had stored up for a good tirade left his body harmlessly. He even managed a small smile.

"Nice," he said, throwing his hands in the air. "I'm being nice. Have to be, seeing as I'm surrounded by cops and attorneys and reporters." He shot a nasty look in Felix's direction.

Felix looked away. His eyes traveled around the hall, look-

ing for someone new to alienate. They lighted on Don Logan
but moved away, probably remembering the last encounter.
Then he saw Avery Haskell inspecting the buffet.

Felix would have jabbed me in the ribs again, but I was
across the table from him. Instead he nudged Wayne.

"Avery Haskell," I heard Wayne whisper. I was surprised
that Wayne knew Haskell's name. I shouldn't have been.
Wayne was quiet, but he didn't miss much.

Felix turned to look at Haskell again. Haskell looked back,
treating Felix to his zombie stare. Felix averted his own eyes
quickly. He surveyed the room once more, then whispered to
Wayne, loud enough for my ears, probably loud enough for
the whole table.

"Are you sure this place isn't a lunatic asylum?"

That was enough for me. I had finished the food on my
plate. Even Wayne had done justice to his vegetarian plateful.
It was time to go.

"Wayne, ready for that walk I promised you?" I asked
pointedly.

Wayne rose from his seat on cue. Felix rose too, but Wayne
pushed him gently back into his seat with one large hand.

The two of us left quickly, passing Fran and Bradley at the
counter.

"Please, honey—" I heard her say.

Bradley let out a piercing laugh.

I pushed the glass doors open frantically. What if Felix
was right? What if Spa Santé was a lunatic asylum? And the
staff were the lunatics? What if the Beaumonts and Avery
Haskell belonged to some kind of cult that lured visitors down
and then—

Wayne's gentle voice interrupted my what-ifs as we walked
out onto the porch. "It's okay," he said.

He put his hands on my shoulders and bent down to look
into my eyes. "Kate?" he asked softly.

"I'm all right," I answered. And suddenly I was. The idea of
a lunatic cult seemed absurd in the sunlight. I kissed Wayne
lightly; then we walked down the stairs into the bright afternoon.

We wandered without a destination, following the dirt paths
as they led through and around the spa. We stopped occasionally to admire Fran's landscaping and restoration efforts,
or sometimes to squint at dilapidated buildings in the sunlight. The contrast of the beauty and the deterioration was

disturbing. The more we walked, the more I began to wonder if my what-ifs had been so farfetched. Two people had been brutally murdered. That was real. I stopped walking and turned to Wayne.

"I'm scared," I admitted softly. "It's too damn spooky here. If it weren't for Craig, I'd be out of here in a shot," I reached for Wayne's hand. "Do you think I'm crazy to stay?"

He stood and considered before answering. "I'm afraid of this place too," he said slowly. "Don't know if I can protect you from whoever's doing these things."

I flinched. I didn't like to think I was using Wayne for protection. What if he was hurt protecting me?

He saw my reaction and put up his hand.

"I know, I know. You haven't asked for my protection. But I wouldn't feel right, leaving you here alone." He paused. "And you don't feel right leaving your husband to face this alone—"

"Ex-husband," I corrected automatically.

"Ex-husband?" he asked.

"I got the final divorce papers Wednesday," I replied absently.

I felt, rather than saw, the sudden hurt on Wayne's face. Then I looked up into his eyes.

"You didn't tell me," he said quietly.

"I'm sorry. With the murders and all, I never thought to," I said. My voice had gone high with guilt. I squeezed his hand and asked, "Does it matter?"

"Of course it matters," he said, scooping me up into his arms. "Don't you see? We can get married now!"

Married? I held my arms tight around Wayne's neck in a panic. I loved Wayne dearly. But I didn't want to get married. Wayne sensed my panic and set me back on the ground. I peered into his troubled eyes. How could I make him understand?

"Kate?" I heard my name called.

I turned and saw my ex-husband, Craig, jogging up the path. The man I had also once loved, then married, then hated. The man I had only learned to like again once we were separated. Marriage. Damn.

Craig landed in front of me, his face sweating.

"What's up?" I asked.

- Sixteen -

"THE COUNTY SHERIFFS are here," Craig said. "They want to interview everyone again." A muscle twitched under the tight skin covering his jaw. "In the dining hall. Now," he finished glumly.

I turned to Wayne. His face was closed to me. Marriage? I never would have imagined I would welcome another interrogation but I did. I needed time to think, or not think, about Wayne's proposal. Assuming that was what his words had been.

"I said I'd find you and bring you back," Craig said anxiously. Was he afraid he'd lose his brownie points if he didn't? Afraid they'd arrest him if he failed to find us? Suddenly, I had no sympathy left for Craig's fears.

"Fine," I said curtly. "You found us."

"You are coming back with me?" he prodded. His voice rose to a whine. "Aren't you?"

I turned on him. "Give me a break!" I shouted.

Craig flinched from the sound. Then he hung his head. "I'm sorry Kate," he mumbled. "I just thought—"

"It's all right," I sighed. It wasn't his fault he was a bad advertisement for marriage. "We'll come with you. Won't we, Wayne?"

I swiveled my head back to Wayne, catching the look in his eyes unexpectedly. It was a look of pure hatred and it was directed at Craig! I wouldn't have believed Wayne possible of such enmity if I hadn't seen it myself. Wayne would apologize if he tripped a mugger. (Not only would, but did, one memorable day in San Francisco.) His compassion knew no bounds. I corrected myself. There was a boundary. And Craig was now beyond it. Damn.

Wayne lowered his eyes. "Let's go," he growled.

We walked along the dirt path in silence for a few steps. Wayne's face was closed again, his footstep hard as it hit the dirt. Craig's shoulders were slumped as he shuffled along in front of us. Had he seen Wayne's look of hatred? I reminded myself that Craig's shoulders hadn't been straight for most of his stay here at Spa Santé. No wonder, with his girlfriend murdered. A spark of sympathy warmed my vocal cords.

"So, who's there for the grilling?" I asked in the friendliest tone I could muster.

Craig's head came up. "Everyone," he answered over his shoulder. "Ruth and Terry. Fran and Bradley. Avery Haskell. Don Logan." He paused in his stride so that Wayne and I could catch up with him. "They sent two officers for Nikki."

My chest contracted with pity when I thought of Nikki. But what could I do for her? Nothing, I reminded myself. So I kept on talking. "How about Felix?" I asked.

"Felix was already gone. He zipped out of there after you left. Said something about calling in his story before the deadline." Craig flashed a nervous glance at Wayne as he spoke. Damn. He *had* seen Wayne's look. "And they asked Eli to leave. His name wasn't on their list."

"Was Wayne's?" I asked.

"I think so," answered Craig, with another glance at Wayne.

Wayne grunted.

"Listen," Craig burst out shrilly, suddenly stopping in his tracks. "I didn't mean to get anyone in trouble. If you guys want to leave, leave!"

Wayne and I came to a halt, too. I looked from Wayne's sullen face to Craig's agitated one and back again.

"First off," I said. "I don't even know if they'll let me leave—"

"Kate will do what she needs to do," announced Wayne in a low, menacing voice.

"Well, that's up to her," Craig retorted. "Not you."

The two men faced each other like gunfighters.

"Stop it, you two!" I ordered. Both turned to look at me with identical startled looks on their dissimilar faces. "We're not going anywhere anyhow," I continued. "Not until the Sheriff's Department is finished with us."

Wayne looked at me sheepishly. "On point as usual," he murmured. I flashed him a quick smile. The smile he gave me back was full of such sweetness that marriage seemed possible to me for an instant.

Craig wasn't finished, though. "But—" he began.

"March!" I ordered, exasperated.

Wayne and I marched forward in step. Caught unawares, Craig didn't follow us immediately. Then I heard his footsteps catching up behind us, pattering like a frantic sheepdog's.

We were almost to the main building when Wayne touched my arm. Felix was standing on the porch chatting with a blond woman dressed in a Lakeside Sheriff's Department uniform.

The three of us clattered up the stairs. Felix looked at us quickly, then turned away. Should we pass him by without comment? Leave his low profile intact? I looked at Wayne. His eyes were straight ahead now, ignoring Felix. Maybe Felix would get something useful from the woman. Something to help us resolve this mess. I turned to Craig. *His* eyes were fastened morosely on Wayne. Had he even noticed our friendly reporter in action? We walked by Felix as if he were a stranger, and entered the main building.

Before we were halfway through the lobby, I was straining my eyes to peer through the glass doors into the dining hall. There, standing before the assembled suspects, were Chief Orlandi, the two men who had spoken with him earlier, a deputy in a county sheriff's uniform, and a distinguished, silver-haired gentleman in a well-cut navy blue suit. The distinguished gentleman was busily straightening his silk burgundy necktie with one hand and gesturing toward the men with the other.

The two men I had seen earlier with Orlandi nodded, never changing expression. Though one of these men was blond and fair, the other black-haired and dark-skinned, their expressions were identically grim. The deputy in uniform had a more easygoing, freckled face. He spotted us through the glass.

"Ms. Jasper and Mr. Caruso?" he inquired, pushing open one of the doors.

"That's us," I replied. Wayne merely nodded.

"Have a seat with the others," he ordered in a friendly voice. He looked past us at Craig. "And thank you for finding them, Mr. Jasper," he added.

I looked at Craig. He smiled tentatively, a dog who thinks he's been praised but isn't quite sure.

The suspects were sitting at the long communal dining table, facing the police. Fran was in the center, flanked by her husband, Bradley, on the left and Avery Haskell on the right. Don Logan was wheeled up next to Haskell. And Ruth and Terry sat on the far left by Bradley. I sat down next to Terry. Wayne and Craig both hustled to fill the seat nearest to mine, but Wayne was quicker to get his bottom down. With a martyred sigh, Craig settled into the remaining chair by Wayne's side.

"Is this all of them?" the distinguished gentleman asked Chief Orlandi.

"All but Ms. Martin," Orlandi replied, his voice uncharacteristically subdued.

"Well, let's begin then," the gentleman said. He cleared his throat and smiled with all the warmth of a politician.

"I am Chief Deputy Sheriff Yeager of the Lakeside County Sheriff's Department," he said, and paused as if for applause. After a moment of silence he continued. "This is Sheriff's Sergeant Kelly." He indicated the blond man who nodded briefly. "And Sheriff's Sergeant Alvarez, also of the Lakeside County Sheriff's Department." The dark-haired man nodded in turn. Neither of the sergeants smiled.

I fidgeted in my chair. At this rate, we could be here all day.

"Chief Orlandi of the Delores Police Department has asked for our assistance," Yeager went on. He beamed a smile at Orlandi. Orlandi smiled wanly in return. "Please note, Chief Orlandi will continue to have primary responsibility for this case. But, of course, we are only too glad to help." Another smile at Orlandi. This time, Orlandi couldn't dredge up a return smile. He looked down at the tops of his shoes.

Yeager turned his benevolent gaze back to the audience of suspects. Then his tone became stern. "Sergeants Alvarez and Kelly will question each of you. You will be asked to answer many of the same questions again. And I am sure you will all cooperate."

I looked down the table to my left, checking for signs of assent. Fran was the model of cooperation. She was nodding attentively, her head thrust forward with the eagerness of a good citizen. But that was about the extent of it. Bradley was watching something invisible move in the space between the rafters. Terry glared at Yeager defiantly. Ruth was frowning, lost in thought. And Don Logan had caught Avery Haskell's expression. They both stared through the Chief Deputy Sheriff with blank zombie eyes.

"Thank you," Yeager said, with a repeat smile, as if we had all pledged our cooperation. "We also request that you stay in Delores until this matter is resolved—"

"Well I'm not staying!" came Nikki's voice from the door. She marched into the dining hall, trailed by Officers Guerrero and Dempster. Her cocoa-colored skin had turned to ash, and her large eyes were red and circled by dark rings. But she stood up straight as she spoke. "I've lost enough here!" Her voice thickened. "Everything, do you hear! Everything! Jack was . . ." She put her hands over her face and began sobbing.

"We will take Ms. Martin first for questioning," announced Chief Yeager brightly. He nodded at the two sergeants.

"I'm not going to stay!" Nikki screeched. Sergeants Alvarez and Kelly moved in on her, one to each side, guiding her gently back to the door.

"Right on!" Terry shouted from his seat. "Remember your rights!"

Chief Orlandi quietly followed Nikki and the two sergeants out the door.

Chief Yeager turned back to us with his smile in place. "So, please be patient," he continued. "And thank you once more for your generous cooperation."

With his last thank-you he turned and left the room.

Once Chief Yeager was out the door, everyone had something to say.

"Listen up, folks," began Terry. "We've got to stick together, protect our rights—"

"I hope they don't further traumatize poor Nikki," said Ruth, the brows above her black button-eyes pinched together with concern. "She shouldn't stay here—"

"That guy Yeager makes Orlandi look good," whispered Craig. The whisper carried. "I hope—"

"I liked him," confided Fran. "He's so . . . so . . ."

"Presidential," I offered.

"That's it," agreed Fran. "Presidential. He'll be able to take care of—"

Officer Guerrero stepped forward. "Keep it down, you guys," she ordered. Behind her, Officer Dempster patted the butt of his gun nervously.

The table went silent. Even Terry stopped his tirade, limiting himself to a muttered "goddamn Gestapo" under his breath. Once satisfied by our silence, Officers Guerrero and Dempster walked over to join the freckled deputy at one of the corner tables.

I let out a long sigh and turned to see how Wayne was handling the whole thing. His face was expressionless when I turned to him. But then his eyebrows twitched. Silently he nodded at the doors to the dining hall. I swiveled my head around in time to see Eli Rosen enter. Eli scanned the hall quickly through his thick glasses, located the officials and walked over to their table.

"May I be permitted to sit with the others?" he asked.

"Who are you again?" queried Officer Guerrero, looking up.

"I am Elias Rosen. Suzanne Sorenson's uncle."

"The dead woman's uncle?" Guerrero's brows rose in surprise. "Why didn't you mention that before?"

"No one asked," said Uncle Eli with a gentle smile. "I would be glad to offer my assistance. Perhaps there are some questions I might answer."

"Have a seat," Guerrero said as she stood up. "If you're her uncle, they'll want to talk to you." She walked briskly from the dining hall to knock on Fran's office door.

Uncle Eli walked just as briskly over to our long table and took a seat across from the rest of us. One against nine. I wouldn't be comfortable in that position. But Eli was an attorney, I reminded myself, who was used to facing juries. He was interested in one juror in particular, I noticed. He had chosen a seat directly across from Ruth Ziegler.

Uncle Eli smiled softly at Ruth, apparently oblivious to the rest of us. When Ruth saw his smile, the troubled look on her own face melted away, leaving a goofy grin in its place.

She reached her hand across the table to him. He took the hand she offered and held it, his eyes misting up under his glasses. Romance. It brought a smile to my face, too. In fact, there were quite a few smiles at the table.

To think that after all these years they would find each other. And both unencumbered by spouses. What luck! But what if it was all an act? The question poked at my mind unexpectedly as Eli gently patted Ruth's hand. What if the two were not the strangers they pretended to be? What if they were already lovers, but needed to hide their relationship? What if they were conspirators?

It was easy to think of the motives Eli might have had to murder Suzanne. The inheritance for one. Maybe there was more to Suzanne's estate than the secretary had known. Or blackmail. Suzanne could have dug up any number of sleazy secrets while working for Uncle Eli. I looked at his lovelorn face. What memories lurked behind those Coke-bottle glasses, under those grizzled grey brows? All he lacked was opportunity.

I glanced at Ruth's adoring face. Ruth hadn't lacked opportunity. She had been right here at Spa Santé when Suzanne was killed. And all she lacked was motive.

Ruth and Eli slowly released each other's hands, then looked around as if only now noticing the rest of us at the table.

But why would Eli show up at Spa Santé if they were hiding their relationship? All he had to do was stay put in Marin. The theory began to crumble. If only I could discuss it with Wayne. I turned to him. His face was crumpled in misery. In the second it took me to ask myself what could have upset him, I remembered his words about marriage. I felt the *clunk* as my heart instantly gained ten pounds of guilt.

"Where is Nikki Martin?" a loud voice demanded from the doorway. A young black man in a grey pinstripe suit stood there, clutching a briefcase. His large, wide-set eyes were beautiful. And very angry.

Officer Guerrero stood up. "She's being interviewed by the Sheriff's Department," she answered coolly.

"Here?" asked the man.

Guerrero nodded reluctantly.

"Without benefit of counsel?"

"Well . . ." Guerrero mumbled.

The man glared.

"I'll go check," she said quickly. "You wait here."

As she passed him in the doorway, he said, "Tell Ms. Martin her attorney has arrived." He made no move to seat himself, but stood resolutely where he was.

"Right on," Terry whispered.

I nodded agreement.

Softly spoken comments traveled around the table. "I hope she's okay." "God will watch over her." "As if she hasn't been through enough."

Officer Dempster approached our table nervously, his hand inching toward his gun once more. "You're not supposed to talk—" he began.

A bloodcurdling yowl behind him cut off his warning. Dempster whirled around, drawing his gun as he did. Roseanne yowled again, then sauntered past him, past all of us, into the kitchen, her tail straight with dignity.

After a few startled gasps, people began to laugh. It felt good to let loose. Dempster even offered an embarrassed chuckle before holstering his gun and returning to his seat. But our laughter was cut short when we saw Officer Guerrero lead Nikki back through the doorway.

As soon as Nikki saw the man in the pinstripe suit, she threw her arms around him and pressed her face to his chest, weeping loudly. Guerrero tiptoed off quietly to her table. The man stroked Nikki's hair ineffectually with one hand for a few moments, then dropped his briefcase and put both his arms around her. He held her tight until her weeping dissolved into a random series of whimpers and sniffles. Finally, she brought her head up.

"Nikki?" the man inquired, releasing her from his arms. "Have they hurt you?" He looked into her eyes.

She shook her head and sniffed. He handed her his handkerchief. She buried her face in it.

"Do you want to go now?" he asked.

"I . . . I want to talk to Kate first," she murmured through the handkerchief.

My body stiffened when I heard my name.

"Who is Kate?" the man asked gently.

Nikki lowered the handkerchief and pointed at me. "Kate," she called, her voice growing stronger. "Come here."

I looked at Officer Guerrero for permission. Guerrero shrugged her shoulders and sighed. Permission granted? I walked stiffly over to Nikki, feeling the combined weight of all of the eyes in the room upon me.

"This is my brother, Nathan Martin," Nikki said.

"And Ms. Martin's attorney," Nathan added, with a hasty glance at the police table.

"Nathan will help me with the cops," Nikki said with an affectionate glance at him. Then she fixed her large reddened eyes on mine. "But I need more than that."

I nodded. She drew her face closer to mine.

"Find out who killed Jack," she hissed.

Stunned, I began to nod once more. Then, the meaning of her sentence got through to me. She wanted me to investigate.

"But I—"

"I'm counting on you," she interrupted, then pulled away her eyes. "Do you have a card?" she asked her brother.

He nodded hesitantly, but opened his briefcase.

"And a pencil," Nikki added.

He found both and handed them to her. Nikki scrawled a number under NATHAN MARTIN, ATTORNEY AT LAW and handed the card to me.

"That's my number," she said. She fixed her eyes on mine once more. "Call me if you need any information. Or," she lowered her voice, "if you find anything out."

"I—" I began.

"I've got to know," she said, her eyes holding mine fast.

I couldn't say no to that. She did have to know. But I didn't think I was going to be the one to find the answer for her. I shrugged my shoulders helplessly.

"Right," I said.

She pulled me to her for a brief but intense hug.

"Thank you," she breathed as she let me go.

Then she turned to her brother.

"Take me out of here, Nathan," she said softly.

He put his arm around her and guided her out the door, never turning to look back. Surprisingly, the police officers offered no objections.

I watched the couple leave through the lobby, wondering if Nikki Martin had just done the acting job of her career. I would have bet almost anything that her grief was real. Anything, that is, but a life.

I shrugged my shoulders, ready to return to my seat, when I saw a large woman enter the lobby. She must have weighed at least two hundred-fifty pounds, and she was gorgeous. Black hair, sparkling blue eyes, and cream-colored satin skin. Instant proof that buxom can be beautiful. Who was she?

Before I could voice my question, Paul Beaumont shuffled into the lobby. He looked at the unmanned registration desk and shook his head in confusion. I walked back to my seat as he came through the dining hall doors.

The freckled sheriff's deputy spoke to him the minute he came into the room. "Paul Beaumont?" he asked.

"Yeah," Paul squeaked. His head jerked back and his eyes opened wide.

"Just take a seat, son," the deputy said. He kept his tone relaxed, but Paul's features seemed frozen in panic. "We just need to talk to you."

Paul scanned the room and settled his terrified eyes on my face, clearly asking me whether I had told the police about his attack on me. I shook my head frantically, trying to send him the message that I hadn't. But he just looked all the more frightened.

"Mom?" Paul said to his mother, his voice pleading.

But Fran's eyes were looking through the glass doors into the lobby, where more large people were gathering.

"Oh, my God," she gasped. "The Slim 'n' Fitters!"

She jumped from her seat and ran to the door. Officers Guerrero and Dempster exchanged startled glances, hopped out of their own seats and ran after her.

– Seventeen –

FRAN DIDN'T RUN far. Her sprint took her into the lobby and behind the registration desk, where she smiled frantically at the group of good-sized people who had gathered there. The people in front of the desk were a mixed group of men, women and teenagers whose only similarity was size. Each member of the group weighed somewhere in the range of pleasantly plump to dangerously obese. Fran appeared oblivious to the presence of Officers Guerrero and Dempster, who had followed her behind the desk. She opened her mouth to address the crowd.

But Fran couldn't ignore the police any longer when Officer Guerrero grabbed her arm. In a last-ditch effort, she mouthed some polite words to the group, words that I couldn't hear clearly through the glass doors, and then allowed herself to be led back to the dining hall. Everyone at the suspects' table watched as she returned. Terry shook his head in disgust. At the police, I assumed. Ruth's eyes looked worried despite Eli's presence.

"I've got to take care of business," Fran was pleading tearfully as she came through the doors. Guerrero looked at Dempster. Dempster looked back. "Those people have to be checked in and I have to explain the program. Bradley, tell them!"

Bradley cocked his head and smiled, but said nothing.

"You shouldn't run like that," said Dempster, but his heart wasn't in the reprimand. He avoided Fran's teary eyes. Bradley giggled shrilly.

"I'm sorry," said Fran softly. Bradley's giggle seemed to

have taken the fight out of her. She hung her head. "I won't do it again," she promised.

Guerrero threw her hands into the air and sighed theatrically. "I'll go with her," she said to Dempster.

Together, Fran and Officer Guerrero went back to the registration desk. I could hear bits and pieces of Fran's spiel though the doors. "Reduce body fat . . . healthful eating . . . increase energy . . . lasting results." Guerrero stood woodenfaced next to Fran. Fran was glowing with enthusiasm.

The group responded to her enthusiasm, nodding and asking questions, seemingly accepting Guerrero's presence as the norm. They were filling out the forms that Fran had handed them when Paul shuffled up to the dining hall doors. Dempster and the freckled deputy looked up.

"Gotta help my mom," Paul mumbled.

"Wait a minute—" began the deputy, rising.

But Paul was into the lobby before the deputy could finish. He walked toward the registration desk purposefully, then veered away at the last moment. He darted out the front door just as the deputy began his own walk into the lobby. The deputy broke into a run and was out the front door after him in seconds. All of us at the long suspects' table strained our necks observing the deputy's pursuit, but for all our straining, could see no further than the front door.

A beat behind, Officer Dempster jumped up and hurtled toward the dining hall doors, then stopped in his tracks halfway through. He looked back at us suspects, went through a head-oscillating flurry of indecision that was painful to watch, then dragged himself back to his table. The sole officer left in the dining hall, he was doomed to baby-sitting.

I took a deep breath as Dempster sat down. Why was Paul running away? I turned to Wayne, with unvoiced questions. Was Paul running because he was afraid the police knew about his attack on me? Or because he was guilty of murder? Or for some other reason entirely? Wayne shrugged his shoulders as if he had heard me. Paul wasn't going to get very far. The spa was infested with sheriffs. Where did he think he could go? And what about his mother? Did Fran have his escape in mind when she made her own move into the lobby? I turned to look out the glass doors at Fran. And saw Sheriff's Sergeant Kelly walking to our table.

"Ms. Jasper?" he asked.

"Here," I answered, raising my hand. A tremor traveled from my stomach into my chest. Would they ask me about Paul? How did I answer?

"Follow me," Kelly said.

I followed him into the lobby just as the freckled deputy sheriff opened the front door and dragged Paul through by his handcuffed wrists. Damn. Paul's eyes were streaming tears.

"I didn't do anything," he whimpered. "I didn't do anything."

The group of Slim 'n' Fitters in the lobby turned to look. Fran looked, too. A look of incredulity spread over her face.

"Paul?" she whispered.

But Paul's eyes were fixed on me. "She's lying," he shouted. He tried to point, but the deputy yanked his hands back down before he could raise them to accuse me.

Chief Orlandi came out the door of Fran's office as Sergeant Kelly led me in. Orlandi was no longer subdued. His eyes were lit with determination as he strode in Paul Beaumont's direction. Kelly shut the office door, cutting off the panorama with a decisive *thunk*.

"Please sit down, Ms. Jasper," ordered Sergeant Alvarez from behind Fran's desk. His voice was soft and polite, if not friendly.

I sat as ordered. Kelly sat by the side of Fran's desk, his notebook open. Neither of them smiled as they introduced themselves. Alvarez began the interrogation.

His questions were concise and courteous. And very thorough. There were no Orlandi histrionics, no accusations. Instead, Alvarez adopted the tone of questioning that a disinterested doctor might use to elicit the details of an embarrassing illness. He took me through the last few days' events detail by detail. I had grown more bored than afraid by the time the office door flew open.

Orlandi barreled through the doorway like a small tornado. "So what did the kid do to you?" he demanded, not bothering to sit down.

"He . . . he jumped at me," I mumbled.

"And?" Orlandi glared down at me, not satisfied with my answer.

"His hands landed on my . . . my chest," I said. "But that might have been a mistake."

"And?" Orlandi prodded once more.

"And what?" I answered. "That was it."

"Okay," he said, now pulling up the only remaining chair in Fran's cramped office. "Let's go through it from the top."

So we went through it. And as I gave the full account of the incident, I realized there really wasn't much to it. Even Orlandi finally seemed satisfied. He rose from his chair abruptly, took a step toward the door, then turned back to me.

"Why didn't you tell me before?" he asked softly.

"The kid's got enough problems," I answered.

"Do you want to press charges?" he wanted to know.

I shook my head vigorously.

Orlandi moved his head closer to mine and glared. "Is that why you asked if Miss Sorenson had been sexually assaulted?"

I nodded. He drew back his lips and flashed me his old crocodile smile. "Thought so," he said and left.

Sergeant Alvarez's questions seemed especially mild after Orlandi left. Deceptively mild? I was almost dozing by the time he finished with me and told me I could go.

I walked out of Fran's office into the lobby. Fran's group of Slim 'n' Fitters were still there, listening as she explained how they were to monitor their food intake while at Spa Santé. "No calorie-counting here," she told the group enthusiastically and went on to explain a food-tracking system that I imagined only a mathematics professor could understand. But most of the Slim 'n' Fitters nodded their comprehension. Some even asked questions and took notes. Officer Guerrero merely glowered.

I wondered where Paul was. I looked through the glass door to the dining hall. There was no sign of Paul, but the rest of the gang was there. I waved at Craig and Wayne. They both waved back. So did Bradley. Bradley was grinning. What was wrong with the man? Hadn't he seen his son run? Seen his son caught? Terry, Ruth, Eli, Don Logan and Avery Haskell remained motionless. What were they all thinking?

As I stared through the glass, I considered waiting in the hall with the rest of the suspects until Wayne was interviewed and released. Would that help me to detect? My stomach churned its answer, begging me to leave. Then a sudden pain in my temple chimed in, ordering me to get out and get out now!

I turned and left, passing Fran and the Slim 'n' Fitters on my way out the door. Standing on the porch in the sun, I breathed deeply. My stomach and head felt better out here, away from the dining hall. And away from the people in it. Or was my body reacting to just one of those people? To the murderer? If only my friend Barbara was here to do some psychic translation. Were the nausea and headache merely the result of tension and fatigue, or bad vibes? Or were they important messages from my unconscious? I shook my head in frustration, wishing to see Barbara's face.

Instead I saw Felix's. He walked up the stairs to the porch, an ingratiating smile under his mustache.

"What's new?" he asked.

"Nothing," I answered cautiously, wondering if he had seen Paul run. I plopped down in the redwood bench, tired despite all the sitting I had done.

He sat down next to me. "Kate," he said, his voice serious. "I think we can figure this thing out."

"How?" I asked hopelessly.

"Talk it out," he prodded. "Why Suzanne? Why Jack?"

I was hooked by his questions. I sat up a little straighter. Maybe we could figure it out. "Why both of them?" I asked softly. "What did they have in common that got them killed?"

"Now you're talking," he said, his mustache twitching. "What *did* they have in common?"

"Nothing I can think of," I answered, slumping again.

"No," he insisted. "They had to have something in common."

"Different sex," I said. "Different ages. She must have been ten or fifteen years younger."

"Both Californians," Felix pointed out.

"One from Marin and one from Los Angeles," I countered. "Not much of a connection."

"Both here with lovers," he added, undeterred.

"True." I considered that fact for a moment. "And neither of their lovers was happy with them."

"Yeah?" prodded Felix eagerly. Damn. I knew I shouldn't have talked to him.

"All right," I snapped, rising from my seat. "That's enough."

"Come on, Kate," Felix said, tugging at my arm. "We're getting some place."

"What place?" I asked, plopping back down on the bench. "Felix, these guys were totally different! Jack was a sweet man with an alcohol problem. In the music world. Suzanne was a lawyer. An ambitious, insensitive . . ."

"Bitch?" offered Felix.

"I didn't say that." I had been seeking a euphemism.

"Did they know each other?" Felix asked, as if the thought had just occurred to him.

"I don't think so," I answered slowly. "But I don't know. I don't know much about Jack at all."

"How about his girlfriend? I'd like to interview—"

"Don't you dare!" I shouted, glaring at Felix. "She doesn't need you bugging her after all she's been through."

"Jesus, Kate," Felix objected. "I'm not a vampire! Give me credit for some sensitivity."

I ignored him, thinking. "How about Jack's brother?" I said finally. "Talk to him."

"I might just do that," Felix said. He winked at me as he rose from his seat. "Catch you later."

"Felix!" I shouted as he walked down the stairs. "Tell me what you find out."

"Sure," he said, turning to me. "Just as soon as you tell me what you've found out." His mustache twitched in a quick smile. Then he walked away.

I sat in the afternoon sun, thinking. Did Suzanne and Jack have something in common? Something worth murdering over? They were both white. They were both single with significant others. If that was enough for the murderer, a good portion of the population was in trouble. I was still searching for further commonalities some fifteen minutes later when Craig came wandering out into the sunshine. He looked tired. I braced myself for conversation, but he clumped down the stairs without even noticing me.

Twenty minutes later still, I had come up with another earthshaking commonality. Jack and Suzanne both had light-colored hair. Great. I heard the door behind me swing open, and turned to look. Wayne stood silently, peering at me wistfully from beneath his low brows. I felt suddenly shy. We had not been alone together since he had spoken of marriage.

"Hi," I greeted him softly.

"Hi," Wayne replied, just as softly. Then he looked down at his feet, his face closing on the way.

I lurched out of my chair and across the porch, suddenly needing to touch him. I took his hand. "Wayne, I'm not sure about marriage," I rattled off, speaking fast to get it out. "I've been married. It didn't work." Then I took a breath.

His face softened. He put his arms around me and held me tight, then released me and looked into my eyes.

"You need time to think," he whispered.

I nodded, mesmerized.

"Right," he said, his voice back to normal volume. "Meanwhile, I'm getting you out of here. Have a friend with a restaurant in Delores. Arnie's. Let's go."

"But we just ate," I objected. As much as I wanted to leave Spa Santé, something was holding me there, besides the fact that we'd been told not to leave.

"Food isn't the point," he said. "You need out."

"But what about Paul? What about the police? What about Craig?"

Wayne winced when I said "Craig," but he answered the rest of my questions. "I cleared the trip into town with Sergeant Alvarez. Orlandi's still talking with Paul." He paused and looked into my eyes again. "They're not your responsibility," he finished.

That was what was holding me. Responsibility. To Craig, to Nikki, to Paul, to my own need to know the truth. Who had elected me responsible?

"Let's go," I said.

During the short ride into Delores I watched Wayne's serious face as he concentrated on driving, and I wondered. Did I really need time to think about marriage or had I already decided? Decided against marriage? Guiltily, I pushed away the thought.

Wayne was right about one thing. It was good to be out of Spa Santé. I could feel the miasma lift gradually. By the time we got to Delores it was almost gone, leaving me suddenly clear-headed. Downtown Delores wasn't very big, but it looked good to me. A few blocks containing a 7-Eleven, a bar, a gas station, a hardware store, three antique shops and Arnie's.

"Where do you know this guy from?" I whispered as we

walked into Arnie's. The restaurant was dark and smoky, illuminated by a TV at the bar, some backlit beer ads and flickering candles at the tables. The afternoon sunlight disappeared as the door slammed behind us.

"Met Arnie at a restaurant convention," Wayne whispered back. I could just make out his embarrassed face in the dark. "Doubt that he'd remember me. Not exactly a friend."

"Was this a ruse to kidnap me?" I asked.

He nodded.

"Thanks," I said and gave him a quick hug. At least the darkness here was visible. The darkness at the spa hid in the sunlight.

A barely discernible young man seated us at a murky-red leatherette booth and handed us our menus.

"Steak, hamburger or steak," I read aloud, bending over the table to catch the lettering in the candlelight.

"You could get a salad," Wayne suggested sheepishly.

Wayne knew I ate for my health. At least I believed a vegetarian diet had saved my health when I was seriously ill. Maybe it was a faith-healing. And Wayne had wooed me with his own vegetarian cooking. Meatless lasagna, ratatouille, pine-nut dolmas, homemade pasta with eggplant-olive sauce. The man could cook! But he needed meat once in a while. At least he believed he did. Maybe that was a faith-healing too.

"Was the food that bad at the spa?" I asked softly, suddenly sympathetic.

"No," he said. "But the company was." He bent forward in the flickering candlelight. "There are some very sick people at your health spa."

"Who?" I asked. I wanted his impressions.

"Bradley," he answered. "A lot like my mother used to be." I shifted uncomfortably in my seat. Wayne's mother was now completely mad. I had visited her once at the Shady Willows Mental Health Facility, where she sat drooling blankly in front of the TV in the patient's recreation room.

"Worse than my mother in some ways," Wayne continued. "Watched Bradley when his son ran today. Bradley got very excited. Not concerned, just excited. And when the deputy hauled Paul back, Bradley couldn't stop laughing."

I shivered. Spa Santé had seeped into Arnie's.

"Probably his way of dealing with stress," Wayne allowed. "Can't do the boy any good, though. Then there's the guy in the wheelchair."

I looked across the table in surprise. Don Logan hadn't been on my short list for crazy.

"Guy's very angry," Wayne said. "Doesn't know how to deal with it. And Fran. In complete denial about her family. Let her son be interrogated without a peep of protest."

"Did you see what happened with Orlandi and Paul?" I asked.

Wayne nodded solemnly. "First thing Orlandi did was have the deputy take the handcuffs off Paul. Then he asked Fran if he could question her son. 'Of course,' she said. 'We're glad to cooperate.' " Wayne's voice came out in a bitter falsetto as he imitated Fran. "When Orlandi asked if she wanted to be there, Fran said, 'No, no. Of course not.' Began babbling about how Paul was just in 'one of those stages.' How he was 'really a good kid.' Boy was crying the whole time. She just ignored him." Wayne shook his head sadly before going on.

"When Orlandi took the boy away, Fran went right back to her lecture for the weight-watchers. Did her show. Lots of smiles for the crowd."

Wayne shook his head again. I had never heard him so bitter. I reached out for his hand, seeing the empathy in his eyes. Was he reliving his own emotional desertion by a mad and uncaring mother? He took my hand and squeezed it.

"Sorry," he said quietly.

"Sorry for what?" I asked.

But before he had a chance to answer, the young waiter was at our table again. He turned to me for my order.

"Salad, no dressing," I said. "And a baked potato, no butter or sour cream."

"Say," said the waiter, with a friendly smile. "You ought to try that restaurant out at the spa. You'd like it a lot."

– Eighteen –

"SORRY FOR WHAT?" I repeated once the waiter was gone.

Wayne looked up and answered. "Sorry for the gloom. Meant to take you away from it, not bring it here with me."

"But I want to discuss the murders," I insisted. He looked unconvinced. "It's either you or Felix," I said.

"Me or Felix?" He threw his hands in the air. "I'll talk! I'll talk!"

I chuckled. I loved his playful side, a side few people ever got to see. I wanted to tell him so. To tell him, marriage or not, I loved him. But he spoke first. And he was serious again.

"What happened with you and the boy?" he asked.

I related the story of Paul's unfortunate leap one more time. By now it seemed trivial, even ludicrous. But Wayne didn't agree.

"Boy's got real problems," he growled. "Could be dangerous." All of my original fear of Paul Beaumont welled up again, clutching my chest. Kid that he was, and as absurd as it seemed, he had attacked me. And there was no way of knowing how it would have gone if I hadn't pushed him away.

"Damn it!" Wayne exploded, hitting the table with his fist. "Parents ought to take care of him."

The blow scattered silverware, and set the candle to swaying, casting dizzying shadows across Wayne's angry face. I was stunned. I had never seen this gentle man so upset before. Suddenly I wondered if there was more going on than just empathy with Paul. Other anger that needed channeling.

"Wayne," I asked softly. "Are you mad at me?"

He raised his head to disagree, then stopped to consider the idea. Slowly a flush crept up his neck and over his pitted face. "Guess I am," he whispered, a tone of astonishment flavoring the shame in his words. He lowered his eyes to the table, nervously rearranging the scattered silverware.

"It's all right," I said, putting my hand on top of his. "All right for me to need time. All right for you to be angry."

His hand stopped moving. He didn't say anything. Didn't even raise his eyes. My heart speeded up. Had I lost him?

"Friends?" I asked. My voice shook.

"And lovers," he agreed, but he still didn't lift his eyes to mine.

I stood up and leaned over the table to kiss him.

"One green salad, one baked potato and one steak sandwich," came the waiter's voice at my side.

Damn. Do waiters time their entrances to interrupt? To ask how everything is when your mouth is full? I sat back down.

Wayne was quiet as he ate his steak sandwich. Too quiet. He kept his eyes down as he chewed. I felt lonely, far distant across the table. He took a big bite. Catsup and shredded lettuce poured out the other end of his sandwich.

"Moooo," I lowed plaintively as he chewed. Vegetarian humor.

His eyebrows twitched but he didn't look up. He took another bite. I mooed again. No reaction. I sighed and took a bite of my potato.

"Ow, my eyes!" Wayne yelped in a falsetto.

I jumped.

"Potatoes have feelings, too," he said, looking at me finally, with a grin on his homely face. "And eyes."

Carnivorous humor. I fell back in my seat and laughed loudly. Laughing away Spa Santé. Laughing away murder. And, most of all, laughing away the fear that I had lost Wayne. Finally, I reached across the table to him. He grasped my hand firmly.

"Don't worry—" he began.

"Wayne Caruso?" a voice boomed, moving in our direction. "Am I right?"

Wayne turned to the voice. I turned too and saw a stocky balding man in jeans and a cowboy shirt.

"Arnie," said Wayne, standing up, hand outstretched.

"Thought it was you," Arnie said, shaking Wayne's hand.

"Never forget a pretty face." He guffawed. I winced looking at Wayne's nonstandard-issue features. But Wayne was smiling. "Sit, sit!" ordered Arnie.

Wayne slid back into the booth. Arnie pulled a chair up to the end of our table. "So introduce me," he said with a faint leer in my direction.

"Kate Jasper," Wayne said. Then he paused. "A friend," he finished. An inadequate description, I thought guiltily. And I had denied him the use of "fiancée."

"So, what the hell are you two doing down here?" Arnie asked, all set to gossip. I had a feeling Arnie's restaurant wasn't keeping him busy enough in the late afternoon.

"Friend of Kate's is caught up in this murder business at the spa," Wayne answered, his face serious once more.

"Is that right?" exclaimed Arnie, his eyes lighting up. "Orlandi's big case?"

Wayne and I both nodded.

"Well, he'll sure as hell take care of it," said Arnie in a confidential whisper. "We call him Bulldog Orlandi here in Delores."

"Bulldog?" I asked.

"Never gives up," explained Arnie. He leaned back in his chair and laughed. "He's one mean son of a bitch. Once he's got a bite on you, he won't let go. Rather chew off your leg first. Got the name playing football originally. But he earned it as a cop."

He leaned forward to whisper again. "I've got this friend whose kid was selling a little grass here in Delores. No big thing. Just for his pals. Well, Orlandi hears about it and goes ape-shit. Not that Orlandi's got any proof. The kid was too smart for that. But that didn't stop Orlandi. He harassed that kid day and night, parking out in front of his house, talking to his pals, scaring off his sweetie pie. A couple of months of this shit and the kid finally gave it up. No more dealing for him. He's afraid to smoke a Marboro these days!"

Arnie leaned back and laughed again. "Got to admire a son of a bitch like Orlandi," he finished, nodding emphatically.

I sat staring at Arnie, a polite smile on my face, hoping Orlandi hadn't picked Craig to bite into. Or anyone else innocent for that matter.

"Eat, eat!" Arnie ordered.

We ate and Arnie regaled us with Orlandi stories. How Orlandi had worn down "the poor Smith girl" by knocking on her door with a red rose every day for six months until she agreed to marry him. They had three kids now. How Orlandi had busted a burglary ring, figured out who was spraying graffiti on the Meyers' house, and terrorized the town drunk into A.A. meetings—all through pure force of character. How Orlandi was going to solve these murders.

I nodded agreement but my heart wasn't in it. Maybe Orlandi could do it. But he'd need more than force of character.

"Hey, how about a beer?" Arnie asked as we were finishing up. "On the house."

"Thanks anyway," said Wayne, patting his stomach. "Too much good food. Got to go."

Arnie followed us up to the register, where I paid the bill, waving away Wayne's efforts to contribute. It was my turn, after all. As Arnie was making change, I heard the door open behind us.

Arnie whispered. "Must be Slim 'n' Fit Weekend again." He gave a quick nod to the doorway. I turned and saw a heavyset woman in a tie-dye T-shirt approaching. She glanced nervously over her shoulder. "We've gotten a helluva lot of business from the new spa program," Arnie continued with a wink. "This is where they come to blow their diets."

The drive back to the spa was all too brief. As we drove through the gap in the trees that served as the entrance to Spa Santé, I heard B-movie prison doors clanking shut in my mind. Wayne looked over at me, his face full of concern. Maybe he had heard them too.

Wayne parked on the far side of the spa lot, as far away from the yellow-taped crime scene as he could. There was one lone sheriff's deputy there now. He seemed to be guarding the area. Wayne and I sat in the car for a moment.

"Let's see who's left in the dining hall," I suggested.

"Kate, are we investigating?" asked Wayne.

I shrugged my shoulders. Wayne sighed.

"I've got to know who killed them," I answered finally.

"Okay," he agreed quietly and opened his door. He turned to me before he got out. "I'll do what I can to help," he added.

We walked across the parking lot and up the stairs of the main building. Avery Haskell was sitting on the porch.

Wayne strolled over to Avery. "Police still here?" he asked.

"The two sheriff's sergeants and Orlandi are still in there with Fran and Bradley. The rest are all gone, except for the Mexican woman, Guerrero, and the sheriff's deputy," Avery answered. His face was zombie-blank as usual. "For now, anyway," he finished glumly.

"Terrible thing," Wayne said. Suddenly I realized this was his help. He was pumping Avery Haskell. "What do you make of it?" he asked Avery.

"God's will," answered Avery shortly. Then he turned his head away.

"God's will?" Wayne repeated softly.

Avery kept his head turned from us, but he finally spoke again. "Had to be God's will," he said softly. "But neither of those two had given their lives over to God." He turned his head back slowly. "I still can't figure why God wanted them." A look of honest confusion broke through his zombie mask for a moment, but only a moment.

Then he shook his head and the mask became whole again. "It's not my place to question. God works in mysterious ways," he finished. He rose from his seat and moved quickly through the front door before Wayne could ask another question.

I walked up behind Wayne and put my arms around his waist. "Thanks for trying," I said.

"I'll do better next time," he promised. Then he turned to me. "Have I earned a break?" he asked.

Before I could reply, I heard the sound of footsteps on the stairs. I swiveled my head and saw Paul Beaumont approaching.

He shuffled forward, head down and mumbled, "Can I talk to you?"

I hid my surprise. "Sure," I answered. "What's up?"

"Avery said I should apologize to you," he said. He kept his eyes lowered as he spoke. He took a big breath. "I'm sorry I called you a liar," he recited.

"That's all right," I answered, magnanimous now with Wayne at my side for a bodyguard.

"Orlandi said you didn't tell on me." Paul's words tumbled out quickly now. "Not till I told them myself." He finally brought his eyes up to mine. "I didn't know, or I wouldn't have yelled at you," he explained.

I nodded my understanding.

He lowered his eyes again. "Thank you," he mumbled.

Wayne put his hand on Paul's shoulder. The kid jerked his head up, startled.

"You okay?" asked Wayne. Paul nodded.

"Need to talk?" Wayne prodded.

Paul squirmed a little, then shot a nervous glance in my direction. Wayne saw the glance and mouthed "see you later," to me. I got the message. Time for a man-to-boy talk.

"I need something in my room," I fabricated quickly. "A . . . a book."

Sure enough, Paul looked relieved at my prospective absence. I scurried down the stairs, glad that Wayne was questioning the kid. Maybe he could get further than I had. It took me all of three steps up the dirt path to begin worrying. Could Paul be dangerous to Wayne? What if Wayne was hurt while doing my dirty work? I turned and looked behind me as I walked. Paul and Wayne were sitting on the redwood bench side by side. It certainly didn't look like a dangerous situation. I swiveled my head back. And came face to face with the twins bearing down on me.

"Psst," hissed Arletta theatrically, beaming at me through her thick glasses. Edna stood behind Arletta. With her bull-dog scowl, she looked very much like her nephew Vic Orlandi.

"Hi—" I began.

"Shhh," warned Arletta, bringing a thin finger to her lips. She pointed with studied nonchalance over her shoulder, to a bench behind a nearby orange tree. Then she strolled over to the bench. Edna rolled her eyes, but followed behind Arletta.

I scanned the area for a moment, looking to see if anyone was nearby on the path. The only people in sight were Paul and Wayne on the porch. Just as nonchalantly as Arletta before me, I sauntered over to the bench.

"Another murder!" chirped Arletta once I had seated myself in the space left for me between the two women. No greeting. No small talk. "A man named Jack Ireland," Arletta nodded.

"Kate knows *that*," growled Edna.

Arletta ignored her friend. "Have you learned anything new?" she asked eagerly, her wispy white head trembling with excitement.

I sat for a moment, considering. What had I learned?

"I saw the second body," I said finally.

"Oh, my," Arletta breathed, squeezing her hands together in apparent delight.

Edna patted my shoulder sympathetically. "Was it a mess like the other one?" she asked. Her intense stare belied her casual tone.

"Yes," I said briefly, the memory of Jack's body manifesting itself before my eyes. Arletta and Edna watched me closely as I tried to shake off the gruesome image. "There was a mark around his neck. Like Suzanne's," I told them.

Edna nodded in satisfaction. This fact seemed to confirm something for her. But Arletta wanted more.

"What else?" she asked.

"Not much," I said, feeling inadequate. "Suzanne's uncle flew down."

"Before the second murder?" asked Edna sharply.

I shook my head. Edna frowned in disappointment.

"And?" prodded Arletta.

What could I say? "Jack Ireland was full of life. He was playful. Kind. And probably an alcoholic. Now he's dead." Arletta continued to look at me expectantly. "His girlfriend seems to be completely broken up over it," I finished.

"What about the others?" Arletta asked.

Bits and pieces of the morning and afternoon flashed through my mind. Bradley Beaumont's shrill giggles. Ruth's flirtation with Eli. Paul Beaumont's flight. But none of these pieces had any true evidentiary value.

"It's hard to tell," I answered finally. "No one acted like an obvious murderer." I shrugged my shoulders. "I'm afraid I haven't detected much," I admitted.

"We have," Arletta whispered.

Edna rolled here eyes once more.

"Well, we *have*," Arletta insisted. She looked around us for nosy ears, and finding none, began to speak in a low whisper:

"We've researched the Beaumonts," she said. "Bradley's doctor told Edna that Bradley is close to another breakdown. He's been institutionalized before." She looked at me to see if I was impressed. I nodded her on impatiently. I didn't need her to tell me that Bradley was near a breakdown.

Arletta went on. "And the child, Paul. He's a problem student in school. Poor dear. He doesn't have any friends in school except for the Sullivan boy, and God knows that child's no role model. Poor thing can barely read—"

"Arletta," Edna interrupted. "Kate doesn't care about the Sullivan boy."

Arletta blinked for a moment, said "Sorry, dear," to Edna and continued. "Paul is failing most of his courses and plays hooky two days out of five. Miss Nagel—that's his teacher—is worried to death about him."

"Tell her about Fran," Edna prompted.

Arletta's face lit up. "I had a little talk with Charlotte Ortega, the teller at Fran Beaumont's bank. Charlotte's a good girl, used to visit the library every week when she was in school. She was only too happy to share what she knew about Fran. She told me that Fran was quite wealthy when she first came to Delores, but now she's nearly down to her last penny. Fran asked the bank for a loan earlier this year, but they refused her."

"I didn't know that," I whispered. No wonder my room was covered in psychedelic wallpaper. Fran couldn't afford to replace it, or finish the work on the dilapidated buildings that dotted Spa Santé's grounds.

Arletta looked gratified. "There isn't any way you could know, dear," she said smugly. "And there's no way you could find out the state of Avery Haskell's account either," she added enticingly.

"Tell me," I ordered. I would have to be careful with this woman. If she could pry confidential information from bank employees, who knows what she could wheedle out of me.

"Mr. Haskell's bank account is another matter entirely. He also came to Delores with a small fortune. And it would appear that he has invested his fortune wisely. He banks his dividends regularly. He told the people at the bank that he received the money as an inheritance." Arletta cocked her head in a knowing look. "I wonder if the young man was telling the truth."

"Where do *you* think he got the money?" I asked.

But Arletta's frail body had gone rigid. So had Edna's sturdy one. I followed their gaze to the dirt path. Wayne stood there, peering quizzically around the orange tree that stood in front of our bench. I rose to greet him.

In the time it took me to walk the few steps to Wayne, the twins disappeared. I turned to introduce them, but they were gone, invisible.

"Who were those women?" Wayne asked.

"The twins—" I began, but stopped short as I heard new voices coming down the dirt path. A quick glance confirmed that the voices belonged to Ruth and Eli. The twins' spy routine had rubbed off on me. I put my finger to my lips and pulled Wayne behind the tree onto the bench.

"Let's listen," I whispered.

"And then?" we heard Eli ask.

"And then I decided I had wallowed in self-pity long enough," Ruth replied. "I turned my back on the past and began to write."

"Ah," said Eli. "*The Things We Do For Love*. I read this book, you know. I thought you must have been the Ruth Ziegler who wrote it, although there was no picture of your lovely face on its cover."

Ruth giggled. "You're incorrigible, Eli Rosen," she admonished, then went on in a low voice. I couldn't hear the rest of her words as she and Eli moved away from us down the path.

"They certainly sound like they're meeting each other after a long separation," I said to Wayne as I rose from the bench.

"You wondered?" he asked as he stood up himself.

I turned to him. "They might have been conspirators—" I began.

"His motive, her opportunity," he finished with a frown.

"You thought of it too!" I said in excitement. "Well?"

Wayne's brows were so low I couldn't see his eyes as he thought it over. "Probably the first stages of romance and nothing more," he said finally. But his face was still troubled.

"Speaking of romance," I said, putting my arm around him. "How'd you like to come up to my room for a while?"

Slowly the trouble lifted from his face, pulling up his brows on the way. He bent and kissed me. Then he drew back with a smile.

"At least you've got some of your priorities straight," he whispered.

We walked down the dirt path holding hands, temporarily oblivious to the spa's unhealthy aura. But, as the path twisted, we saw Don Logan sitting alone in his wheelchair. Instinctively Wayne and I dropped each other's hands and moved apart. It didn't matter. Logan didn't see us. He stared out into space, his face bitter as he watched something no one else could see. I reached out again for Wayne's hand, feeling suddenly cold. I wondered then if the insanity of Spa Santé was infectious.

When we got to my room Wayne lay down on the salmon bedspread and opened his arms. I threw myself full length on top of him and kissed him until I was breathless, inoculating myself against the insanity of the spa.

The knock on the door jolted us both.

- Nineteen -

WE HEARD ANOTHER knock on the door, then Craig's voice shouting, "Kate, are you there?"

Craig. I should have guessed. I didn't need to see the look of martyrdom on Wayne's face to know how he felt about the intrusion. I felt the same way myself.

I rolled over on the bed and shouted back. "What do you want!"

Then I heard Felix's voice. "I told you they were in there," he said.

Wayne got up slowly, his face and body taking on the intimidating characteristics that had earned him an early career as a bodyguard. Brows pulled low, obliterating his eyes. Head thrust forward. Muscular shoulders hunched around his thick neck. After all our time together the look still scared me. He strode to the door and opened it.

"What?" he asked in a low voice full of menace.

Craig shrank back from Wayne's look but maintained his footing. Felix, on the other hand, simply ignored Wayne and slipped past him into the room, leaving Craig and Wayne locked in a scowl-to-scowl battle.

"We looked under every orange tree in the friggin' spa," Felix complained. "Where have you two been?"

"Out," I snapped, walking cautiously toward Wayne and Craig.

"Dinner buffet's on," Felix continued from behind me.

Slowly I inserted myself between Wayne and Craig. They ignored me. I waved my hand between their scowling faces. They stared through it. I pulled my hand back, surprised it wasn't lasered through from the energy the two were putting out. Suddenly I was tired of the posturing.

"Wayne!" I shouted. "Cut it out!"

He blinked, then looked down at me, his features resuming their natural state, homely and only mildly threatening.

"Sorry," he said softly. I squeezed his hand quickly. It wasn't his fault he was here.

I turned toward Craig. He looked away, avoiding my eyes. I shrugged my shoulders. I didn't know what to say to him.

"Do you guys want dinner or not?" Felix demanded.

"The buffet sounds good," I said slowly. My stomach was gurgling for food, unimpressed by the undressed salad and potato I had eaten earlier. Tension makes me hungry. I looked up at Wayne hopefully. "How about you?"

"Fine," he answered, his curt tone contradicting his reply. No doubt he was full after his steak sandwich. And still angry with Craig to avoid being angry with me. Damn. I wanted out of this angry psychedelic room!

"Let's go," I said, grabbing Wayne's hand and tugging.

The expedition to the dining hall would have been a silent one if it hadn't been for Felix. Wayne and Craig walked on the far edges of the dirt path, carefully avoiding either touching or looking at each other, much less speaking. Felix didn't seem to mind the atmosphere. As we walked past a roped-off stucco building that had fallen in on itself, he enthused over the journalistic potential of the spa.

"My editor is happier than a pig in poop," he crowed. "Here I am, Johnny-on-the-spot, for not only one murder but two. A possible series. This might be as big as the Hillside Strangler!"

"Wonderful," I drawled.

"But it is," he insisted eagerly. "There might be more murders. And if we figure out who did it first—"

"We've got to get organized!" I cut in loudly, stopping short in the middle of the dirt path. The three men stopped walking too.

Their faces turned to me. "Organized?" asked Felix.

"We're going about this all wrong," I said slowly. "No plan. No organization. I've talked with all the suspects, but with no specific list of questions in mind. Craig's chatted with everyone. Even Wayne's been trying." I gave Wayne a smile, remembering he was only down here to help me.

"And Felix," I said, turning to him. "If I know you, you've interviewed half the female members of the Lakeside County Sheriff's Department by now."

Felix blushed. I reconsidered my last statement. He had probably interviewed *more* than half of them.

"But we haven't pooled our information," I continued, serious now. "We haven't organized our research. We haven't even figured out what we want to learn."

"It's simple," offered Craig. "We want to know who the murderer is."

"Right," I agreed. "But what are the questions we should be asking to figure that out? And who should be asking them of whom? Let's do this efficiently."

Wayne was nodding slowly. "Probably help to brainstorm," he contributed.

"That's the idea!" I said, pumping enthusiasm into my voice. I felt like a cheerleader. I hated cheerleaders. But I was fairly certain this approach was what it would take if the four of us were going to solve the murders.

"I'll go for it," said Felix, catching my enthusiasm.

"Will you promise to keep the confidential stuff out of your stories in the meantime?" I asked quickly.

His enthusiasm drained visibly. He turned his head away from me and said, "I guess so."

"Not good enough, Felix," I pressed. "We can't do this right if we're worried about censoring ourselves in front of you. Either you're in or you're out."

He stroked his chin for a few moments, then laughed. "You're a mean-ass negotiator," he commented. I glared at him. He put up a hand. "Okay, okay! Don't get uptight. You win. I'm in."

"And . . ." I prompted.

"And I'll keep the confidential stuff under my hat," he recited. "But I still don't know who elected *you* God," he grumbled as I turned from him.

I ignored the grumbling and asked Wayne and Craig, "How about you two?"

They looked at each other cautiously. I could see their gears turning. What would be lost by cooperation? What would be gained?

"I'm in," Wayne agreed quietly after a moment. I reached over and hugged him.

Craig immediately added his own assent. He got a brief nod in reward. After all, this was his problem in the first place.

"When do we meet?" asked Felix, rubbing his hands together with anticipation.

"Tonight, after dinner," I whispered conspiratorially. We resumed our walk up the dirt path.

As we climbed the stairs to the main building I was feeling good. We had a plan. And a truce. I sneaked a quick glance at Wayne and Craig, who were still avoiding each other's eyes, and hoped the truce would last.

Bradley was behind the dining hall counter. The blackboard behind him read "Welcome Slim 'n' Fitters!"

"One lady and three gentlemen for the buffet?" he asked with a meaningless giggle.

"Nothing for me," said Wayne. "Pay for Kate, though." He pulled his wallet from his pocket.

"No," said Craig, pushing in front of us. "I'll pay."

Wayne's eyebrows came down. I cut in before he could work himself up again. "What's for dinner?" I asked Bradley.

"Funeral baked meats," Bradley replied, his luminous eyes staring through me. "But the meats are vegetarian," he mused. Then he let loose a shriek of laughter. I jumped back, landing on Wayne's foot. Wayne didn't seem to notice.

Paul hurried up behind his father. "Dad, stop that!" he whispered urgently.

Bradley turned to Paul and motioned him behind the counter with an elaborate bow. Paul looked uncomfortable, but shuffled behind the counter dutifully.

"The king is dead," announced Bradley, arms outstretched as if for the crucifix. "Long live the king." Then he walked purposefully across the hall to stare out a window.

The room was full of people and most of them were watching Bradley. Officer Guerrero squinted at him cautiously from her chair in the back. Ruth, Eli and Terry stared openly from the communal table. Don Logan shot Bradley a quick look of disgust from his table for one. And most of the other diners whose faces I didn't recognize gazed surreptitiously at him over their meals. At least the hall was full. I hope Fran was making money tonight.

"Four buffets?" asked Paul softly.

"Three," I said, turning back to him. His face looked so vulnerable. How could I have found this child threatening?

"And put it on *my* bill," said Craig.

Wayne stiffened behind me. I turned quickly and tugged his ear down to my level. "You're the one I love," I whispered into that ear. I felt his body soften again. He kissed me on the forehead, then turned and walked off to take a seat at the communal table. The rest of us headed for the buffet.

Felix smiled a private smile as we walked over. Was he tickled by the newspaper copy potential of Bradley's performance or just now realizing that he had snagged another free meal?

The buffet was heaped higher than usual. And the food was all Slim 'n' Fitted. There were little signs stuck on toothpicks in each dish. The raw vegetables had bright yellow signs announcing cheerfully: "A = unlimited." The soups were labeled in pink: "B = 1 cup." A platter of broiled tofu and vegetable shish kebabs had a lavender sign warning: "F = 1 skewer." "F" sounded tasty. I took three skewers. Then I heaped my plate with other goodies, mixing up coded food randomly in an uninhibited alphabet stew.

Avery Haskell came out of the kitchen with refills, dressed in white from his sneakers to his tall chef's hat. Once he had freshened the fruit salad, he stood by the buffet in military stance. His zombie glare looked like it ought to scare off any Slim 'n' Fitters who were tempted to take more than their coded share. It was enough for me as well. I took my plate and walked to the communal table.

I could hear Eli and Terry arguing as I approached.

"I agree that the law is not perfect," said Eli, "but I would ask you if there is any better way."

I sat down next to Wayne. Across from me, Ruth smiled good-naturedly as she listened to the debaters.

"Of course there's a better way," said Terry.

Felix and Craig joined us with heaped plates. "If the American people weren't blinded by the deliberate mystification of the legal system," Terry continued, "there would be a mass uprising for change. . . . "

I pulled a piece of tofu from its skewer and popped it into my mouth. Terry's words floated unheard over my head as I chewed. Tasty. A cherry tomato and pepper slice later, Fran came over to the table with a stainless steel water pitcher.

Gone were the tears of the afternoon. Her delicate, moon-shaped face was gleaming with happiness.

"Water?" she asked, smiling broadly.

The ice cubes clinked as she filled our glasses.

She whispered confidentially. "This has been the best turn-out yet for the Slim 'n' Fit weekend."

"Is that what all those little signs are about?" asked Terry, pointing at the buffet. He looked ready to argue the political implications of dieting.

Fran nodded eagerly. "You see, the yellow signs are—"

"Is business looking up?" I interrupted. I didn't want to hear the explanation for the signs. I had a feeling it would spoil my appetite.

Fran seemed happy to be derailed. "Business is great!" she bubbled. "Not only the Slim 'n' Fitters, but a table of six all the way from San Diego just for the dinner." As she pointed out their table, one of the San Diego diners waved at her. Fran waved back. "And a couple from Lakeside, and one from Palm Beach. People are beginning to hear about us."

I hoped that people were hearing about the food at Spa Santé, not the murders. The eager faces of the diners from San Diego looked suspiciously interested in the others in the room, especially in those of us at the communal table.

Ruth Ziegler reached out and patted Fran's hand. "I'm very happy for you, dear," she said, smiling benevolently.

Fran returned the smile and thanked her before turning to go to the next table.

"Fran," Ruth called out after her. Fran turned to face us again. "Before you go, I wanted to talk to you about Paul."

"Paul?" asked Fran, her smile losing some of its warmth.

"Yes. Paul," Ruth continued. "The recent events must have put a terrible stress on him. I'd like to spend some time with him this weekend, if he'd like. Help him put it all into perspective."

Fran's face had lost interest under her smile. "He'll do fine," she replied shortly. "Don't worry about him."

"No charge," Ruth assured her. "Just an ear to listen and a shoulder to cry on. We all need that, especially when we're young."

"I'm sure he'd love to talk to you," Fran agreed. Then she

bent to whisper again. "But I'll need all the help I can get this weekend. Beds to make. Food to prepare—"

Ruth's expression was no longer benevolent. She looked like an angry witch as she interrupted Fran. "Can't your husband help you instead?" she asked, her brows pinched together above suddenly hard black-button eyes.

Fran stepped back, clearly stung by Ruth's question. "My husband helps as much as he can," she replied, her voice high and defensive. Then she bent over to whisper once more. "You see," she explained confidentially, "Bradley is a writer. He needs time to write. And time to be away from people."

Ruth just eyed her coldly. And Ruth wasn't the only one who didn't buy Fran's explanation. Wayne's face was fierce with anger as he stared at Fran. And Don Logan had wheeled up, apparently to join in with his own glare.

"My husband is sensitive," Fran whined, her voice like that of a child who can't understand the injustice of adult rules. "He really is."

She searched the rest of our faces for approval and found none. Eli and Terry watched her without pity. Felix's gaze was interested, but not particularly friendly. And Craig avoided her eyes. I tried to keep my own expression neutral. I had a lot of sympathy for Fran. She was working night and day to keep her spa from going under. But I had sympathy for her son too, totally ignored as he sank further and further into anger and despair. I glanced over at the counter. Paul stood behind it stiffly. I hoped he couldn't hear the conversation.

"Anyway," Fran went on. "Paul doesn't mind the extra work."

"Have you ever asked him?" Don Logan broke in. His voice was low and hard.

"I . . ." Fran's voice trailed off in confusion. She couldn't seem to understand the irrational anger her denial of her son's problems had engendered. I wanted to explain it to her gently, but before I could find the words Ruth spoke again.

"Fran," she said, her voice a thin layer of politeness over fury. "Will you call Bradley over?"

"Bradley?" asked Fran nervously, glancing at the window where Bradley still stood staring.

"Yes, Bradley," Ruth replied. "And come back yourself. I want to talk to both of you."

"But I've got to—" Fran began. The anger in Ruth's eyes cut Fran's protest short. She shrugged her shoulders and walked off to get her husband.

We all watched as Fran approached Bradley and whispered in his ear. He issued his trademark loon's laugh as she tugged at his elbow. He turned to wave at us briefly, then turned back to the window. But Fran was persistent. She walked in front of him and held his arms still as she spoke in a low tone—too low for me to hear what she said to him. I imagined a plea to consider the effect on spa business of refusing a guest's request. Finally, he shrugged his shoulders and followed her over to our table.

"Have I been summoned?" Bradley asked when he reached us, his voice rich with irony.

"Yes," snapped Ruth, unamused. She motioned at Fran and Bradley to sit down. Fran obeyed immediately. She wasn't protesting anymore. And when Fran tugged on Bradley's elbow, he too plopped into a chair.

Then Ruth stood up, regal in her purple caftan. She opened her arms with mesmerizing slowness. Then she shouted:

"Pay attention!"

She got Fran's attention. Even Bradley's. His mouth dropped open and a surprisingly sane look appeared on his face. As if he had forgotten to be crazy for a moment, when faced with someone as outrageous as himself. Unfortunately, Ruth had also earned the attention of the entire hall. She didn't seem to notice, though, so intent was she on Fran and Bradley. I shrank in my own chair, embarrassed for all involved.

Ruth brought her arm up and pointed an accusing finger at the couple, holding the position as she continued.

"You are losing your son!" she hissed angrily.

Fran opened her mouth to speak.

"And what's worse," Ruth continued, cutting off any back talk, "you haven't even noticed!"

Fran looked at Bradley for help, but Bradley's eyes were fixed on Ruth.

"You!" Ruth's pointed finger moved to single Bradley out. "I don't want to hear any more about your fabled sensitivity, when you aren't even sensitive enough to notice your own son's suffering." This from a woman who hadn't noticed the hall full of faces watching her humiliate the Beaumonts.

But Bradley didn't refute the charge. His eyes were suddenly sane as he turned to look at his son behind the counter. Too suddenly sane. I wondered once again how much of Bradley's loon act was self-dramatization.

"As for you," Ruth went on, her arm swinging toward Fran now. "You can't solve a problem if you don't even admit to it, if you don't even see it. Look at your son now." Ruth's voice softened. "Will you think of him only when he's gone?"

Fran squirmed in her seat, glancing quickly at Paul as if to assure herself he was still there. A flicker of sadness appeared in her eyes momentarily.

Ruth opened her arms wide once more.

"You need therapy and you need it now!" she hissed.

Bradley went rigid in his seat.

"No," Ruth assured him. "I don't just mean you alone. I mean all of you, as a family."

Fran broke in. "We don't have the money," she objected.

"If you can't find free counseling, I'll write you the check," Ruth answered curtly. "No more excuses."

Fran shook her head stubbornly, pushing her chair back to get up. She seemed to realize now that she didn't have to listen.

"Pay attention," Ruth said once more, but softly this time. Her black button-eyes had become moist with sadness. "This is your last chance."

– Twenty –

RUTH ZIEGLER'S VERBAL ASSAULT on the Beaumonts had stunned the communal table into silence. In fact, the whole dining hall was silent and tense with anticipation, waiting for her next words.

Suddenly, Ruth seemed to become aware of the presence of the other diners in the room. She scanned the faces staring at her, sank into her chair and put her face into her hands.

Fran snatched her water pitcher from the table, her body stiff with anger. She opened her mouth to speak, then seemed to think better of it. She snapped her mouth shut and turned her back on our table. Then she made her way across the dining hall to fill glasses there.

Whispered conversations among the diners started up again sporadically, then swelled in volume to erase the silence.

Bradley remained sitting at our table. His face was somber as he stared at his son. Finally, he too rose.

"Thank you," he said to Ruth. His voice was so quiet I wasn't sure I heard him correctly. Ruth jerked her head out of her hands to look at him, her own expression surprised. Bradley thanked her again, then took a deep breath and walked over to the counter where Paul stood averting his eyes. I watched Bradley put his arm around his son's shoulder. Then I looked away. Too many eyes were intruding on their privacy already.

"I guess I got a little carried away," Ruth said in a very small voice.

No one offered a second opinion.

"I shouldn't have done that," she sighed. She looked very old and un-Ruth-like as she hung her head.

"You did what needed to be done," said Don Logan in a curt tone.

"But not in public," Ruth replied impatiently. She shook her head and rose from her seat. "I've got to apologize to Fran."

"No, no," said Uncle Eli, motioning her to sit back down. "Apologize later. To do so now might nullify the good that you have done." He tilted his head meaningfully toward Bradley and Paul Beaumont.

"You think I might have done some good?" Ruth asked. Her voice was eager. But her face was still troubled.

"Perhaps," Uncle Eli said. "It is too early to tell." He paused for a moment's thought before going on. "In this country there is a tradition of respect for privacy. One is not expected to interfere with another's family. But you make me wonder if some benefit may come from this, this . . .''

"Involuntary family counseling," I finished for him. Ruth cringed at my description. But Eli twinkled a smile at me.

"Ah, yes," he chuckled. "Very good, that phrase. Involuntary family counseling." He reached over and patted Ruth's hand. His eyes went to hers. "You are a concerned and passionate woman," he said slowly. "An action arising from that concern and passion must have some good in its effect."

Ruth was smiling now, even beginning to glow as she returned Eli's gaze. "You're incorrigible," she said. "Such a silver tongue! You could convince me my actions were all pure and good. Why, I think you could convince me I'm forty years old again!"

"I am an attorney," Eli answered. "It is my job to make convincing arguments." He bowed his head to her. "And your loveliness would do honor to any forty-year-old."

Ruth giggled in delight. Eli's was a silver tongue indeed.

I reintroduced myself to my shish kebab, lying cold and untouched on my plate. As I took a bite of tofu, Wayne spoke up.

"What kind of law do you practice, Mr. Rosen?" he asked. I turned to Wayne in amazement. A full sentence from his mouth was unusual. A conversational gambit was an event. He had to be sleuthing.

"Please, please," said Uncle Eli with a a wave of his hand. "Call me Eli, young man."

"Eli," obeyed Wayne gravely.

"I practice in more than one field of law," Eli answered. "But I do prefer trial work. Civil litigation and criminal defense are my specialities. I leave to the others in my firm most of the family and business law. I must confess that I enjoy the drama of the courtroom."

"Have you ever defended any really big criminals?" asked Felix eagerly.

"Ah," said Uncle Eli, straightening in his chair. "I have defended men *accused* of major felonies. But to ask if any of these men were actually criminals, that is a very different question." He wagged an admonitory finger at Felix. "Thankfully, the accused is not guilty until proven so in this country."

"Lawyers," sneered Don Logan. The look on his face matched his unfriendly tone.

Eli took Don's sneer in stride. "I have heard it said that every man hates a lawyer until he needs one," he joked. Then he went on more seriously. "Other people accused of crimes are seen as 'criminals.' But when one finds oneself on the wrong side of a criminal accusation, suddenly one believes in the rights of the accused."

"And the poor get overworked public defenders," said Terry, leaning forward, ready to argue with anyone who didn't agree. "And the public defenders don't believe in their clients any more than the rest of society!"

With that introduction, Terry was off and running. While he lectured on the inadequacies of the criminal law system, I sneaked another look at Bradley and his son. They were standing behind the counter talking quietly. Perhaps Ruth's tirade had brought about the desired result after all.

I plowed through shish kebab, curried rice, cornbread and fruit salad as Terry and Eli agreed and disagreed at great length about the American legal system. Ruth offered a cheerful opinion once in a while, apparently now over her brief period of self-abasement. Don Logan, on the other hand, whirred away his wheelchair in disgust when she suggested that counseling might be more appropriate for convicted criminals than punishment.

I ate the last bite of cantaloupe on my plate, and whispered to Wayne, "Time to leave?"

The grateful look he gave me melted my heart into a pool of guilt. The poor guy. Why was I putting him through this? I squeezed his shoulder. Then I remembered that it had been *his* idea to visit. He had wanted to protect me. Now I wondered what exactly he had wanted to protect me from? The murderer? Or my falling in love with my ex-husband again? I glanced at Craig playing with the rice on his plate despondently. There was no way I was going to fall in love with him again. Fourteen years had been enough. But how did I explain that to Wayne?

I rose to go as quietly as possible. I didn't want to interrupt Terry's commentary on certain judges who were former prosecuting attorneys and still prosecutors at heart. Wayne rose silently as well. We crept off toward the glass doors, huddling close together. Close enough that I could feel the heat radiating from Wayne's body.

I put my arm around his waist.

"Hey, wait a minute!" called Felix. He pushed his chair back and jogged across the dining hall to catch up with us. "How about our meeting?" he demanded in a whisper.

I looked up at Wayne. He shrugged his shoulders massively and sighed.

"We don't have to," I whispered. "We could do it later."

"Now," he whispered back. He looked down at me with the eyes of a martyr. "Get it over with."

I turned back to Felix. "Get Craig," I ordered.

We decided to meet in Craig's room. I was tired of paisley. So was Craig. Wayne reserved comment. But he raised his heavy brows in appreciation when we came through the door of Craig's room, taking in the white walls, Monet poster and peach and aqua accents.

"Well, fearless leader," said Felix, flopping into one of the aqua easy chairs. "What's the plan?"

I sat down on the edge of Craig's bed, then thought uncomfortably of the possible implication. Me on my ex-husband's bed. I grabbed Wayne's wrist and pulled him down next to me. Now I was comfortable. Craig sighed softly and lowered himself into the remaining easy chair.

Felix watched me expectantly. He didn't have to remind

me that this meeting was my idea. So, I asked myself, what did we do now?

"First," I said, arranging my face into a look of competence, "I'd like to hear everyone else's theories."

Felix's eyes lit up. Of course. He was probably chock full of theories.

"Go for it, Felix," I ordered.

"You heard her," Felix said, straightening in his chair.

"Heard who?" I asked.

"Ruth," he replied, his voice thick with pleasure. He stroked his mustache. Then he recited, " 'This is your last chance.' That's what she said to the Beaumonts tonight."

"And . . ." I prodded.

"Jeez! Can't you see? The woman's the good fairy of death! If everyone doesn't relate to each other like good little sensitive human beings, then ka-powie! They're dead."

Craig was shaking his head in disbelief.

Felix turned to him. "Suzanne was giving you a hard time before she got it, wasn't she?"

Craig winced at his words, then nodded sadly.

"And Jack Ireland was refusing to stop doing drugs and be a good little boy. Then he got it! Don't you see? It's a pattern."

We sat quietly for a few moments, absorbing Felix's theory. He was right. There was some kind of pattern there. Was Ruth making the world a more loving place by selective homicide? I found myself shaking my head. I just couldn't imagine Ruth killing anyone.

"All right," I said finally. "It's a possibility." Then I turned to Craig. "Who do you see as the murderer?" I asked.

Craig took a big breath. "Avery Haskell," he announced. He ducked his head guiltily. "I'm not saying that Haskell did it, though. I'm just saying he might have."

I nodded my understanding. "Why do you think it might be Haskell?" I asked.

"He's a religious fanatic," Craig answered. Then he shivered. "The way he quotes Scripture." Craig deepened his voice to a fair approximation of Avery Haskell's. " 'Let not mine enemies triumph over me,' " he intoned. "It gives me the creeps! And he didn't like Suzanne. Maybe he convinced himself she had to die for being unwomanly or something." He sighed and shook his head.

"And Jack?" I asked.

"Jack's easy," Craig answered. "Drinking, drugs, fornication. To a religious nut, Jack must have seemed like the devil incarnate."

I nodded. I could imagine Haskell killing both Suzanne and Jack all too easily. I shook off the image of his unchanging zombie face as he slowly throttled Suzanne. I wanted to keep my mind open.

I turned to Wayne, who sat next to me on the bed, his eyes hidden under lowered brows.

"Lots of possibilities," he growled. He raised his eyebrows, revealing troubled eyes. "Eli for instance. Easy to breach the code of legal ethics. Would Suzanne have blackmailed him?"

"But he wasn't even here when Suzanne died," objected Felix.

"No," agreed Wayne. "But he could have hired someone."

Felix nodded slowly, considering.

"Someone who needed the money," I murmured, thinking of Fran.

"And the hired killer had to kill Ireland because Ireland saw something," Felix finished. "I like it," he said with a smile. "But who—"

"Lots of other possibilities too," Wayne said before Felix could go on. "I agree with Craig about Haskell." Craig looked up in surprise. Wayne continued. "Bradley Beaumont's insane. Don Logan's angry. The Beaumont boy's unstable." Wayne scowled down at his hands. "But nothing really clicks," he finished.

"How about you, Kate?" asked Felix. "Who's your choice?"

I shrugged my shoulders. "I'm with Wayne," I answered. "Too many possibilities."

"Come on," prodded Felix. He leaned forward attentively, an ingratiating smile on his face. Was this the method he used to pump policewomen? "You must have a favorite," he purred.

"Okay," I said slowly. I didn't like putting the thought into words. But that was what this meeting was for. "I'd add Fran to the list. She's in financial trouble." Felix's eyes lit up like a pinball backglass. This was obviously new information to him.

I turned from his eager eyes and went on. "And she's put her life into the spa. Fourteen-hour days, eighty-hour weeks. I know what it means to put that kind of time and energy into a business." I paused, then finished in a spurt. "I have a feeling she would kill to keep it."

Felix was excited now, nodding enthusiastically and bouncing in his chair.

"But," I admonished, holding up my hand. "Outside of the improbable case of her being a hired assassin, I can't imagine how killing Suzanne, or Jack, would have helped her in any way."

"Eli could have hired Fran," Felix whispered half to himself. His gears were turning audibly.

"Doesn't really work," Wayne pointed out brusquely. "How would Eli know she needed money. How would he know to put the proposition to her? Can't see her name being listed in *Soldier of Fortune.*"

Felix slumped back into his chair, his face scrunched up like a spoiled child denied an ice-cream cone.

"Wayne is right," I said. "Lots of possibilities, but no sure fits."

We sat in glum silence for a while.

"So what are we going to do now?" Felix asked peevishly.

"Organization time," I answered. When in doubt, make a list. "Who's got some paper?" I asked.

Craig went to the desk and pulled out a yellow legal pad. As he walked back to his chair his eyes filled with tears. "Suzanne's," he whispered. "She never went anywhere without paper."

"Do you want to be secretary, honey?" I asked him softly. The endearment just slipped out, made of pity and old habits. I swiveled my head around to Wayne quickly. Too late. The damage had been done. His eyes were filled with antipathy as he glared at Craig.

But Craig was oblivious to Wayne's glare as he sat down and prepared to take notes. He pulled a pen from his pocket and touched it to the top page in readiness.

"All right," I said. "We do categories. Motive, means—"

"Wait!" shouted Felix, jumping out of his chair. He

snatched the yellow pad from Craig's hand. Craig jerked back in surprise.

"Suzanne might have written something important on this pad," Felix explained as he scanned the top page. But his eyes were puzzled when he looked up.

"What?" I asked impatiently. When Felix didn't answer, I got up and took the pad from his hands.

I looked down. Printed across the top of the page in block letters was: SUCCESS IS MINE. I turned the page. The sentence was repeated on the next page and on all of the pages left in the pad. I held up the pad to Craig.

"Is this Suzanne's writing?" I asked gently.

He nodded sadly. "That was her affirmation," he said, taking the pad. "She said it thirty times every morning and every night. She wrote it on the top of every notepad, on every sheet in the calendar. She . . ." Craig's eyes brimmed over. "She tried so damn hard," he sobbed.

I sat down and glued myself to the edge of the bed. It took all my willpower to keep from putting my arms around Craig as he sniffed back tears miserably. Suzanne *had* tried hard. I could almost see her in the room now, tall and proud, her long shining blond hair rippling as she moved against the white backdrop. Suzanne's determination to succeed had been palpable when she was alive. I could feel it even now that she was dead, emanating from her written affirmation on the yellow legal pad. No wonder Craig had been drawn to her. And for all of her drive to succeed, she had been cruelly murdered.

Beside me, I felt Wayne fighting his empathy for Craig. First he averted his eyes from Craig's tears. But he could still hear the sobs. He crossed his arms and shifted uneasily on the edge of the bed as Craig brought himself under control again. Finally he cleared his throat.

"Want me to take the notes?" Wayne asked Craig gently.

"No!" snapped Craig, holding the yellow pad to his chest as if it were a baby about to be stolen. "I'm fine." He settled the pad in his lap and began writing. "Motive, means. What else?" he asked. His voice was rough with the residue of tears.

"Opportunity. Character," I answered briskly, willing to pretend we hadn't experienced the brief intermission. "And a column for more information needed."

"Let's start with motive," suggested Felix eagerly. He seemed cheerful again. What had he made of Craig's breakdown?

"All right. Motives first," I agreed. "Any ideas?"

It took us over three hours to compile a list of possible motives. Among others, we catalogued lust (Paul Beaumont), lunacy (his father), and lucre (his mother). We even listed love (Ruth Ziegler, a.k.a. the Good Fairy of Death), jealously (Nikki), and political assassination (Terry McPhail). Then there was the possibility of resisted blackmail (almost anyone), silencing a witness (God knows who) or revenge (your guess is as good as mine). Or just plain irritation! Irritation was on all of our minds. After three hours each one of us was getting cranky.

"Opportunity" went faster. In ten minutes we had agreed that everyone had opportunity. Even Eli, if you considered the hired-gun theory.

Then we got down to means. Between them, the victims had been strangled, smothered, dragged and bludgeoned.

"It had to be someone strong," said Craig softly. I looked into his unfocused eyes and wondered if he was seeing Suzanne's body again.

"That lets out Ruth," said Felix, disappointment evident in the slump of his shoulders. Ruth was still his favorite choice for murderer.

"Not necessarily," I argued. "Just because she's old and female doesn't mean she's weak." I was in favor of an equal opportunity approach to this murder.

My approach seemed to cheer Felix up. He straightened his shoulders and went on. "How about Don Logan?" he asked. "At least we can rule him out. He couldn't have done it from his wheelchair."

"Upper arms are strong, though," Wayne pointed out.

I agreed with Wayne. "Fran said Don works out every day in the gym," I said. I wasn't standing for discrimination against the disabled either. "He may be stronger than anyone else for all we know."

Craig had written down every motive we'd discussed on Suzanne's yellow pad, along with pro and con arguments. The room was silent as he flipped another page to note our most recent comments on opportunity and means.

"Last page," he said without looking up. His voice was tired.

"How about a conclusion?" suggested Felix.

"Well," said Craig, flipping through the pages. "Adding up all of the data, it seems like . . ." He looked up at me, his face as aged and hopeless as those seen in an old folks' home.

"What?" I asked.

"It looks like anyone could have done it," he finished glumly.

"But we still haven't talked about character," I insisted. "Or figured out what other information we need."

"We need to know who killed Suzanne," Craig replied. He lowered his eyes. "And I don't think we're going to find out."

"But—" I began.

"Let's call it a night," said Wayne softly. He rose up off the bed and stretched out a hand to me. "Discuss the rest tomorrow."

Unwillingly, I let him pull me up to my feet.

"Check you out *mañana*, guys," said Felix, jumping out of his chair and jogging out the door with suspicious energy. "Adios," he added as he clattered down the stairs.

Wayne put his arm around my shoulder. I turned toward the door, feeling as old as Craig looked.

"Wait!" yelled Craig.

"For what?" asked Wayne, continuing to steer me to the door.

"I . . . I need to talk to Kate," said Craig. I felt Wayne's arm stiffen around my shoulders.

I turned back in Craig's direction. He rose from his chair and approached me hesitantly.

"Kate, I want you to know I've been thinking some more," he said. He lowered his puppy-dog eyes. Then raised them again quickly to see my reaction.

"We've all been thinking, Craig," I answered gently, hoping to deflect what I was afraid was coming. I could feel Wayne as he turned to face Craig. I didn't have to look to see the angry expression on his face.

But Craig was undeterred. He reached out for my hand and held it. "I've changed a lot in these last few days. And I want . . . I want to give our marriage another chance. I'm serious this time," he said. "Don't answer me now. Just think about it. I . . ." He glanced nervously at Wayne, then went on anyway. "I love you, Kate."

I pulled my hand back. "Don't—" I began.

"You," said Wayne slowly, his deep voice shaking with tension. He stepped forward and leaned his fierce face into Craig's. "You have ruined the whole idea of marriage for Kate. Isn't that enough?" The last words were so low they were barely audible.

But Craig heard them. He stepped back as if he had been struck. His face was paper-white.

"Craig, I—" I began.

"Go," he said shrilly. "It's okay. Just go."

So I went. And Wayne came after me. I stomped angrily out of the Orange Blossom building into the dark. Why were Craig and Wayne arguing? It was my decision whom to love. Whom to marry. I could hear Wayne following me silently down the dirt path. I knew if I turned to him he would tell me he was sorry. And I would probably forgive him. But I wasn't ready yet. I needed to walk off my anger. After fifteen minutes of random stomping I realized I was lost. I could just see the brick structure I was approaching in the moonlight. It was the mud bath where Craig had found Suzanne.

I heard a low groan and stopped short, my muscles tensing. Had I conjured up Suzanne's ghost? I turned to Wayne, suddenly glad he was there. But he was already running past me. It was then that I realized it wasn't a ghost I had heard. I sprinted after Wayne, circling the brick wall. The yellow tape that had blocked off the opening of the mud bath lay on the ground, cut into pieces.

I peered past Wayne, down into the mud bath and saw a body sprawled on its side. Oh God, I thought. Please, not another dead body. Then the body moved.

– Twenty–One –

WITH ANOTHER GROAN, the body heaved itself on its back. Then it lay still, settling only a few inches into the surface of the mud. The mud didn't look very deep, contained by a sunken enclosure not much bigger than an ordinary bathroom tub. A flat tiled edge ran around the rim of the bath, butting up against the surrounding brick wall.

Thank God for peat moss, I thought, remembering Fran's boast about the superior density of the spa's mud baths. Whoever's body it was, it was alive, sprawled out on the top of the mud, like a drunk on an overly soft sofa. The body looked almost comfortable, except for its legs, which were twisted up at an unnatural angle onto the tiled edge. A faintly sulfurous odor emanated from the mud. I shivered, sweating in the cool night air.

"Don't know if we should try to move him," Wayne's low voice whispered in my ear. I looked at his anxious face and shook my head helplessly. Didn't safety courses tell you not to move an accident victim? Frantically, I tried to remember my first-aid rules as Wayne stepped down onto the tiled stairs that led into the mud.

When Wayne's foot hit the mud-smeared stair it made a slurping sound that sent me into another panic. In my adrenaline-fried brain the mud sounded like quicksand. I moved quickly through the opening into the bath, ready to haul him out if the mud sucked him in.

Wayne took another slurping step down. I reminded myself it was only mud. But I stepped onto the edge of the bath, at the top of the stairs, just in case. From that vantage point I looked down and recognized the body sprawled on its back. It was Eli Rosen, now a ghostly moonlit collage of mud-smeared flesh, hair and cloth. His glasses were gone. And his eyes were closed. Was he even breathing?

"Eli!" I called out loudly, suddenly afraid that he was dead after all. Or dying.

He groaned again, the sound echoing eerily in the brick enclosed bath. But his eyes remained closed.

Wayne squatted down and touched Eli's twisted leg carefully. He shook his head hopelessly.

"Eli!" I called again, even louder this time.

Eli's mud-smeared eyelids pulled up slowly. His eyes were unfocused beneath them.

"Wo bin ich?" he murmured softly.

"What?" I answered. Was he speaking English?

"Ach du Scheisse," he rasped. Definitely not English. But he was talking. He was alive.

Wayne climbed back out of the bath carefully. Then he walked around the edge of the bath like a tightrope walker. When he reached the spot on the edge closest to Eli's head, he squatted down again and put his hand on Eli's chest.

"Breathing's okay," he whispered. "Can't see any bleeding either."

Eli's eyes focused on Wayne's face above him for a moment. "Something around my neck," he rasped. Then a tremor shook his body. He raised a muddy hand to his neck, then dropped it again. His eyes fluttered closed.

"Don't see anything," said Wayne, moving his hand gently up Eli's neck. Then he peered closely. "But there's a mark," he said in a low voice.

Wayne pulled his head up to stare at me, his face tight with anger. Angry at whoever had done that to Eli?

Eli's eyelids popped open suddenly, revealing the terror in his eyes.

"My face was in the mud," he whispered urgently. "I was smothering in the mud!" Then his voice calmed. He asked wonderingly, "Did I turn myself over?"

"Must have," said Wayne brusquely. Then more gently, "You're okay now. We're with you."

"Thank you," murmured Eli, closing his eyes once more. "Thank you."

A few moments passed. Eli looked far too still as he lay there. And why didn't he straighten out his legs?

"Shall I try to help you out of the mud?" Wayne suggested.

"Am I still in the mud?" Eli answered dreamily, his words barely audible. He didn't bother to open his eyes. Damn. He may have been breathing and talking, but it was obvious that his faculties were seriously impaired.

"You are in the mud," answered Wayne, his deep voice taking on a soothing tone. "But you're on your back. You're fine now. Just fine."

"Who did this to you, Eli?" I asked softly. Eli didn't answer. And as I asked that question, a related one blossomed in my mind. Where was the person who did this to him? I looked over my shoulder anxiously, seeing no one through the opening in the brick wall. But I wasn't reassured. However long it felt, I knew we had been with Eli only a few minutes at most. Was the would-be murderer waiting nearby? All I could hear was my own heart pounding as I strained for the sound of someone in the dark. I felt a trickle of fresh sweat drip down my face.

"My glasses," rasped Eli, breaking the silence. "Where are my glasses?"

Wayne felt around in the mud, but pulled his hands out empty.

"It's all right," I told Eli. "We'll get you another pair of glasses." He murmured an inaudible reply.

"Do you remember who did this to you?" I asked once more, raising my voice as much to give myself courage as to get Eli's attention.

His eyes fluttered open briefly. "Someone did this to me?" he asked.

I restrained myself from cursing aloud. So much for a quick identification.

It was time to get help. And I doubted anyone would hear our shouts this far away from the main building. Except, perhaps, the murderer. I would have to go on foot.

"I'd better get an ambulance," I said to Wayne. I looked out the brick opening toward the dark path I would have to take, and shivered. "And the police," I finished.

I turned to go quickly. I had wasted enough time.

"Wait!" Wayne called to me. He lowered his volume to a

whisper. "Could still be out here." However incomplete his sentence was, I knew he meant the murderer.

"One of us has to stay with Eli," I said, an unwelcome quiver in my voice belying the decisive tone of my words. "The other has to get help."

I turned to see Wayne's strained face in the moonlight. I knew he wanted to choose the more dangerous task for himself. But which was more dangerous? Going as a messenger? Or staying as a guard? The murderer might be waiting on the dirt path to kill the messenger. With the messenger dead, the murderer would be free to pick off Eli and his guard leisurely. My hands began to tremble. But maybe the murderer was only interested in Eli, just waiting until the messenger left, to attack Eli and his only remaining guard. The trembling spread to my legs. Once Wayne and I split up, neither of us was going to be as safe as we were together. But we couldn't leave Eli alone.

"I'll run to the dining hall," I announced, cutting short the menacing babble in my mind. If my body trembled any harder, I wouldn't be able to move at all. "It's not far," I added. "Probably less than a half a mile."

Wayne stood up on the edge of the bath. He reached out a hand to me, then realized that it was too far away to touch and drew it back. He glanced down at Eli, lying peacefully in the mud.

"I'll yell my head off if I so much as see anyone," I promised. Wayne nodded. "And you do the same," I ordered. He nodded again.

I turned once more to go. "Kate," Wayne whispered. I looked over my shoulder.

"What?" I asked.

"Can't lose you," he answered gruffly. "Take care of yourself. Please."

"I will," I said and left.

Jogging down the dirt path in the moonlight, I tried to take care of myself. I strained my ears to hear any sound that was out of place. But all I could hear was my own labored breathing and my feet slapping the dirt. I scanned the path ahead for movement, seeing only unrelieved darkness. But I felt something. A presence. Was someone watching me? Or was the presence my own fear, taking palpable form? I ran faster.

And thought of Suzanne. Had she been running when the murderer had caught her?

I was almost to the dining hall when I saw the figure on the porch. I couldn't see who it was, only the tall shadow silhouetted by the porch light. Sweat bathed my entire body. I stopped short and took a deep breath. It was time to yell.

"Help!" I screamed. "Get the police! Get an ambulance!"

The figure raced down the stairs toward me. Oh God. Should I turn and run?

"Help!" I screamed even louder.

Finally I saw who was coming toward me. It was Officer Guerrero. And she had her hand on her gun. My body convulsed with relief. Then my legs gave out. I flopped painfully down onto the dirt path, jolting my tail bone. Impatiently, I forced myself to stand again.

"What's happened?" Guerrero demanded. I saw my own fear reflected in her wide eyes. "Are you okay?" she asked.

"Eli Rosen, in the mud bath!" I raced the words out. "He's hurt."

"Dead?" she asked tightly.

"No, he's alive," I answered. Suddenly I was very grateful. Eli was alive. The murderer had made a mistake. "But he needs an ambulance."

Guerrero motioned me to go on.

"We've got to hurry," I insisted. I wasn't taking any more time to be grateful. What if the murderer was there at the mud bath now? "Eli's alone out there. Him and Wayne."

"Hold on," said Guerrero, putting her hand on my shoulder. "Is Wayne your boyfriend?" I nodded impatiently. "And he's hurt too?"

"No," I answered. "Only Eli is hurt. Wayne's guarding him." Guerrero nodded slowly. Why wouldn't the woman hurry up? "But the murderer could find them any minute. We've got to protect them!"

"Did you see the assailant?" Guerrero asked.

I shook my head frantically.

"Okay. Tell me Mr. Rosen's injuries, and I'll call it in," she said. "Then we'll go."

"I don't know what his injuries are," I yelped. I told myself to calm down. "He was strangled, I think. And put in the mud bath to smother. His legs are twisted—"

"Is he conscious?" asked Guerrero.

"He was," I answered. "But barely."

"Okay," she said. "I'll call it in." She turned to the stairs, then turned back. "Wait here for me," she ordered.

"But—"

"I don't know the way," she explained. "Wait. I'll be right back." Then she turned back to the stairs, ran up them and through the front doors. At least she was hurrying now.

So I waited, hoping this wait wasn't something I would regret for my entire life. I doubted I could hear Wayne yell for help this far away. And even if he yelled and I heard him, could I get there in time? And what would I do anyway? I needed Guerrero with me. Her and her gun.

I heard steps behind me. I swiveled my body in the direction of the sound quickly. I saw Fran. She was scurrying toward me, dressed in a chenille bathrobe. She fiddled with the sash around her waist.

I stepped back, watching her hands on the sash. Was chenille strong enough to strangle a person? This person? I wouldn't bet my life it wasn't. I resisted the urge to turn and look over my shoulder for Officer Guerrero. I kept my eyes on Fran and her hands.

"Oh, Kate," she greeted me breathlessly. Her face didn't look murderous, only softly concerned. "Has something happened? I heard you screaming. There hasn't been another . . . ?" Her words trailed off. She looked down at the ground. Was she still unable to pronounce the word "murder"?

"No, there hasn't," I snapped.

I heard more footsteps. I glimpsed a brief look of fear on Fran's face as she turned toward the sound. But the approaching footsteps belonged to her husband and her son. Bradley Beaumont was in his bare feet and striped pajamas. His son Paul, however, was fully dressed in jeans, T-shirt and Adidas running shoes. I asked myself why he was dressed at this hour. Then again, I was fully dressed too.

"We heard a yell," said Bradley, his voice unusually resonant in the darkness.

I breathed deeply, trying to center myself. The three Beaumonts stared at me as if I were an abstract painting they were trying to comprehend. Their faces seemed preternaturally pale in the moonlight, their eyes dark pits. The word "vampire" flitted through my mind. I wished it hadn't. I took three more steps backward, reminding myself that the marks on the victims' necks didn't look anything like vampire marks. As far as I knew. I took another step backward. The Beaumonts continued to stare.

Then I heard Officer Guerrero's footsteps clattering down the stairs behind me. "Ambulance and backup will be here in a few minutes," she announced briskly.

"Ambulance?" asked Fran, her voice small and frightened.

Guerrero ignored her question. "Who knows the way to the mud bath?" she demanded.

"The outdoor one?" Bradley asked, stepping forward.

Guerrero turned to me for clarification. I nodded.

"We all know the way," Bradley answered.

"Good," said Guerrero. Then she snapped out orders to the Beaumonts. "You three stay here. One of you bring the paramedics when they arrive. Whoever's left can bring Chief Orlandi and any other officers. Got that?"

The Beaumonts nodded as a unit.

Guerrero turned to me. "Go!" she ordered.

I sprinted up the dirt path to the mud bath. How long had I been away? Five minutes? Fifteen? My time sense had been swallowed by the events. I listened to the comforting sound of Guerrero running behind me and concentrated on speed. I hadn't run in years. My lungs were burning with the effort. But I kept the pace up. Only when we were almost there did I allow myself to think of Wayne. *Please let him be all right*, I chanted in my mind, praying to a god my agnostic soul had never been introduced to.

Once the mud bath came into dim view I shouted out, "Wayne!"

"Here!" he yelled back.

Wayne was alive. My feet slowed down, fear no longer propelling them forward. I sucked in air. Guerrero sped past me. I watched her disappear into the opening in the brick wall as I jogged the last few yards. Then I was through the opening myself, panting and weak.

Guerrero was squatting down next to Wayne, talking to Eli. Only Eli wasn't answering. He lay as I had left him, sprawled out on the mud, eyes closed. Guerrero grabbed his arm and felt for his pulse. Then she turned to Wayne.

"You can leave now," she said softly. "We'll take care of it from here on in."

Wayne stood up slowly, and gazed at me across the mud bath.

"But don't go too far," Guerrero warned. "The Chief will want to talk to you two."

Wayne grunted his assent, but kept his eyes on me. His homely face was smeared with mud. So were his hands and arms, his shoes and his knees. They all bore the muddy imprint of his care for Eli. But Wayne was alive. He looked beautiful to me. Unexpected tears welled up in my eyes. I wiped them away impatiently and smiled. Wayne reached his arms toward me briefly. Then he tightrope-walked quickly around the edge of the tub so that he could actually touch me.

"Okay?" he asked gruffly when he reached me. He put his hands on my shoulders.

"Perfect," I replied.

He looked down at his hands, still gripping my shoulders. "Filthy," he said, as if noticing for the first time, and pulled them back.

His eyes were serious under his low brows as he whispered, "Sorry."

A laugh burbled up and escaped my lips. We were alive and he was sorry for the mud. I pulled him to me and pressed myself against his mud-smeared body. I felt his arms come around me hesitantly. Then the strength entered them and he squeezed. Mid-squeeze, we heard the sirens.

We jumped apart guiltily, caught embracing while Eli might still need us. I swiveled my head in Eli's direction. He still lay unmoving on the mud, his eyes closed. Officer Guerrero was gently massaging one of his hands, her face anxious.

"Is he—?" I began.

"Don't think about it," Wayne whispered. "He'll be fine."

He put his arms around me again. We held each other until the sound of approaching footsteps burst into the silence.

A blur of figures came rushing down the dirt path in the moonlight. Bradley was in the lead, still clad in his striped pajamas. Two uniformed men were close behind him. One of them carried a folded stretcher. He dropped the stretcher and unfolded it at the entrance to the mud bath, then entered on the heels of the other man. Officer Dempster was next, running up the path with his gun pointed upwards. Orlandi jogged up last, his belly heaving as he gasped for air.

The uniformed men emerged from the mud bath within moments, carrying Eli Rosen. They laid him carefully on the stretcher, then lifted it to transport him back down the dirt path. I looked at Eli's still form and fought back tears.

"Hold it!" ordered Orlandi, wiping his face with a white handkerchief. The men stopped. "Is he alive?"

The man in the lead nodded his head impatiently.

"Is he conscious?" Orlandi demanded.

"No," the man replied curtly. My stomach tightened. Was Eli going to die, after all?

"Take him away, then," snapped Orlandi, shaking his head. Then he spotted Bradley Beaumont. "You!" he barked impatiently. "Get out of here! Go back to the dining hall and stay there."

Bradley did as he was told. Without a word, he turned and followed the men who carried Eli's unconscious body.

Officer Guerrero emerged from the mud bath as Bradley and the stretcher-bearers disappeared from view. Orlandi marched toward her angrily. "What the hell is going on here?" he demanded.

"Ms. Jasper and Mr. Caruso," she began patiently, pointing to us, "discovered Mr. Rosen—"

"Not that Jasper woman again!" Orlandi bellowed.

- Twenty-Two -

ORLANDI TURNED SLOWLY to face us. His eyes surveyed my figure, then Wayne's. Gradually his lips drew back, exposing his teeth in the old crocodile grin.

"Been doing a little mud wrestling?" he inquired unpleasantly.

One glance down my body told me what he meant. Half of the mud that had covered Wayne had somehow transferred itself to me. My legs and arms were liberally smeared. I reached my hand up to my face and felt something wet there too. Then I dropped my hand, realizing I was probably adding more mud to my face by touching it. I could just see Wayne out of the corner of my eye. His face was flushed under its muddy mask.

Officer Dempster trotted over to join the action. His gun was still in his hand, though now pointed at the ground. His eyes were slits of suspicion.

Orlandi's grin disappeared as he registered the officer's presence.

"Dempster!" Orlandi shouted, never taking his eyes from Wayne or me. "Stop playing with your gun! And stay with Rosen. Follow those paramedics."

Dempster's eyes widened in confusion.

"Someone has to be there if Rosen regains consciousness," Orlandi explained slowly, with a show of infinite patience. I shivered at his use of "if." *What if Eli didn't regain consciousness?* Orlandi went on: "Write down anything Rosen says. It might be important. Once he's up to answering questions, ask him what happened."

Dempster saluted as he spun around to chase the paramedics. He sprinted down the dirt path.

"And call me, whatever happens!" Orlandi shouted after him.

Then Orlandi grinned at us again. I prepared myself for further intimidation.

"So, you two found another body," he began conversationally.

I nodded.

"Wonderful," he said, injecting a full syringe of sarcasm into the word. "And I suppose you two walked all over the crime scene."

I nodded again and found an unexpected smile tugging at my lips. Somehow Orlandi's sarcasm had served to cheer me this time around. His sharp tone felt very homey, as comforting as a roaring fire on a cold day. We were standing in the dark, covered in muck, but I was no longer afraid. Even Eli's prognosis seemed more positive, with "Bulldog" Orlandi barking at everyone in sight.

Orlandi spotted my smile and shook his head in ponderous disgust. "Stay right there," he ordered brusquely. "Don't move a muscle."

Then he turned to Officer Guerrero. "Have a look around," he told her. "See what you can find."

"What am I looking for?" Guerrero asked, head bent forward earnestly.

"How the hell do I know, Guerrero?" Orlandi snarled. Guerrero's head snapped back. "Footprints. Weapons. Lurking suspects. Monkeys in the trees! Use your imagination."

"Yes, sir," she replied crisply and turned to go.

"And, Guerrero!" Orlandi barked.

"Yes, sir," she said, halting mid-step.

"Have you sketched the scene as it was when you arrived? Position of the body?"

"No, sir."

"Well, do it, then!" Orlandi ordered impatiently. "And take down some notes while it's fresh in your memory."

"I don't have my notebook, sir," Guerrero informed him. I thought I saw a glint of malicious satisfaction in her eye as she spoke.

Orlandi heaved a massive sigh. "Well, get your notebook, check out the area and be back here pronto," he commanded.

"Someone has to secure the area until the technicians get here"—he paused and jerked his head toward Wayne and me—"though these good citizens have probably destroyed most of the evidence already."

Guerrero ran down the path as Orlandi turned to us, escaping before he had anything more to say to her. She was fast, probably in better shape than I was. And certainly in better shape than Chief Orlandi.

Once she was gone, Orlandi resumed his questions.

"So, you didn't see the assailant?" he asked, as if hoping we would change our minds.

"No," Wayne and I answered simultaneously.

Orlandi sighed, then asked, "When did you find the victim?"

Wayne and I looked at each other for answers. But neither of us had kept track of the time. I shrugged my shoulders.

"Maybe twenty minutes, a half hour ago," Wayne said slowly.

Orlandi looked down at his watch. "Twelve-thirty?" he asked.

Wayne shrugged.

Orlandi sighed once more. What was it about this spa that produced so many sighs? I looked around in the darkness and shivered. Sighs were the least of it.

"Tell me what happened," the Chief ordered finally. "Everything."

Wayne and I told our story in tandem. We covered nearly every moment from the time we found Eli's body until Orlandi arrived on the scene.

Then Orlandi pressed us for details. By the time we had been over the story twice, Officer Guerrero was back.

"I couldn't see anything out of place in the dark," she reported. "Sir," she added, seeing the scowl on her boss's face.

Orlandi told her to secure the area until the technicians arrived, then motioned to Wayne and me over his shoulder.

"You two come with me," he ordered, beginning down the dirt path to the dining hall. "I'll have more questions for you later."

We followed Chief Orlandi down the path quietly. He stomped along without speaking, deep in thought. Wayne and I walked close enough together that our arms bumped every once in a while. That was a comfort. But some of my fear began to creep back as we walked, despite the escort. The path was too dark, too quiet. Suddenly, I imagined someone watching us. Or was it only my imagination? I peered into the darkness nervously, but I couldn't see anyone. Or very much of anything, for that matter.

When we were almost to the hall Wayne asked Orlandi if we could wash up.

"Not a chance," was Orlandi's muttered reply.

"But we're covered in mud," I objected. A whine had entered my voice without permission. I tried to correct it. "We really are dirty," I said in a lower voice.

"That mud may be evidence," Orlandi barked.

Wayne and I exchanged worried glances as we continued to walk. Did Orlandi really think we had pushed Eli Rosen into the mud bath, then called the police to rescue him? Wayne and I shrugged in unison. I wiped my hands on my pants. The mud was beginning to dry now. Some of it flaked off as I wiped.

I was briskly dry-cleaning my hands by slapping them together when the main building came into view. Someone had turned on all the outdoor lights, transforming the porch into a stage, complete with actors.

I dropped my hands, my attention captured by the spectacle before us. Bradley Beaumont stood straight and tall in his striped pajamas, his arm around his son's trembling shoulders. He stared out into the shadows with a soulful expression of angst worthy of Sir Laurence Olivier. Paul's face was less subtle, a study in pure wide-eyed fear. Fran sat on the porch bench in her chenille robe, her arms wrapped around herself, her head drooping forward. Two uniformed men, both tall and dark, stood off to the side. One was burly, the other thin. The stage was set, frozen in readiness. But no one spoke their opening lines.

We were almost to the stairs when the stillness was broken by the whir of Don Logan's wheelchair behind us. "I heard the sirens," Logan explained softly.

Orlandi shot him a quick glance and grunted in reply. Logan seemed to be fully dressed, up to and including his cowboy hat. Another night owl? As we mounted the stairs, Logan wheeled up the ramp.

Suddenly the actors on the porch began to move. Fran's

head pulled up. Bradley and Paul turned to us. And the thin uniformed officer marched forward.

"Deputy Nerviani," he introduced himself. And with a nod at his burly partner, "Deputy Jordan, County Sheriff's Department. Here to assist."

"Glad to have you," said Orlandi. "This is a hell of a mess. I'll fill you in."

He looked at the rest of us on the porch and barked, "Stay here!"

Then he led Deputies Nerviani and Jordan down the stairs for a whispered consultation. While the police consulted, the Beaumonts stared at Wayne and me. We stared back at the Beaumonts. And Don Logan stared at all of us. After a few minutes Orlandi's normal speaking voice came floating back up the stairs.

"Nerviani, you round up the ones who aren't here." Orlandi looked up at us on the porch. "Not too many left. Ruth Ziegler, Terry McPhail, Craig Jasper, Avery Haskell—"

"I'm here," came a low voice from the shadows.

Orlandi's head swiveled around, startled. Then he glared into the shadows where the voice had come from.

Avery Haskell emerged from behind an orange tree, his zombie mask intact. How long had he been there listening? Was he the watcher whose presence I had felt? He was dressed, but barely. He wore no shoes, no socks, only jeans and a sweatshirt.

Orlandi squinted at Haskell suspiciously, then turned back to Nerviani. "That leaves Jasper, Ziegler and McPhail," he said. He motioned to Fran. "Can you give Deputy Nerviani their room numbers?"

"I'd be happy to," replied Fran, her face brightening at the request. She led Nerviani into the lobby, chatting cheerfully. I wished I had something to do. I was exhausted, and sleepy, too, in the aftermath of the night's events.

"Jordan," Orlandi ordered, turning to the burly deputy. "Take the rest of them into the dining hall. Don't let them talk. I'll take them one by one for interviews."

Jordan herded us into the building. Orlandi followed. We were halfway through the lobby when Avery Haskell spoke again.

"Correction is grievous unto him that forsaketh the way," he declared.

Orlandi marched past Jordan and jerked Haskell away from the rest of us by his elbow. Haskell turned to face him slowly. "And he that hateth reproof shall die," Haskell finished, his face still wooden.

"That's very interesting," said Orlandi, flashing his teeth in a brief crocodile grin. Then his voice hardened. "What does it mean?" he demanded.

"It's the Lord's word," replied Haskell.

"It is, is it?" barked Orlandi.

"The Lord's word is always of comfort to the saved," Haskell explained slowly. The impact of the words might have been friendly, if only he had been smiling. But he wasn't.

"Fine," said Orlandi, baring his teeth again. "You're first. Come with me."

He led Haskell off to Fran's office while the rest of us moved into the dining hall. We all sat down at the communal table as if we had been ordered to. Wayne and I took one side, Bradley and Paul Beaumont the other. And Don Logan wheeled up to the end.

A minute later Fran came in, still smiling after helping Deputy Nerviani. She sat down next to Bradley.

When Deputy Jordan began the "don't speak among yourselves" spiel I tuned out. His voice became a warm buzz as I leaned against Wayne sleepily. All out of adrenalin, I thought. My eyes were refusing to focus properly. There seemed to be two sets of Beaumonts. With a blink they wavered into one set again, but then lazily separated once more into twins. I closed my eyes gently and wondered if I was sitting at the table with a murderer. Even if I was, I decided, I wanted a little nap.

A phone rang in the hall. My eyes popped open to see Bradley Beaumont's eyes frankly studying my face. The phone rang again. Fran turned to Deputy Jordan. He nodded his permission to answer the phone. She went to the counter and picked it up, murmured a few words, covered the receiver and told him breathlessly that it was for Chief Orlandi.

I sat up straight in my chair. My foggy mind struggled for alertness. Was the phone call about Eli? Was he conscious? Or dead? I turned to Wayne. His brows were low on his worried face.

Deputy Jordan walked to the phone and grunted into it a

few times. Then he hung up and trotted through the dining room doors to find Orlandi.

I looked across at Bradley. Why had he been staring at me? Was it the mud? His eyes were lowered now, shielded from mine. Then I heard the dining hall doors open again. I turned, expecting to see Deputy Jordan. But there were two people coming through the doors, Edna Grimshaw and Arletta Ainsley.

"Psst," hissed Edna loudly. Everyone at the table turned to her. Her jowly face reddened. Arletta waved a frail hand at me and smiled.

"How did you—" I began.

"Shhh," Edna warned. She put her finger to her lips and motioned me over.

What the hell, I thought. Deputy Jordan was gone. I got up, feeling the curious eyes of everyone present, including Wayne. I gave his shoulder a quick squeeze and walked over to the twins.

As soon as I reached them, Arletta chirped, "We heard it on the radio."

"Police band," explained Edna in a curt whisper. Her eyes traveled down my body. "Why are you covered in mud?"

I sighed. I was so tired. It was easier to explain truthfully than to hold out on them.

"We found another body," I whispered back. "In the mud bath. But he's alive—"

"Out!" boomed a voice from behind the twins.

I jumped, then looked up into Chief Orlandi's angry face. I had been so intent on my explanation that I hadn't heard his approach. Deputy Jordan trotted up behind him.

Edna Grimshaw was not intimidated. "Vic Orlandi," she growled, pointing a beefy finger in his face. "Don't you ever speak to me that way."

Orlandi rolled his eyes up to the ceiling. When he brought them back down he turned on Deputy Jordan.

"Don't leave these people alone again," he snapped.

Deputy Jordan flinched but managed a quick nod.

Then Orlandi turned back to Edna and Arletta. He drew back his lips and grinned. "Would you ladies be so kind as to accompany me?" he asked, sweeping his hand toward the lobby.

Edna narrowed her eyes. Arletta giggled. Orlandi drew his

lips back even further, straining his face into a grinning skull. Finally Edna hunched her shoulders forward and marched into the lobby as requested. Arletta bobbed dutifully behind her.

I watched them all disappear out the front doors. Then I heard Orlandi bellow, "And stay out!" After the echoes died down, he stomped back through the lobby and into Fran's office.

Deputy Nerviani brought in the rest of the crew as Jordan was steering me back to the communal table. Ruth, Terry, Craig and Felix came through the dining room doors. Felix?

Craig rushed over to me. "You're okay!" he exclaimed. Then he took a better look at me. "How'd you get that mud all over—"

"That's enough," warned Jordan. After Orlandi's reprimand he wasn't going to allow any loose lips to flap. That was clear.

I took my seat next to Wayne. Craig flopped down beside me and Felix next to him. Felix had a big grin on his face, having infiltrated the inner circle of suspects. I wished he could have taken my place. All I wanted was to take that little nap I deserved. Jordan was reciting his speech again to the newcomers. I dropped my eyelids as Terry and Ruth took seats across the table.

"We have a right to know what's going on here!" Terry shouted. I opened my eyes again to look at him. He must have dressed in a hurry. His T-shirt didn't have any words printed on it.

Jordan opened his mouth to respond. But Orlandi beat him to it as he walked through the door. He must have finished with Haskell.

"Keep quiet," he snapped at Terry. "We can discuss your rights later."

"But—" insisted Terry.

"Enough!" bellowed Orlandi.

Volume triumphed over free speech once more. Terry slumped back in his chair and crossed his arms angrily. But he kept quiet. Ruth looked around the room anxiously. Had she noticed that Eli was missing? I wanted to reassure her, to tell her that Eli wasn't dead. But Orlandi's surly presence was enough to keep my mouth shut, even if common sense wouldn't have been.

Orlandi pointed at Felix, who was still grinning. Was Felix already composing his story about Orlandi's tactics?

"Who's he?" Orlandi demanded. Felix's grin flickered.

"He claims he's a witness," answered Nerviani.

"To what?" demanded Orlandi with a scowl. "This man's a reporter."

Felix winced and gave up on his grin altogether. Nerviani led Orlandi over to the corner of the dining hall, where they conversed in muted grunts and whispers. I wondered what it was that Felix claimed to have witnessed. I let my eyes close. He probably just wanted a chance to talk to Orlandi. But I was curious enough to push my eyes back open when Orlandi returned to our table.

"Mr. Byrne, come with me," he ordered Felix. His face was serious.

As Felix followed Orlandi out into the lobby I wondered if he really had seen something. And, if so, what was it?

I leaned my head against Wayne's shoulder, catching a glimpse of a frown on Craig's face as my eyes closed again. I didn't fall asleep right away. I could hear the rustling of bodies shifting in their chairs and Terry's muttered "stormtroopers" as an image of Eli Rosen's muddy body floated into my mind. I tried to summon up a picture of a flowery meadow instead, but that vision came complete with Jack Ireland's bloody head, floating over my meadow like an angry sun. Then his head smiled and I drifted away.

I awoke to my name being called. I blinked and saw Chief Orlandi before me. It seemed to me that I had been dreaming about him too. But the dream was gone.

"Your turn, Mrs. Jasper," Orlandi said softly. At least he wasn't shouting. Or grinning. His face held a natural smile. Something must have improved his temper. I stifled a yawn and returned his smile as I rose to follow him to Fran's office.

Orlandi began his interrogation as soon as I was seated across from him at Fran's desk. He wasn't posturing this time. Just asking straightforward questions. Maybe he was as tired as I was. It was nearly two in the morning by the clock behind him. On the other hand, maybe this was a new trick to gain my confidence.

We went over what I had told him at the mud bath earlier. Then he asked me where I had been previous to finding Eli.

The tension in his face told me that this was an important question.

"We were walking," I answered hesitantly. From the look on Orlandi's face that wasn't the right answer.

"Where were you walking from?" he asked patiently. A forty-watt bulb turned on in my tired brain.

"From Craig's room," I answered eagerly. "Wayne and I were with Craig and Felix until we left!" An alibi. All four of us had an alibi! "Felix left about a minute before we did," I added.

I frowned at a sudden thought. Could Craig have attacked Eli in the few minutes that Wayne and I wandered around the spa. Not likely, I assured myself. A sixty-watt bulb turned on. This is what Felix had witnessed. Our alibis.

"What time did you leave?" asked Orlandi.

"Somewhere after twelve," I guessed, looking at my lap and figuring. "Just a little while before we found Eli."

With a jolt I remembered actually finding Eli. I sucked in my breath, seeing his twisted legs on the edge of the mud bath once more, and his still body being carried away on the stretcher. I lifted my face to Orlandi's.

"Was that phone call about Eli?" I asked. I didn't expect Orlandi to answer, but I had to ask the question.

He nodded, surprising me.

"And?" I asked as meekly as possible.

"Rosen's regained consciousness," Orlandi replied. His eyes were intent on my face as he spoke. Looking for a guilty twitch of surprise?

I sat back in my chair and let my breath out in relief. Eli was alive. Warmth came into my cold hands.

"Will he be all right?" I asked quickly. Consciousness was not necessarily good health.

"Probably," answered Orlandi softly. Then suddenly his face turned angry. He bent forward and slammed his fist on the desk. "Rosen's been through too much for an old man! Hit over the head. Strangled. And his legs are all bashed up! Whoever tossed him in that mud bath didn't even bother to throw him far enough to clear the edge."

- Twenty-Three -

ORLANDI SAT BACK in his chair, his sudden anger dissipated. "The doctors say Rosen will survive," he finished softly. "Most likely, he won't be permanently injured."

I clapped my hands together in an instant of celebration. Then I slumped in my own chair, exhausted by relief. The strings of tension holding me up like a puppet had been cut. I could relax now. The murderer had failed. And Eli Rosen would live.

But would Eli be able to identify his attacker? Tension pulled me up straight in my chair again.

"What does Eli remember?" I asked quickly, taking advantage of Orlandi's talkative mood.

Orlandi shook his head in disgust. "Eli Rosen remembers walking Ruth Ziegler to her room around eleven o'clock," he recited, "then starting back to his own room."

Orlandi bent forward again, peering into my eyes. Finally, he nodded his head as if having made a decision. "That's all he remembers," he finished brusquely.

"That's all?" I repeated, unbelieving. "Doesn't he even remember Wayne and I talking to him?"

Orlandi shook his head. "Concussions can do that," he told me. "Maybe he'll remember more later. But for now, that's all we've got."

Damn. Maybe the murderer was safe after all. He—or she— had probably attacked Eli as he walked back from Ruth's room at eleven o'clock—

"Craig was with us at eleven o'clock! He couldn't have done it!" I burst out triumphantly.

"You sound surprised," said Orlandi, raising his eyebrows. Renewed interest glimmered in his eyes.

"No, no. Not surprised at all," I sought to assure him. I calmed my voice. "Just pleased that the evidence clears him."

"Whoa," Orlandi warned. "The evidence doesn't clear Mr. Jasper." Orlandi watched me intently as he spoke. "You're assuming Rosen was attacked at eleven. Maybe he was. But maybe he wasn't. He could have met his assailant after twelve, right before you and your boyfriend got to the mud bath. If he ran ahead, your ex-husband would have had enough time."

I shook my head vigorously. "You don't really believe that, do you?" I asked.

Orlandi stretched his lips back in his old grin for an answer. Damn.

"How about me?" I asked nervously. "Am I cleared?"

He shrugged his shoulders, still grinning.

"Can I at least wash the mud off?" I begged.

Orlandi lowered his gaze to the papers on Fran's desk. Had he even heard my plea? He wrote something in a notebook. I told myself that the spa mud was healthy mud. It was probably good for my skin. But my clothes? Finally Orlandi raised his head again to look at me.

"I guess it can't hurt," he muttered dispiritedly. "You've already admitted being at the mud bath."

I left Orlandi in Fran's office after a few more halfhearted questions. He seemed to have lost interest in me. In fact, he seemed thoroughly depressed. I didn't think he really suspected Craig any longer. But I wasn't sure.

I marched straight to the restroom off the lobby to clean up. There is only so much you can do for caked mud with paper towels and water. I did it. If nothing else, the cold water on my face woke me up. Then I strolled out onto the lit porch to wait for Wayne. I certainly wasn't walking back to my room without him.

I sat down on the porch bench and thought. Why had Eli Rosen been attacked? What did he have in common with Suzanne Sorenson and Jack Ireland? Questions I should have considered from the moment I saw Eli's body in the mud bath.

The sound of movement in the nearby trees distracted me

from my belated consideration. Suddenly, I felt vulnerable on
this lit porch. I rose to go back inside. Then I heard a sharp,
"Psst."

Arletta and Edna hurried out from under an orange tree to
stand at the foot of the stairs. I let out a relieved laugh. At
that late hour, the twins—with their sharply contrasting faces
and figures—seemed to me especially comical. Edna stared
up at me, her jowly face set in an unappreciative frown. I
tried to get serious. Arletta smiled at me serenely, as if sharing my amusement.

"Come on up," I whispered.

Edna jerked her head over her shoulder just as I heard a
new set of footsteps. Damn. Edna and Arletta scurried back
into the grove of orange trees. My shoulders tensed.

"Howdy hi, Kate," came the voice before I could see the
body attached to it. I flopped back down on the bench. It was
only Felix.

He danced up the stairs and sat down next to me. His eyes
were glistening with excitement. "Who got it this time?" he
asked, his voice low with pleasure.

"No one," I answered. Technically, I was telling the truth.
Eli was alive. And I wasn't sure what I should tell Felix.
Besides, Felix was fun to tease.

"Come on," he whined, his eyes narrowing. He was not
amused. "There's a whole herd of crime-scene people down
at the outdoor mud bath where Suzanne got it, and cops
crawling all over the spa. Something's happened. Something
big. Something Craig needs an alibi for."

He thrust his glaring face at me. "Tell me this, little Miss
Wise-ass, if no one new got it, why is Orlandi so friggin'
interested in who I was with between eleven and twelve?"

"What's the hurry?" I asked sweetly. "Got a story due?"

"Come on, Kate. I'm your friend." He pulled his head
back and softened his tone. "Don't put my nuts through the
wringer on this one, okay? Tell me what happened." His mustache vibrated anxiously. He looked like an intellectual rabbit,
I thought sleepily. I've always been a sucker for rabbits.

So I told him. After fifteen minutes he had squeezed all
the details from me and chewed them over thoroughly. I told
him he'd better not write anything about Eli's memory lapse.
If the murderer hadn't figured it out yet, I wanted to keep it
that way. Felix assured me he wasn't entirely stupid. That's

good to know, I thought and yawned. Then I came up with my own question for Felix.

"How'd you know you were an alibi?" I asked.

He smiled smugly before answering. "I moseyed on back to Craig's room about fifteen minutes after you guys left. I wanted to throw around a few more ideas." Poor Craig. Alone at Felix's mercy. But at least Felix's presence strengthened Craig's alibi.

"I was still with him when the deputy came to take him in," Felix continued. "So I did the right thing. I told that deputy that I'd been with Craig most of the night."

"Congratulations," I said. "A real coup."

Felix nodded complacently, then frowned. "Only Orlandi threw me out as soon as he sucked the details out of me. Wouldn't answer *my* questions. Noooo!" He drew out the word in disgust. "Friggin' vampire!" he concluded, shaking his head angrily.

I chuckled. The pot was calling the kettle black. Felix settled back on the bench and looked out into the darkness of the spa.

"Who did it, Kate?" he asked suddenly.

I jumped a little, startled out of my chuckle. Damn. That was still the question, wasn't it? Eli might be safe, but the murderer was too.

"I wish I knew," I answered slowly. Suzanne, Jack, Eli. If only Jack had been a lawyer, it might have made more sense.

"What if Jack was incidental—" I began. Then I heard the door open behind us.

I turned and saw Wayne walk through. Most of the mud was gone from his face and hands. I guessed that he had made a trip to the restroom, too. I stood up to go to him. But he hung his head the instant he saw me.

"Wayne?" I inquired anxiously. What was wrong with the man? Had Eli died after all?

He looked down miserably at me, his sorrowful eyes not even halfway visible below his brows. I closed the distance between us in a few urgent steps.

"Been thinking," he growled softly. "About Craig, me, you."

I nodded my head cautiously, feeling a chill that didn't

come from the night air. This was about us, not murder. Had I finally lost him?

"Been a real jerk," he finished glumly. He shook his head. "Sorry."

"That's all?" I burst out. I wrapped my arms around him and pressed my cheek to his still muddy chest. "I love you, you . . . you big jerk," I said.

He raised my chin and looked me in the eye. "Really?" he asked.

"Really," I answered. I put my arms around his neck and kissed him gently.

"Jeez, you guys!" whined Felix.

Wayne returned my kiss with passion. I held on tight.

"We've got a murderer to catch!" Felix reminded us impatiently. "Break it up, okay?"

Wayne removed his lips from mine slowly. I gave him one more quick kiss on his cauliflower nose, for luck. Then we joined Felix on the redwood bench.

The three of us sat there and talked in the cool night air. About the spa people. Then we talked some more. About motives. And more. About backgrounds. And still nothing clicked. I was getting sleepy again. But it felt safe and comfortable there on the porch, so I just leaned against Wayne and listened to Felix spin bizarre scenarios.

Felix had almost convinced himself that Suzanne was Avery Haskell's illegitimate daughter, when Don Logan came wheeling by. Felix lifted his hand in greeting. But Logan rolled down the ramp without returning the gesture.

I sat up abruptly, remembering the thought that had tickled my mind earlier.

"Eli and Suzanne," I said. "They had a law practice in common!"

Felix turned to me. "So?" he asked sourly.

"What if the murders have to do with one of Suzanne's cases? All Suzanne's cases were Eli's cases too. He was her boss. So what if one of those cases—"

"What about Jack Ireland?" Felix interrupted. He could rattle on indefinitely about his own theories, I thought angrily, but I mention one of mine and he torpedoes it.

"I don't know about Jack," I snapped. "Maybe he saw the murderer do it or something. But the point is Suzanne and Eli."

I was wide awake now, excited. I stood up and wagged my finger at Felix. "And this is a theory we can check," I told him. Then I began to pace. "If we can get Eli's permission, we can call his secretary. Have her go through all the cases Suzanne has handled. Find the link—"

This time it was Wayne who interrupted me. "Won't work," he said softly. "Case files are confidential."

Damn. I stopped in my tracks. But I wasn't finished with the idea yet. "How about Eli?" I proposed. "We could tell him the theory and have *him* go through his cases."

Wayne shook his head gently. "You heard how Eli feels about his clients. Man's not going to give out incriminating information—"

"And anyway," Felix broke in. "If the murderer is one of Suzanne's clients, don't you think Eli would have realized it by now? He knows the names of all the people at the spa. He's got a functioning brain. Don't you think he would have checked them out against his files?"

"Not necessarily," I answered defensively. "And maybe the murderer isn't a client! Maybe the murderer's a friend of a client, a child of a client, maybe even someone on the other side—"

As the door behind us opened I realized I had been shouting. I snapped my mouth shut and turned to the door.

Ruth sprang toward me, her gypsy face now wizened with distress. "They told me Eli was assaulted!" she cried. "But they wouldn't tell me his condition." She twisted her hands together as she spoke.

I wanted to comfort her. To tell her Eli was conscious and well. She may be the murderer, I reminded myself. I shouldn't tell her anything. I looked into her anxious eyes. Did she know I knew Eli's condition?

Finally, I compromised. "I'm sure he'll be all right," I murmured gently.

"But I've got to *know*," she insisted. "I have to face whatever's happened." Her voice grew calmer as she said this, as if she'd been hypnotized by her own words. Her eyes lost focus. "I've figured out where he is. I called the hospitals. He's at Lakeside General. I'm going to see him there."

"Will they let you see him?" I asked.

"I'll find a way," she answered, her voice regaining determination. She was a formidable woman. She probably would find a way.

She grabbed my hands and sandwiched them between her own. "Wish me luck," she ordered, smiling.

I smiled back. "Good luck," I whispered, and hoped she wasn't the murderer.

She dropped my hands and rushed across the porch to the stairs, a hurricane in a purple caftan.

"Ruth, hold on a minute," I called, remembering Eli's first words in the mud bath. "I want to ask you something."

"Walk me to my car," she shouted over her shoulder.

I shot Wayne a quick glance. He stood up, but I motioned him back down. I would have better rapport with Ruth alone. And the parking lot wasn't far.

I trotted down the stairs in her wake and caught up with her at the edge of the graveled lot. I could still hear Felix's voice expounding a new theory from the porch. I could even hear the whir of Don Logan's wheelchair, sounding only yards away. It's strange how sound travels in the silence of the night.

"My car's at the far end," Ruth said. She kept on walking as she pointed into the darkness of the parking lot. "What did you want to know?"

"Do you know if Eli speaks German?" I asked. I thought that was the language he'd spoken when he first awakened in the mud bath, but I wasn't sure.

"German?" was Ruth's distracted reply. She shot me a quick glance. Admittedly, it was an odd question.

"I have a reason for asking," I assured her. And I did. What if Eli was part of a Nazi spy ring? I can only blame Felix's influence and the hour for my flight of imagination. It had to be past three o'clock in the morning.

"German," Ruth repeated, scrunching up her face in thought. "Now I remember," she said finally. Her face relaxed. "Eli was born in Germany, I think. His father was German. It seems to me he was a boy when he and his mother escaped the country. They got out before the worst of it. But his father died in the camps."

"Then Eli is Jewish?" I asked stupidly.

"Is the Pope Catholic?" she returned my question. I took that for a confirmation. So much for my Nazi spy theory, I thought, now embarrassed by my own imaginings.

"Here's my car," Ruth said, pointing to her ancient Volvo

looming menacingly before us. I wished she hadn't parked so far away. It was dark out here, with only the moon for light. And quiet. I couldn't hear Felix anymore.

She opened her door and hopped in. Then she rolled down her window. "Thanks," she said.

"For what?" I asked.

"For helping me with my perspective," she answered. Her Volvo erupted into noisy life before I could ask what she meant.

"Give my love to Eli," I called out.

She blew me a kiss and drove away.

It seemed even darker in the parking lot without Ruth. And once she was gone I felt the watcher's presence again. Forget it, I told myself. But I couldn't stop the trembling that took over my body. Just exhaustion, I assured myself, rubbing my arms vigorously. *Get back to the light* now, my mind screamed. I inhaled deeply, then turned and took a step back toward the safety of the porch.

I centered myself as I took my next step, stepping heel first as in tai chi. That was better. Stronger. My mind stopped shrieking fear.

Then I felt something slip lightly over my head.

– Twenty–Four –

IT GRAZED THE tip of my nose before settling down around my neck. I knew in an instant that it was a rope. And that it was tightening from behind me. And in that instant I could hear my tai chi teacher's voice telling me not to resist. Telling me to go with the movement.

I stepped backwards quickly. And kept stepping, toe-heel touching the gravel lightly, until I felt the rope go slack. I took three more long steps for good measure, then turned to face the murderer.

Don Logan sat in his wheelchair, a few yards away from me in the moonlit parking lot. He gazed at me cheerfully. I could just see the broad smile on his face under the shadow of his cowboy hat. The other end of the rope that was looped around my neck was grasped firmly in his hand. He gave the rope a slight jerk that rippled up to my neck but didn't tighten the loop. I stepped closer. Now I could see his eyes too. I estimated a yard or so of slack in the rope between us. I took a good look and saw that it was the same white nylon rope that was strung all over the spa to cordon off the construction areas.

"You're not as stupid as the others," Logan drawled. He whirred his wheelchair a few inches closer to me, then continued. "They all struggled against the lasso. I hardly had to jerk it, they were so quick to choke themselves. Stupid as a bunch of cows." He laughed. He hadn't looked this happy since I'd met him. "Lucky these wheelchairs come with seat belts," he added with an sardonic wink. "The way the bitch struggled, could have pulled me right out of my chair."

I brought my hands up to the loop of rope around my neck.
The smile left his face.

"Don't touch it!" he warned in a low whisper, jerking the
rope again. The knot slid around to the front of my neck.
Then the loop contracted. "I can pull it tight before you ever
have a chance."

I dropped my hands and looked up toward the porch. Was
anyone watching? My heart was beating in my ears. I could
feel sweat prickling all the pores of my body.

"And don't scream either. They'd never get here in time."
His eyes were glued to my face as he wrapped the rope around
his hand, taking up the slack.

I returned his look, all the time wondering if I could lift
the loop over my head fast enough to beat him. I just wasn't
sure. It was still fairly loose around my neck. I was sure it
would clear my head if I lifted it. But how fast could he yank
it tight? His upper body was powerful. He was quick too.
And I was no cowboy. Then I realized. Don Logan was.

That first day on the porch, Logan had even told me that
he worked a ranch. And the cowboy hat! Why hadn't I ever
put it together? Cowboys, roping. All the victims had been
lassoed. If you can't reach someone easily from a wheelchair,
what a great way to catch them.

"Isn't quite like calf-roping," Logan mused. "A little
more challenge. But I can handle it."

He smiled as he explained. "See, you ease out the rope,
then jerk it!" He gave the rope around my neck an illustrative
jerk, tightening the loop a half inch more, then laughed. A
trickle of sweat ran into my eyes. I hoped the amount I was
sweating would make the rope slippery.

"Then you play the rope while they struggle," he continued cheerfully. "The bitch struggled so much, I was afraid
I'd tip over. But I just kept moving my chair, synchronizing
with her movements. This chair's a lot like a horse in some
ways."

Logan focused on my eyes to see if I appreciated his lecture. If it kept him from yanking that rope tight, I'd be glad
to listen to him all night long.

"What about Jack?" I asked.

He smiled broadly. "I thought he would be a mite more
difficult. So I waited till he started his bike. Then I roped
him and pulled him clean off it. The bike stalled, but that

was no problem. I roped it too, and pulled it over on him. Thought they might think it was an accident.''

"But his head—'' I began.

"Oh, that.'' He whooped and slapped his knee merrily. "They leave the damnedest things out around here. Rope all over the place. Even hammers.'' He paused. "I used a hammer on him before I pulled the bike over. Didn't feel like toting him over to the mud bath.''

I shivered and sweat some more. Couldn't someone hear us out here? But I didn't dare look up at the porch to see.

I raised my voice slightly to ask the next question, hoping that Wayne or Felix would hear me. "How'd you get the other two into the mud bath?''

"It wasn't easy,'' he answered ruefully. He shook his head. "I could only get so close to the bath. Then I gave them the old heave-ho. But there's only so much you can do from a wheelchair. That old man didn't land right. He was too heavy.''

I remembered Eli's twisted legs. Logan was peering into my face now.

"You found the old man, didn't you?''

I nodded my head slowly, carefully.

"He's still alive, isn't he?''

"Yes,'' I answered. Then I spoke with more bravado than I felt. "And he'll remember you once the shock wears off.''

"Not likely,'' answered Logan. He cocked his head as if considering the possibility. "First of all, I got him from behind. And his glasses went flying right off. By the time I dragged him over to the mud bath he was already unconscious. No, he never knew what hit him.''

Logan eyed me seriously. "You're the only one I have to worry about,'' he said. His voice had a hint of regret. He jiggled the rope lightly. I thought up another question fast.

"Why?'' I asked. I wasn't just playing for time. Afraid as I was, I was still curious. "Why did you kill them?''

He looked down at his own crippled legs in answer. Then he brought his eyes back to my face. But his eyes were out of focus now.

"You wouldn't believe how your life can entirely change in a moment,'' he said. His voice was low and bitter. "Two years ago we were heading back home from the in-laws. Over the Golden Gate Bridge. My wife was driving. She was in the center lane, trying to make time. There aren't any dividers on that bridge, you know.'' He focused his eyes on mine momentarily. Then he looked through me, and went back to his story.

''My son was sitting between us in the front seat, playing with his baseball cards. I was half asleep. Then I heard my wife shout. It was the last thing I ever heard from her.'' He paused and swallowed. His eyes were shining, either with rage or insanity, or both. ''I looked up and saw what she was shouting about. A Lincoln Continental had crossed the center line. It was coming at us, full speed. She swerved, but it was too late.''

Logan brought his shining eyes back to mine. His voice was hard as he spoke. ''It was a long time later before I found out anything about the drunk that hit us. They kept me doped to the gills at first. I figured out my legs were paralyzed pretty quick. It's hard to miss when they keep asking you if you feel anything and you don't.'' His bark of harsh laughter rang out like a shot in the silent air.

''Then they told me my wife and kid were dead. Just like that. I wanted to die, too.'' He paused. Then a trace of a smile twisted his lips. ''But I found a reason to survive. A reason to go through the torture they call 'physical therapy.' A reason to live in this goddamn wheelchair.''

He bent forward, peering into my eyes. ''Do you want to know what I found to live for?'' he asked.

I nodded.

''Revenge,'' he whispered. His smile broadened. I shivered, shaking the sweat from my forehead into my eyes. I reached up a hand to wipe the sweat away.

''I told you not to do that,'' Logan snarled and gave the rope another jerk. This time I felt the loop tighten more than an inch. I wasn't sure that it was still loose enough to clear my head—if I decided to chance lifting it off. At least it wasn't choking me. Not yet anyway. Logan bent his head up at me, glaring.

I took a big breath. ''Why Suzanne?'' I asked.

He smiled and relaxed in his chair. ''I thought you'd figure it out,'' he teased. ''You were on the right track.''

I shrugged my shoulders.

''Want a clue?'' he asked.

''Please,'' I answered softly.

"It was one of that bitch's cases. You were right about that." He gave the rope a playful tug. This time I moved my head with it so that the loop didn't tighten. But with my head forward, I was off balance. "Can't you figure it out?" he asked.

Suddenly I had it. "Drunk driving," I whispered. "She defended drunk drivers."

"Bingo!" he answered, infusing the word with all the good cheer of a game show host. "When I first got moving again I thought I'd kill the drunk. But he had already died in the accident. Then I thought of the drunk's fat wife. But she was a pitiful woman. There wouldn't have been any point to it."

Logan sighed heavily, then continued. "So I sued the estate. The wife came waddling up to me afterwards in the courthouse corridor. She said she was sorry. She blubbered all over me. Told me she'd do anything she could to help." He shook his head in disgust.

"Pitiful," Logan repeated. "But she did do something for me that day. This tall blond bitch came walking by, all dressed for success. The wife said the bitch was Suzanne Sorenson, the one who had saved her husband's license with some fancy legal bullshit."

"And you killed Suzanne for that?" I asked in disbelief. I shouldn't have spoken.

"Isn't that enough?" Logan snarled. He looked into my eyes angrily as if it had been my fault. "The bitch got him his license back two weeks before he hit us! Two weeks before he killed my wife and kid!"

"I'm sorry," I murmured. I really was. I wasn't sure if Logan heard me, though. He jerked his eyes away from mine and stared out into the darkness over my head.

I listened to the sound of my own heartbeat in the silence. Then I thought I heard another sound. Something in the trees. My eyes wanted to look, but I knew that would be a mistake. I strained my ears but the sound wasn't repeated. Had Logan heard it? He was still staring past me.

"Did you come here to kill her?" I asked. If there was anyone moving out there, I wanted to cover the sound.

Logan turned his eyes back to me slowly. Then he shook his head. "No," he answered. "I came here to get away. To get past the anger. Doctor's advice." He laughed harshly again.

"And there she was, the bitch who'd killed my wife and kid, bragging about getting people's licenses back for them.

"I couldn't decide whether or not to approach her. To tell her what she'd done. So I went for a little wheelchair ride." Logan's eyes were out of focus again, lost in the memory. "I had found some rope lying on the ground and I was fooling around with it—I can still do a lot of trick-roping even from this chair—when the bitch came jogging by. I waved at her but she didn't stop. She just kept running on those long healthy legs. So I got her! Around the neck."

He looked up at me, eyes focused now. "The bitch struggled against the rope, fighting me. And losing. That felt good. She might have been a winner in court, but she was a loser against my rope." He smiled triumphantly. "She won't help kill anyone else."

Then he dropped his eyes to the ground and scowled. "I blew it on the old man, though. Who knows how many people have died because of him? Goddamn lawyer!" He spit the last words out.

I heard another rustle. This time I was sure of it. I just hoped it was human. Logan lifted his head and glanced at the trees.

"Why Jack?" I asked quickly.

"Why Jack?" he snapped, jerking his head back. "You heard him. 'Get high and fly!' Who was he going to kill, out there stoned on his motorcycle? Who was he going to cripple? I could give a shit if he killed himself. But what about the others?"

Logan made a fist of his rope-wrapped hand and banged it down on his knee. The loop tugged on the back of my neck, nearly pulling me off my feet. I scuffled my feet forward a few inches, hoping Logan wouldn't notice.

"I ought to get an award," he muttered, unseeing. "Wheelchair Avenger, clearing the state of scum!" He took a breath.

I heard something scuff the gravel on my right. But Logan didn't seem to hear it. He was too wrapped up in his own words. I kept my eyes on him. He smiled again.

"I covered myself well. No one will ever find my bloody jeans. I even erased my wheelchair tracks with a branch, Indian style."

Logan gave the loop around my neck a friendly tug. I took

a full step forward. He didn't object. I was within two yards of him now, and there was a little slack in the rope again.

"But you," he whispered. "You had to figure out that it was one of her cases. Why didn't you leave it alone?"

Good question, I thought. A drop of sweat trickled into my eye. I didn't reach up to wipe it. I blinked. And heard the crunch of gravel on my left. Logan kept his eyes on me. I couldn't believe he hadn't heard the sound.

"Listen," I said loudly. "I don't drink. I don't defend drunk drivers. I'm as innocent as your wife was."

"My wife was no whore!" he shouted at me. Damn. He hadn't been this angry at me a minute before. Was this what it took to work himself up to kill me?

"You and all your 'friends,' " he snarled. "Don't compare yourself to my wife!"

I breathed deeply and centered myself. I took a slow step toward him, to put more slack into the rope.

"You—" he began.

"Hold it right there," a gruff voice warned at my left.

"We've got you covered," another voice chirped at my right.

The twins. I glanced quickly to my left. Edna had something clenched in her upraised fist, but it didn't look like a gun. I looked back at Logan. He had turned his head away from me to stare at Edna. I inched my hands toward the loop around my neck.

Logan turned to Arletta next. After one look at her frail form, he leaned his head back and roared with laughter.

His mouth was still open when Edna drew back her arm and heaved the contents of her fist at him. Her aim was good. Gravel bounced off his hat and face, some of it even making it into his mouth. Startled, Logan spit and pulled up his arm to shield his eyes, jerking the loop of rope taut around my neck again. I stepped toward him quickly, slipping my hands into the taut loop as I did.

Arletta fired her handful.

I yanked at the rope, loosening it as her load of gravel peppered Don Logan's head and body, and mine. I was two feet away from him now. I looked into his eyes and saw resignation there. Or was it relief?

Edna was scooping up another handful when I pulled the loose rope over my head and tossed it away from my body.

As Edna took aim I began to scream.

- Twenty-Five -

BY THE NEXT afternoon I was pretty embarrassed about all the screaming I had done the night before. The minute I had let out the first shriek Don Logan had whirred away, trailing rope behind him. But that hadn't been enough to ease my fear. I had kept on screaming, unable to stop.

The screaming had brought Wayne, so it had served a purpose. He had been on his way down the stairs, wondering why I was taking so long, when he had heard the first shriek. Poor guy. He had thought that shriek was my death cry. It was the sight of Wayne's frightened face as he came running toward me that had shut my mouth. I don't know which of us was comforted more when I wrapped my arms around him.

By that time, everyone was streaming into the parking lot. Felix had followed Wayne down the stairs. Chief Orlandi and the two sheriff's deputies were next. The two deputies, with a lot of yelling and pointing assistance from the twins, had apprehended Don Logan as he tried to maneuver into his van. Craig, Terry, Avery Haskell and all the Beaumonts had come down the stairs in a group. Then miscellaneous police officers, technicians and sleepless Slim 'n' Fitters had swarmed over the parking lot.

But all that was history. At least that's what I kept telling myself. It was Saturday afternoon and I still felt pretty shaky. Wayne and I had slept through the remaining morning hours huddled in each other's arms. Now we were back in the dining hall, picking over the remnants of our final vegetarian feast.

"Don't you see?" Ruth was saying. She bent across the communal table, her gypsy eyes sparkling. "Your screams were the perfect feeling response." She took my hand and squeezed. "You did great!" she congratulated me.

Terry McPhail sat at Ruth's side, unimpressed by her words. He crossed his arms over his "Split Wood Not Atoms" T-shirt and rolled his eyes toward the beamed ceiling.

"Well, I won't need psychotherapy for a few years," I muttered quickly. I could feel my face burning with embarrassment. "I think I got all my feelings out until 2016."

"Won't need to buy a primal box either," Wayne teased gently. His voice was soft and low. A voice you could climb into. I squeezed his knee gratefully.

" 'Feeling response,' " snorted Terry, ignoring our comments. "Screaming isn't action. It doesn't do anything constructive."

"It brought the police," Craig pointed out. He sat on Wayne's other side, looking amazingly fit. He had jogged five miles that morning. There was new color in his bony face. And light in his eyes. The light beamed in my direction. Damn.

"No, no. I didn't mean Kate's screaming for help," Terry corrected Craig impatiently. "I meant all this garbage about screaming to get your feelings out. It's Pablum," he finished. "A substitute for action."

"Feelings are not garbage," Ruth snapped. "If Don Logan had screamed a little more, he might not have needed revenge. But he couldn't let go of what he'd lost. He couldn't get beyond his anger."

"Spare me the psychological analysis," Terry drawled. "The man's a psychopath! Sure he suffered a tragedy that put him in a wheelchair. But did he do anything constructive? Did he work on legislation against drunk driving? Did he work for the rights of the disabled? No, he went around killing people!"

Terry shook his head in disgust. His sympathy for the accused obviously didn't extend to Don Logan. "You'd think the man would have been sensitized by the experience," he finished.

Ruth hit the table with the palm of her hand. And she hit it hard. If she had wanted attention, she got it. I sat up straight. Terry blinked nervously. Ruth turned her fierce glare on him.

"Why is it that people expect someone to suddenly become a saint when they're put in a wheelchair?" she demanded. "Would you?"

Terry lowered his eyes. "I guess I wouldn't," he mumbled. "But—"

"Well, nor would I," Ruth assured him. She softened her tone as she continued. "I've talked to Don Logan. He was a man who was used to having things his way. I'll bet that he was an angry and violent man before he was crippled. And his losses just made him even angrier and more violent. He didn't know how to pass through the anger. He couldn't complete his mourning. So that's where he got stuck. In a morass of rage and hatred."

I shivered, remembering that rage only too well.

The swinging doors of the kitchen opened before Ruth could say anything more. Fran trotted to our table, wiping her hands on her apron as she came. Her soft face was shadowed with fatigue, but she was smiling.

"Oh, Kate," she bubbled. "I knew you could do it. I'm so impressed that you found our murderer. Bradley says—"

"I didn't exactly find the murderer," I interrupted, feeling my face flush again. "He found me."

"Well, anyway," Fran chattered on happily. "We're so grateful. We have a little surprise for you. So don't you go anywhere." She rushed on to the next subject without taking a breath. "Nikki called again for you this morning. Did you get a chance to talk to her?"

"Yes," I answered briefly. I had called Nikki back the first thing after kissing Wayne good morning. Wayne and I were going to drive out to talk to her before we went to the airport. I wasn't looking forward to it. My stomach tightened. Would she ever be able to get over losing Jack? I moved closer to Wayne, touching my arm to his, assuring myself he was still there.

Fran warbled a few more cheery words of thanks, then walked around the table to give Ruth a big hug before returning to the kitchen. The moment the swinging doors closed behind Fran, Ruth reached across the table to put her hand on top of mine. As I looked at her, I felt myself being sucked into her intense gaze.

"Nikki will get through it," Ruth pronounced slowly and clearly. "She is a survivor. She knows there is more to look forward to in her life. Her mourning will be brief." I found myself nodding, convinced by Ruth's certainty.

"Thank you," I whispered. She patted my hand, then released it.

"And Eli," she continued, her black button-eyes softening into those of a moonstruck teenager. "He'll be fine too. I'm going to stay down here until he gets out of the hospital." She sighed. Then her face became a wise gypsy's again. "Craig's already on the road to recovery," she added briskly.

Craig blushed and lowered his puppy-dog eyes for a moment. Then he turned his eyes back to me.

"How about Fran?" I asked quickly, avoiding his gaze. "What's with the big hug? Has she forgiven you for lecturing her?"

Ruth pulled herself erect in her chair, her mouth curved in a smug smile. "She has not only forgiven me, she's going into family counseling with her husband and son." She bent forward and whispered, "And guess who's going to pay for the therapy?"

"Avery Haskell?" I ventured.

Ruth's smug smile faltered.

Terry chuckled. "You're not the only mind reader around here, you know," he told her.

Ruth leaned back in her chair and laughed. "Yes, Avery Haskell," she confirmed. "And he's investing in Spa Santé too—"

"He's confessed!" came Felix's shout from the dining room door, cutting off Ruth's sentence. He raced to our table. "Don Logan's confessed to everything! And I got my story in first!"

"Logan's going to need one of those lawyers he hates," commented Terry dryly.

"He's already got one," Felix answered, pulling out a chair on Ruth's other side. "Looks like they're going to go for an insanity plea."

There was an uncomfortable silence around the table as Felix sat down. Insanity? Was Logan insane? For all his rage, he had seemed calm and methodical to me. But to kill two strangers? Weren't his actions intrinsically insane? Then I re-

membered his look of resignation. Or had it been relief?
Maybe he had been glad to have been stopped. I hoped so.

The sound of the kitchen doors swinging open once more
came as a welcome interruption to my thoughts. Fran marched
to our table holding a layer cake out in front of her. Bradley
and Paul Beaumont followed her through the doors. And
Roseanne brought up the rear, tail high, eyes on the cake.

"For Kate Jasper, our own detective," Fran announced
formally. I stood up and opened my mouth to object to "detective" but Fran wasn't finished yet.

"It's applesauce oatmeal with a tofu-cream frosting," she
stage-whispered. "A new recipe. Bradley made it up this
morning—"

"We wanted to express our thanks," said Bradley. His eyes
were clear today. And somber. "All of us appreciate what
you did."

Avery Haskell came through the kitchen door and handed
a piece of paper to Paul as Fran set down the cake. Avery
nudged the boy.

"And a certificate for two weeks free stay at Spa Santé,"
Paul recited, his eyes on the paper. "Any time you want to
use it." He lifted his eyes to mine and smiled uncertainly.

Two weeks at the Spa of Sighs. Damn. Roseanne yowled
plaintively. My sentiments exactly. But I made the effort and
stretched my face into what I hoped was an appreciative smile.

"I—" I began.

"Psst," I heard from the dining hall doors.

Edna and Arletta stood in the doorway, gazing at me fur-
tively. Edna's shoulders were hunched forward defensively.
Arletta fidgeted behind her.

"Wanted to say goodbye," Edna growled.

"We don't want to intrude though," chirped Arletta from
behind her.

"Intrude?" I asked loudly, striding toward them. "Like
you intruded last night?"

Edna and Arletta exchanged puzzled glances.

"You guys," I sighed affectionately as I reached them.
"You saved my life last night. You have my permission to
intrude whenever you want to!"

Arletta's face lit up. I gave her a quick hug, not wanting
to damage her frail bones. Then I squeezed the stuffing out
of Edna. She was solid enough to withstand it. Both women

were blushing by the time I led them over to the rest of the group.

"These are the real heroes," I announced, introducing the twins. They shook hands all around, first with Ruth and Terry, then with Wayne and Craig, and finally with Avery Haskell and the Beaumonts.

"Arletta Ainsley and Edna Grimshaw," I proclaimed. "True detectives."

They blushed even more deeply. Edna sputtered out disclaimers while Arletta giggled.

Craig rose from his seat and beamed his chairman-of-the-board smile down at the twins. "If there is ever anything you need," he said, "feel free to ask. I can't thank you enough for what you did last night."

The man has charm. I can't deny it. Arletta simpered becomingly and Edna let out a girlish snort of pleasure.

"Listen," I said to them, not to be outdone. "Why don't you come visit me up in Marin? I'd love to see you again."

"Oh, that would be lovely," Arletta chirped. "But we couldn't impose."

"No problem," I assured them. "We'll get you a motel nearby. I know just the one. All the amenities. A private whirlpool tub, in-room movies, the works." I turned and locked eyes with my ex-husband. "And I'm sure Craig will be only too glad to treat you," I finished.

Craig's mouth dropped open. As I winked at Wayne, the dining hall filled with laughter.